praise for *the secret of life*

D1334768

praise for rudy rucker

"Rudy Rucker should be declared a National Treasure of American Science Fiction. Someone simultaneously channeling Kurt Gödel and Lenny Bruce might start to approximate full-on Ruckerian warp-space, but without the sweet, human, splendidly goofy Rudy-ness at the core of the singularity." —William Gibson

"One of science fiction's wittiest writers. A genius . . . a cult hero among discriminating cyberpunkers." —*San Diego Union-Tribune*

"Rucker's writing is great like the Ramones are great: a genre stripped to its essence, attitude up the wazoo, and cartoon senti-ments that reek of identifiable lives and issues. Wild math you can get elsewhere, but no one does the cyber version of beatnik glory quite like Rucker." —*New York Review of Science Fiction*

"What a Dickensian genius Rucker has for Californian charac-ters, as if, say, Dickens had fused with Phil Dick and taken up surfing and jamming and topologising. He has a hotline to cosmic revelations yet he's always here and now in the groove, tossing off lines of beauty and comic wisdom. 'My heart is a dog running after every cat.' We really feel with his characters in their bizarre tragicomic quests." —Ian Watson, author of *The Embedding*

"The current crop of sf humorists are mildly risible, I suppose, but they don't seem to pack the same intellectual punch of their forebears. With one exception, that is: the astonishing Rudy Rucker. For some two decades now, since the publication of his first novel, *White Light*, Rucker has combined an easygoing, trippy style influenced by the Beats with a deep engagement with knotty (or 'gnarly,' to employ one of his favorite terms) intellectual conceits, based mainly in mathematics. In the typical Rucker novel, likably eccentric characters—who run the gamut from brilliant to near-certifiable—encounter aspects of the universe that confirm that life is weirder than we can imagine." —*The Washington Post*

"Rucker stands alone in the science fiction pantheon as some kind of trickster god of the computer science lab; where others construct minutely plausible fictional realities, he simply grabs the corners of the one we already know and twists it in directions we don't have pronounceable names for." —*SF Site*

"Reading a Rudy Rucker book is like finding Poe, Kerouac, Lewis Carroll, and Philip K. Dick parked on your driveway in a topless '57 Caddy . . . and telling you they're taking you for a RIDE. The funniest science fiction author around." —*Sci-Fi Universe*

"This is SF rigorously following crazy rules. My mind of science fiction. At the heart of it is a rage to extrapolate. Rucker is what happens when you cross a mathematician with the extrapolating jazz spirit." —Robert Sheckley

"Rucker [gives you] more ideas per chapter than most authors use in an entire novel." —*San Francisco Chronicle*

"Rudy Rucker writes like the love child of Philip K. Dick and George Carlin. Brilliant, frantic, conceptual, cosmological . . . like lucid dreaming, only funny." —*New York Times* bestselling author Walter Jon Williams

by rudy rucker

FICTION

the secret of life

a novel by

RUDY RUCKER

night shade books
new york

THE OTHER SIDE OF DARK

JOAN LOWERY NIXON

When Stacy McAdams wakes in a hospital room to discover she has been in a coma for the past four years, her problems are only just beginning.

An innocent thirteen-year-old trapped in the body of a mature seventeen-year-old, Stacy has a lot of catching up to do. She yearns for the familiarity of her previous world.

Stacy is heartbroken to discover that her mother has been killed. Murdered by the same stranger who shot Stacy four years ago – and she is the only eye-witness. The only eye-witness to a murderer who hasn't been caught...

LIGHTNING

SAFE, STRONG AND STREETWISE

HELEN BENEDICT

SAFE, STRONG AND STREETWISE takes a bold look at some of the problems faced by teenagers today. What is sexual abuse? How can you defend yourself against it? Who can you turn to for help and advice? How should you react if you are physically attacked? All these important questions and more are answered in a realistic and constructive way, using accounts given by young people about difficult situations they have had to face.

"It's the ultimate street-safety guide."
  Lenny Henry

LIGHTNING

contents

Part III

Part IV

sartre and the meaning of life
an introduction by kim stanley robinson

By the time I met Rudy Rucker, sometime in the early 2000s, he was a mellow professor from San Jose State University. Most traces of his wild past had seemingly disappeared, but I had been reading his books for many years, so I was alert to any signs of strange brilliance, and it didn't take long to see them. Rudy was relaxed but intense, spaced but focused, casual but gnomic, quick but slow, startling but reassuring. How did he manage all these things at once? You'll have to ask him; I don't know him that well. I do know, after many pleasant encounters over the years, including one unforgettable Oakland Raiders game that Cecelia Holland took us to, that he's a lot of fun to hang out with. I'm grateful to our mutual friend Terry Bisson for introducing us. These two crazy Kentuckians, one beatnik, one hippie, are now two great Californians, and we who have lived here all along are the luckier for it.

The first of Rudy's books that I read was *Wetware*, which I greatly enjoyed. The influence of Kerouac on Rudy was not hard to see, and it occurred to me right away that we therefore had a kind of connection, as I had been much influenced by Gary Snyder, Kerouac's friend. That the successors to those very different existentialist dharma bums turned out to be science fiction writers made sense to me. Both the beats and science fiction writers are outsider artists who see America from the skeptical angles of the existential beyond. We've stayed mostly outside the literary establishment, partly because of the establishment's disdain for us, partly by way of our prideful renunciation of them. This outsider status has been good for us; there has never been an establishment American writer worth a damn—maybe that's not true, but it's definitely true that all the greatest American writers have been outsider artists. So we're lucky to be under the mark of Cain, and hopefully it will always stay that way.

Rudy's non-fiction masterpiece is *The Lifebox, the Seashell, and the Soul*, a sort of culmination to all his previous mathematical writing. It includes his account of his own philosophical journey, so possibly it's "transreal nonfiction." It's a book I found tremendously helpful for understanding our world.

Rudy's masterpiece in fiction, for me, is *As Above, So Below*, a great historical novel about Peter Brueghel. In its character pattern and its plot it has a lot of correlations with Rudy's wonderful science fiction novel *Spaceland*, a riff on Edwin Abbott's famous story *Flatland*, which Rudy wrote at about the same time as his Brueghel book. Another wonderful novel from these same years is *Jim and the Flims*, perhaps his greatest non-transrealist sf novel. Rudy's Californian writing has been rich and productive.

The one you're holding, one of his very best, is an early example, maybe the first example, of what he later came to call transrealism. Rudy's written a lot about this method of his, so I won't go into it much myself. Essentially, I take it to be a matter of using the various tools and concepts of science fiction to write stories roughly based on your own life experiences. This is a great way to escape the trap of autobiographical fiction, which ate up both Kerouac and Hemingway, among many other writers. Those guys were too literal, and having quickly written down their youths, they then went out looking for more adventures to turn into fiction, which led them into doing stupid things and destroying their lives. Rudy's transrealism is a better way. For one thing, he alternates his transrealist stories with other kinds of novels, so he isn't entirely reliant on his own life, probably a good thing for a man who has been mostly a college professor and computer scientist; for another, the trans in his transrealism makes his novels into something more interesting than autobiography usually is, turning them into works of art with a larger reach.

Transrealism is a kind of symbolist poetry. All the various ideas common in science fiction are easily understood as metaphors for things already present in our world. Spaceships are cities, robots are workers, on it goes through the whole genre: lots of metaphors and symbols. Using them as such gives them more power. So in the case of *The Secret of Life*, without going into too much detail in an introduction, we can say that as an existentialist text written under the impact of Jean-Paul Sartre's *Nausea*, it is pretty clear that Rudy is playing some games with the idea of alienation. And "the secret of life" could just as well be called "the meaning of life." Sartre famously said there's no such thing, that we have to make that up if it's going to exist at all; that process of making is what this novel does. And the main character's special gift is also easily tranrealized into Rudy's description of his coming into being as a science fiction writer, a very powerful form of alienation indeed. Yay for all of us that this happened!

It should also be said that *The Secret of Life* has a realist twin that Rudy wrote around the same time, called *All the Visions*. By reading them both you can see very clearly what Rudy is up to, in terms of his early life and his discovery of his method. He clearly intends you to see this pairing; the first sentence of *All the Visions* is, "I was sixteen when it first hit me: someday you'll be dead," while the first sentence of *The Secret of Life* is, "Conrad Bunger was sixteen when it first hit him: someday you'll be dead." Clear enough? Yes. Having been clued in like this, it's easy to follow all the subsequent parallels, and interesting to read as an exercise in comparative literature. And now this paired set is complemented by Rudy's later autobiography, *Nested Scrolls*, which retells the story from a much later perspective. It's good to have that angle too, creating a triangulation that is maybe Rudy's non-Euclidean geometry of deep time, a kind of whole sight. They all make it clear: Rudy was lucky to find Sylvia, and we are lucky he found science fiction.

the secret of life

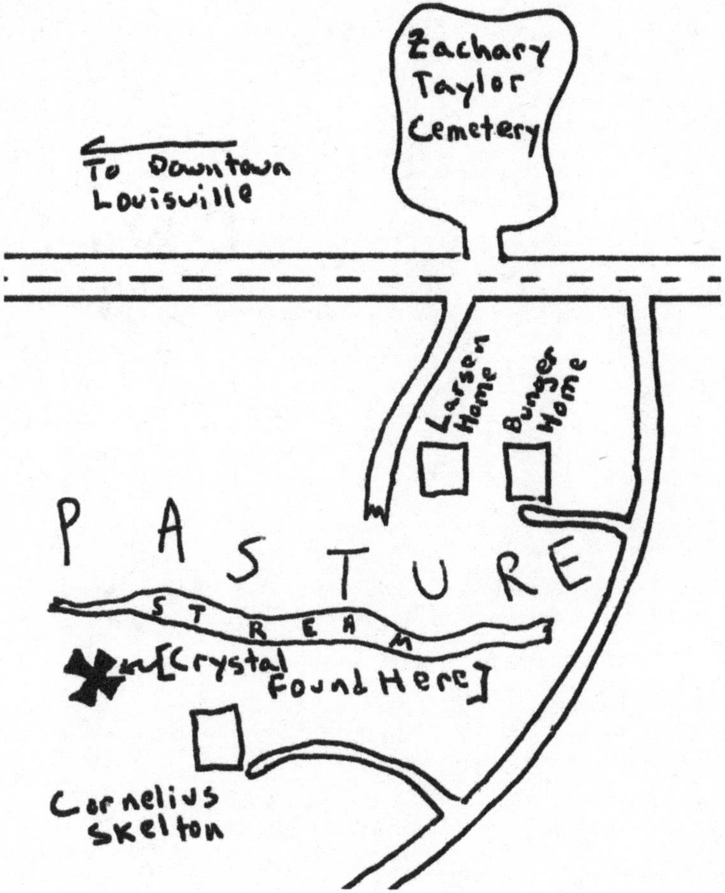
Zachary Taylor Cemetery
To Downtown Louisville
Larsen Home
Bunger Home
PASTURE
STREAM
[Crystal Found Here]
Cornelius Skelton

part one

"I was just thinking," I tell him, laughing, "that here we sit, all of us, eating and drinking to preserve our precious existence and really there is nothing, nothing, absolutely no reason for existing."

—Jean-Paul Sartre, *Nausea*

part one

ONE
monday, december 31, 1962

C onrad Bunger was sixteen when it first hit him: *Someday you'll be dead.*

He was at a New Year's Eve dance at the River Valley Country Club in Louisville. It was a much classier scene than Conrad was accustomed to, though he did know many of the other boys and girls, the rich boys in brand-new tuxedos, the girls in pale dresses with thin straps. Conrad had his father's old tux and horrible lumpy dress shoes; he was smaller than the others, a *brain*, but blending in well enough. His date Linda was dancing with a boy she'd had a crush on since fifth grade, and Conrad was hoping to get drunk.

The coat racks were at the foot of the stairs leading down to the bathrooms. Conrad made his way there and patted down the overcoats, feeling for the happy tumor of a hidden pint. It was easy; the bottles grew as thick as autumn fruit. Conrad drew out a pint of Old Crow and gulped at the strange liquid, vile and volatile stuff that evaporated almost before he could swallow.

With flushed skin, buzzing ears, and the sudden conviction that *he was cool*, Conrad fumbled the bottle back into its velvet-collared overcoat. A brief wave of sickness. He made for the men's room, eyes and mouth streaming, and drank some water from the sink.

The bathroom was empty, all light and white tile. Mirrors, a stack of clean-smelling linen towels by the sinks, and the urinals across the room. "I'm here by the sinks," thought Conrad, "and it seems impossible that I will ever be over there by the urinals." He began to walk. "Now I am moving through space, and time is going on, and now . . ." He unzipped and began to piss. "Now, although it seemed inconceivable before, I am on the other side of the room." His mind felt unbelievably clear. "Last year I never thought I'd be drunk at a dance, yet here I am, just as surely as I've crossed this tile floor."

As he started back toward the dance floor, the wider implications hit him. "I can't conceive of being in college, but that will come, too, and when it comes it will feel like *now*. I will go to college, and marry, and have children, and all the time it will be me doing it, me doing it in some mysteriously moving *now*. And then I'll die. It seems impossible, but someday I will really die."

Linda wasn't interested in all this; Linda was a tennis player. She and Conrad had gone steady for almost a year, and now all of a sudden at the New Year's Eve dance he was interested in the problem of death. Babbling about it on the dance floor, Conrad wore a heavy, glazed expression that made Linda suspicious.

"Are you drunk? You're acting funny."

"What difference does it make? What difference does anything make? Oh, beautiful Linda, why don't you sleep with me before we die."

"That is just a *little* out-of-the-question, Conrad. Maybe you should sit down."

Instead he dug back into the coat racks. There were some older boys down there now, but, hell, everyone was drinking, why should they care if he took a little?

"Get out of here, Bunger. What are you, a pickpocket or something?" It was Preston, a party-boy with cratered skin and a black burr-haircut. He was sipping from the very same pint that Conrad had sampled earlier.

Conrad attempted a smile. Suddenly he wasn't cool anymore. "Happy New Year, Preston. Can I have a slug?"

"Christ, and give me syphilis? Get your own!"

It was still only 10:30, and those few gulps of whiskey were wearing off fast. The boys in the cloakroom glared at Conrad. He found his way back upstairs.

Linda was still dancing, laughing and light on her feet. Her partner was Billy Ballhouse, a real snowman. Ballhouse was talking about love, no doubt, love and kissing, dance steps and new clothes. Watching Linda dance, Conrad felt very old. Who was he to badger this gay young thing for sex? With death so near, and the night so young, how could he find a bottle?

The answer came to him as the song ended. *Steal some wine from the St. John's sacristy!* He told Linda he'd be back in a few minutes and hurried out into the hall.

There were some younger boys without dates out there, smoking and horsing around. Right now they were having a belching contest, bouncing the gurpy sounds off the oaken walls. One of them, Jim Ardmore, was a pretty good friend of Conrad's. They belonged to the same high-school fraternity, a club called the Chevalier

Literary Society. Some of the Chevalier members were fairly cool—though Conrad himself had been initiated primarily because his big brother Caldwell had been a member before going off to college and the army.

"Hey, Jim," cried Conrad. "You want to help me steal some wine?"

"How decadent," said young Ardmore, his mouth twisting. He was skinny, with a heavy shock of dry black hair hanging into his sallow face. "Decadent" was his favorite word, though right now he was using it with a certain irony. "Are we going to rob a liquor store?"

"No, no. Just come with me. We'll get *two* bottles."

The other boys cheered, and Ardmore went on outside with Conrad. Conrad's mother had lent him her new blue Volkswagen. It shook a lot in first gear. They drove along River Road for a while, then up a long hill to St. John's. It wasn't far.

Just two years earlier, Conrad's father had suddenly taken it into his head to be ordained as a deacon in the Episcopal Church. He worked as an assistant at St. John's, and Conrad was a regular acolyte. Sometimes Conrad would light and extinguish the candles, and sometimes he would be in charge of getting out the bread and wine. As a result, he knew (1) where the locked closet with the communion wine was and (2) where to find the key. The church itself was always unlocked. Conrad's father felt very strongly about leaving churches unlocked—he made a point of leaving a note saying, *"A locked door, an unfaithful act,"* on any locked church door he encountered.

Conrad and Ardmore hurried in, got the liquor closet unlocked, and gazed down at a full case of cheap California port. High high-school laughs. They each took a bottle and tumbled back into the VW.

Conrad was a little leery of bringing stolen church wine into the party, so he and Ardmore drove around for an hour, chugging at the stuff. Lights swept past, stores and cars, and the evening began to break into patches. Conrad could hear himself talking, louder and more eloquently than ever before.

"We're going to *die*, Jim, can you believe that? It's really going to stop some day, all of it, and you're dead then, you know? It's going to happen to you personally just like when I was at the dance and walking across the bathroom, how at the sink I thought I'd never be at the urinals, and then I was there anyway. I can't stand it, I don't want to die, time keeps passing."

Ardmore laughed and laughed, never having seen Conrad so animated. They realized they weren't going to be able to finish even the first bottle and headed back to the dance. Linda met Conrad in the hall.

"*Where* have you been? You stood me up!" It was past midnight, and people were slow-dancing inside. Conrad was eager to share his new wisdom.

"Linda, oh, tennis Linda, with your pretty new dress. Only the present matters, did you ever think of that?" Conrad fumbled out a cigarette and lit it. An ashtray caught his attention. "Look at that ashtray, Linda. It exists. It doesn't need us to exist. It resists our will and insists on disk-hood!" Conrad picked up the flat glass ashtray and emptied the butts onto the floor. "Holiday snow! Cuban missile crisis!"

"Conrad, if you ever want to go out with me again . . ."

"But I don't!" brayed Conrad, realizing somewhere inside himself that this was true. "I don't want to go out with you anymore, Linda, because you don't understand death."

A few onlookers had gathered. For the first time in Conrad's life, people were looking at him with interest. He'd been a weenie long enough. Get drunk and talk about philosophy! That was the ticket! He groped for a concept.

"God is dead!" he shouted, suddenly understanding the dry phrase. "All is permitted!" With a whoop of laughter, Conrad threw the ashtray into the air and watched it shatter on the marble floor.

Next came a darkness, voices, and rough motion.

"Take it easy, Bunger, you've got puke all over yourself. Is this your house?"

"Uh, uuuuuh."

"Yeah, that's his house. Park his car, ring the doorbell, and let's get out of here. Be sure to get that other bottle of wine."

"Right."

The dark forms disappeared, the house door opened, and there was Conrad's father in his bathrobe.

"Shouldn't wait up for me," muttered Conrad. "Lea' me alone, you old bastard."

There was yelling. His parents put him to bed, he threw up again, lights and more yelling, his mother screaming, *"Pig! Pig!"*

Finally he was alone. The bed and room began to spin. Conrad fumbled for a way to stop it. There had to be some head-trick, some change of perspective to make the torture stop ... there. He felt himself grow lighter and less real. Dropping off to sleep, he had the feeling he was floating one inch above his bed. And then ... he was in the throes of an old, recurrent dream.

The structure is circular, high in the middle. It could be a circus big top. Conrad is off to one side, watching the thin, bright shapes that move above the center. They are flames, these beings; they are rods of light. The whole enclosed space is filled with moving lights, and they have reached some wonderful, awful conclusion about Conrad's future....

TWO

tuesday, january 1, 1963

C onrad's best friend, Hank Larsen, had gone to a different New Year's Eve dance. New Year's Day, Conrad walked over to Hank's house to compare notes.

"No driving," warned Conrad's mother. "After last night, you can just stay in the neighborhood."

"OK, Mom." Conrad's dog Nina followed him over to Hank's house. Hank was in his room, reading a science-fiction book and listening to one of his radios. Hank's big hobby was electronics—over the years he'd assembled four or five different types of radio transmitters and receivers. He even had a ham license from the FCC.

"The Magnificent Paunch," intoned Hank by way of greeting. Friends for years now, the two had a large number of code phrases, many of uncertain meaning.

"High guineaus, Si," responded Conrad. "I don't feel too peak."

"Got y'self all drunked up, did you, Zeke? Got a touch of that riiind fever?"

"It was great," said Conrad, breaking into normal speech. "Ardmore and I stole wine from the church and got really plastered. I was talking about time and death and some guys drove me home."

"I bet you got caught bigger'n shit."

"Yeah. They were both waiting up. I don't remember too clearly. I think maybe my old man slugged me. I was cursing and everything."

"What'd they say today?"

"Well, nothing, really. But what about you? What happened on your big date with Lehman? Did you finger her again?"

Hank closed his book and stood up. He was tall and blond, and his girlfriend Laura Lehman was crazy about him. Instead of answering Conrad's question directly, Hank nodded his head warningly toward the hall. "Let's roll out."

"OK. Let's walk over to Skelton's pasture. Nina's here too."

"Bo-way."

It was a cool, gray day. The frozen grass crunched underfoot. Hank's family lived in a subdivision which petered out in a series of large cow pastures. The land all belonged to an old Kentucky gentleman named Cornelius Skelton. In the mid-fifties, Skelton had gotten into the papers for claiming he'd seen a UFO land in his fields. Skelton said it had butchered one of his hogs, and he had a mineral crystal that the saucer was supposed to have left. He wasn't fanatical about it, or anything—he just insisted that he'd seen a UFO. He was a pleasant, courtly man, and most people ascribed this one eccentricity to his grief over the premature death of his wife.

Conrad had been wandering the pastures ever since the Bungers moved to Louisville in 1956. It was his favorite place. Today, Hank and Conrad were walking along a small stream that ran through the pasture bottoms. You could see bubbles moving beneath the clear patches in the ice.

"Did you *fuck* her?" Conrad asked finally.

Hank seemed reluctant to discuss it—like a rich man embarrassed to describe his treasures to a hungry beggar.

"Did you do it in your car?" demanded Conrad.

"No, uh, her mother was out. We used Laura's room."

"Jesus. Did she take off all her clothes?"

"You planning to beat off on this, Paunch?"

"Come on, Hank, I have to know. What does it feel like? Do they like it, too?"

"I felt tingly all over," said Hank slowly. "It was like pins and needles in all of my skin, and I was dizzy. The first time was real fast, but the next one took longer. She was crying some of the time, but squeezing me real tight. I would have done it a third time, but I only had two rubbers. Just when I was leaving, her old lady came home. 'Was it nice at the dance, children?'"

"God."

They walked on in silence for a while, following the stream. Nina ran ahead, sniffing for rabbits. At the crests of the hills on either side you could see houses, new split-levels like the one Hank lived in. A crow flapped slowly to the top of a leafless black locust tree and perched there, cawing. Conrad couldn't get over the fact that his best friend Hank had actually managed to get laid.

"You really did it, Hank! That's wonderful. Congratulations." They paused to shake hands solemnly. "You know what I was thinking last month—" Conrad continued, "about the only way *I'm* likely to ever get any pussy? I was thinking that when we have World War Three, there'll be a whole lot of dead women around, you know, good-looking dead women with their clothes all ripped, and . . ."

"Oh, come on, Conrad. You won't be a dry stick forever." Hank poked Conrad and sang an altered bar from *My Fair Lady*: "With a little bit of luck, we'll all fu-huh-uck!"

"Yeah, I guess so, sooner or later. Today's the first day of 1963. I can remember when I was about ten, reading an article in *Popular Science* about all the neat inventions we were supposed to have in 1963. Personal helicopters, self-driving cars. Time keeps passing, Hank, and before we know it, we'll be dead. That's what I was telling everyone last night. We're all really going to die."

"So what, as long as you have some fun first."

"You don't understand."

"You're just worried you'll die a *virrgin*." Hank had a special, nasal voice he used for unkind cuts like this. "The Sacred *Virrrgin* Mary."

"Sure, religion's bullshit," said Conrad, steering back to his chosen topic. "Heaven and hell are just science fiction. But can there really be *nothing* after death? I mean a corpse is the same matter as the living person was. Where does the life go to? Where did it come from?"

"Ghosts," said Hank. "The soul." In the distance, Nina was barking.

"That's right," said Conrad, "I *know* I have a soul. I'm alive, I can feel it. But where does it *go*?"

They were near the end of the pastures now, and Nina was running back toward them. The two boys squatted to wait for her, squatted and watched the bubbles beneath the ice, ice patterned in ridges and blobs, clear here and frosty there. Toward one bank, the ice domed up. A lone, large bubble wobbled there, braced against the flow. Smaller bubbles kept arriving to merge into that big bubble, and it, in turn, kept growing and sending out tendrils, silver pseudopods that pinched off into new bubbles that were swept further downstream.

Nina came panting up, pink tongue exposed. Her breath steamed in the cold air. "Good dog," said Hank, patting her. "Hey, Conrad, let's go back. Lehman's mother's giving an open house today. Maybe your parents will let you come."

"Wait," said Conrad, struck by a sudden inspiration. "The *life-force*. Each of us has a tiny piece of the life-force, and when we die it goes away."

"Hubba-hubba, Zeke, I done lost my life-force up Laura's crack."

"No, listen, I know where the life-force goes, Hank. I've got it figured out. There's a big pool of life-force . . . out there." Conrad gestured vaguely. "It's like that big bubble under the ice, you see. And each of us is a little bubble that can merge back in."

"Like a soul going to heaven." They were walking now, headed back toward the houses.

"And the big thing is that once a little bubble joins the big one, the little bubble is *gone*. The soul goes to heaven, *and then it's absorbed into God.* The drop of life-force slides into the big pool. Isn't that neat, Hank? Your life-force is preserved, but your personality disappears! I've invented a new philosophy!"

Still riding high from his big first fuck, Hank felt no need to burst his friend's bubble. "It'd be cool to major in philosophy next year. Find out all the answers and then become a Bowery bum."

"God, yeah." Conrad felt elated. "Do you think we'll be able to get beer over at Lehman's?"

"Sure. Her old lady don't give a shit. She'll be plowed anyway."

On the way back, Conrad began jumping back and forth over the frozen stream. With his big new idea in mind, he felt light as a feather. The floating feeling from bed last night came back . . . he'd never jumped so far so easily before.

"Look, Hank, I can fly!" As Conrad said it, the feeling disappeared. He landed heavily on the stream bank, and one foot crashed through the ice.

"You'll fly better once we get into Lehman's brew."

But Hank's mother waylaid them before they could make off with the Larsen family car. She was a pleasantly plump redhead with a gentle voice. Conrad had an unsettling feeling that she knew exactly what both he and Hank had done last night.

"Conrad, your mother called. Your father would like for you to come home right away. And, Hank, why don't you leave the poor Lehmans alone for one day? Weren't you supposed to rotate the Valiant's tires this afternoon?"

"Oh, Ma."

"Goodbye, Conrad. And Happy New Year!"

Hank and Conrad exchanged shrugs. Hank was led into his house, and Conrad started back home. His father was waiting in their gravel driveway.

Mr. Caldwell Bunger, Sr., had moved his family to Louisville when Conrad turned ten. He'd gotten two acres of land cheap from Cornelius Skelton, and he'd built a white split-level, a comfortable house set well back from the road. He'd never gotten around to putting blacktop on the long driveway.

Approaching his father, Conrad's mind wandered. *Gravel driveway.* When Hank and Conrad were twelve, they'd had a special game with the gravel. They'd get a shovelful of it, douse it with gasoline, light it, and then throw the burning sand and rocks up into the air. It looked like people made of fire, sort of, and . . .

"Feel pretty silly?" Conrad's father was a solid-looking man with bifocals, and with gold in his teeth. He was wearing his clerical collar.

"I'm sorry about last night," mumbled Conrad. He'd managed to avoid his father so far today.

"You're making a name for yourself, boy. People remember these things. What am I going to tell Holman Barkley when I see him downtown? *I'm sorry my son threw up on your daughter?*"

"I didn't . . ." Conrad broke off in horror as the memory swept back. He *had* thrown up on Linda. On her legs. She'd phoned up her father for help. Ardmore and two other guys had driven Conrad home and . . .

"Have you apologized to your mother?"

"Uh, sure, yeah."

"Conrad, what's the matter with you? Up until just a few months ago we were so proud of you. And now your grades are slipping; every time you get a chance you go out and get your snoot full; you say you're sick of church . . . what's the problem, Conrad? What is it?" His father seemed genuinely baffled.

"Well, Pop, I'm worried about death. If humans have to die anyway, then everything's meaningless, isn't it?"

"So that's it now," sighed Mr. Bunger. "I'll tell you one thing, boy, if you're worried about death, you shouldn't be drinking and driving. Otherwise your life will be over before you know what hit you."

"Some other guys drove me back last night. And it doesn't really matter how long I live anyway. Sooner or later it comes to the same thing: nothing."

"What if I'd felt that way?" said Mr. Bunger, his voice rising. "Look at this house, look at you and your brother. If I'd chickened out young, you wouldn't be here!"

"So I'm supposed to get a job and buy a house and have kids and be just like you? I don't see the point of it, Pop. What's the difference, really, if there's one more or one less nice middle-class family?" Conrad meant all this, though at the same time he was conscious of adopting a pose. The main thing was to get the better of his father—his father who was always so right and so patient. "I hope the Russians bomb us tomorrow and blow all this bullshit away."

That did it. "I ought to paste you one!" shouted Mr. Bunger. "Go inside and do that homework you've been putting off all vacation. *Take*, that's all you know, *take*, *take*, *take*, and if it's not enough, tear everything down. I'll give you the meaning of life—you're not using Mom's car again till you pull your grades back up. School starts again tomorrow, thank God."

"You're just scared to face death," sneered Conrad. "That's the only reason you can believe all that religion crap."

He took off running before his father could react. He made it to his room and slammed the door. *The old people are scared*, thought Conrad fiercely, *but I'm not. I'm not scared to look for the real answers. That's what I'm here for—to figure out the secret of life.*

THREE
monday, january 7, 1963

Although the Bungers were Episcopalian, Conrad attended a big Roman Catholic boys high school called St. X. The idea was that St. X had the best science program in Louisville; and Conrad was supposed to become a scientist. He was one of three non-Catholics among the two thousand students at St. X. During Conrad's four years there, the other boys often tried to "baptize" him. This involved dragging him into a bathroom and slugging him and throwing water or piss on him. By the time Conrad was a senior, he'd formed a real dislike for the Roman Catholic religion. It was even stupider than Protestantism. Purgatory? Limbo? Papal Infallibility? The Virgin Mary's Immaculate Conception and Bodily Assumption? These were all bad enough, but for some reason, the doctrine that bothered Conrad the most was Transubstantiation.

According to the hearty priest who taught the religion class, when the bread and wine are blessed at Mass, they turn into literal, actual flesh and blood. Some of the other boys told Conrad it had to be true, since they'd heard of a kid who'd stolen a consecrated Communion wafer and stuck pins in it . . . and the wafer had *bled*.

"Can you taste the blood when you chew it?" Conrad demanded.

"You're not allowed to chew."

Even more bizarre than the religion classes were the monthly sex lectures that the seniors got. Normally the boys were split into ten different tracks, but for the sex lectures, all four hundred seniors would be herded into the gym together. They'd sit up in the bleachers, and a priest named Father Stook would hold forth like some crazed dictator. Father Stook's chief interests were rubbers and jacking off.

"I've had mothers come to me, boys, come to me in tears because they found one of those things in their son's wallet. Don't break your mother's heart! The use of contraceptives is but one step better than the mortal sin of self-abuse. *Self-abuse destroys the mind!* I knew one poor man, boys, a deranged syphilitic. I was at his bedside when he passed away. And do you know what that pitiful wretch was doing as he died? Do you *know*? *He was reaching down to abuse himself!* What a way to meet your Maker, boys. *In the very act of committing the vilest perversion!* Now, I know that some of you may have heard that certain acts between men and women are perversions. Not so. As long as *the penis ejaculates inside the vagina*, no sin against God has been committed. What you and your wife do *before* ejaculation is strictly your own affair, as long as *the seed is planted in the womb*. Oh, I've heard it's a marvelous thing. I've read that when the woman reaches a certain state of arousal, there are *contractions within the walls of her vagina*. A kind of suction is created. One member of my parish told me, 'Father Stook, if the good Lord made anything better, He kept it for Himself.' There is no inherent evil in sex, boys; sex is God's gift to man. *Perversion* arises only when the seed is *turned aside*. Now, I tell my mothers to be on the lookout for contraceptives in their sons' rooms. And I've heard that some of you fellows are too smart for that. Oh, I know all the tricks. Yes, there was one boy who kept his prophylactics *taped to the inside of his car's rear hubcap*. I said Mass at his funeral last February. For one snowy night, he was out there in the street, with a tire iron in his hand, and his pants around his ankles, and . . ."

On the first Monday after Christmas vacation, Conrad had to hand in a theme for English class. The assignment had been to write a fantastic story of some type. Conrad had chosen to write a science-fiction story satirizing the Roman Catholic Church.

The idea in the story was that an alien energy-creature comes to Earth and takes on human form, so as better to understand mankind's peculiar ways of thought. He has superpowers, of course, and starts out by practicing his power of flight in a deserted pasture. As chance would have it, a group of nuns shows up for a cookout, just as the alien is hovering ten feet above the ground. Most of the nuns think the alien must be a new Messiah, the Second Coming of Christ. But one of the nuns claims the alien is the Antichrist, and before anyone can stop her, she chokes him to death with her rosary. The other nuns decide to cover up their sister's crime by barbecuing the body. It tastes wonderful! "Truly," says one chomping nun, "this is the flesh of God."

The English teacher was a spiritual, literary man named Brother Marion. He glanced up from Conrad's story with such a look of sorrow that all Conrad could think to do was to kick the boy sitting next to him, an effeminate school friend named Pete Jeans. Jeans howled, and Brother Marion reached into the pocket of his black robe.

"Yes, Conrad, I will write you a Jug ticket." A Jug ticket was a small yellow square of paper. It meant that you had to stay after school for an hour.

After class Brother Marion drew Conrad aside. "I'm disappointed by your story, Conrad. Surely you can find more deserving targets than the Church."

"But ... how can you believe all those crazy things? How can you believe in Transubstantiation? A wafer is a wafer, not the flesh of Christ!"

"God became flesh, why should flesh not become bread? Although the *accidental* properties of the consecrated wafer are as bread, its *essence* is Christ's flesh. The *accidental* properties of Christ's body were human, yet His body's *essence* was divine." Brother Marion's hollow eyes glinted briefly. "You should read Aquinas, not blaspheme like a fool."

The brother in charge of Jug was a lean zealot with angry red acne scars on his face. Brother Saint-John-of-the-Cross. Nobody messed with Saint-John-of-the-Cross. You sat there and wrote for an hour, and then Brother Saint-John-of-the-Cross threw your essay away and you could go home. The topic of the essay was always the same: *Why I Am in Jug.*

Taking his pen in hand, Conrad felt a strange surge of power. *Nobody would read this.* He could write whatever he wanted to. It was something Conrad had never thought of doing before—sit at a desk and write whatever you're thinking.

"Stop grinning, Bunger, and get to work. Two sides. *Why I Am in Jug.*"

Conrad began with the stupid way that Jeans always stuck his lower jaw out to look like he was thinking, and then moved right into some confused vaporing about how misunderstood he, Conrad Bunger, really was. *Half a page.* Conrad recounted one of Father Stook's recent tales, the one about the man who'd injured the side of his penis with his electric drill, and who'd then come to Father Stook for permission to wear a condom during intercourse so that the raw spot wouldn't chafe. "All right," Father Stook had said, "but you have to puncture the tip." *A page and a quarter.* Conrad explained about death, and how the secret of life is that we each possess a fragment of the universal life-force. *A page and two-thirds.* He ended by making fun of a St. X administrator called Deforio. Deforio was in charge of issuing late-slips. "Sports fan Deforio's moronic robot scrawl." Here and there a few gaps remained. Conrad filled them in with random curse words. He felt like if he willed it, he could float right up to the ceiling.

"I'm all done, Brother Saint-John-of-the-Cross. Can I go home now?"

The next morning, as he was walking down the hall to his third period mathematics class, Conrad was suddenly struck from behind. Something clamped on to the soft tendons of his neck and dragged him into an empty classroom. It was Brother Saint-John-of-the-Cross.

"Whaddo you mean writing that kind of garbage? You think you're smarter than the teachers?" *Shake*. "I don't want to read about no antics with the Elks." *Shake*. "I want you back in Jug every day this week."

Conrad had once seen Brother Saint-John-of-the-Cross punch a student, a football player, in the jaw. Quivering with fear, he crept off to math class. But as soon as he sat down, the wall speaker crackled into life.

"Brother Albert? Could you please send Conrad Bunger to the Assistant Principal's office?"

The other boys looked at Conrad as he left the silent room. Some smiled, some gloated, some simply looked upset. *Next time it could be me*. Berkowitz, the class clown, squeaked, "*Help!*" from the back row.

The Assistant Principal was a wise-eyed man with big shoulders and a trim gray crew cut. His name was Brother Hershey. If Saint-John-of-the-Cross was a hard cop, Hershey was a soft cop. He had a Boston accent and an air of pained rationality.

"Come in, Conrad. Sit down." Hershey slumped back in his chair and sighed. Conrad's Jug essay was lying on his desk. "Some of the brothers are very unhappy with you."

"Saint-John-of-the-Cross."

"And Brother Marion. *And* Brother Albert. A change has come over you, Conrad. Are you having personal problems?"

"Well . . . it's about death. Life is meaningless. I can't see any reason for any of it." Hershey started to interrupt, but Conrad pressed on. "I've been reading books about it.

Nausea, and *On the Road*. I'm not just making it up. Any action is equally meaningless. The present moment is all that matters."

"I've heard of those books," Hershey said shortly. "Do you think it's your place to ride the brothers about religion?"

"No, sir."

"You say that the moment is all that matters, Conrad. Has this attitude led you into . . . sins of impurity?"

"Uh, no, sir. No."

"You're not a mule, Conrad. I can reason with you, can I not?"

"Yes." Conrad knew what Brother Hershey was hinting at. If you really acted up, Hershey would take you out to the gym and paddle you. A lower-track boy had told Conrad about it at lunch one day. *"He carries that paddle hid under his robe. All the way out to the gym you can hear it bangin' on his goddamn leg."*

"Because I would rather not have to treat a good student like a mule."

"You can reason with me, Brother Hershey. I understand. I'll act better. I can hold out till graduation."

"Fine." Hershey picked up the Jug essay, scanned one side, and then the other. "You misspelled Mr. Delfioro's name."

Pause.

Conrad sat tight. Finally, Hershey crumpled up the essay and threw it in the trash can. He leaned back in his chair and sighed again. "Conrad . . . can I speak frankly?"

"Sure." How long was this going to go on?

"I had doubts, too, when I was your age. We all have doubts; God never meant for life to be easy."

"How do you know there's a God?" blurted Conrad. The pressure of all the things he wanted to say was like a balloon in his chest. "I mean, sure, the life-force exists, but why should there be a God who's watching us? It's wrong to try and explain everything with an invisible God and a life after death. Life should make sense right here and now!"

Brother Hershey leaned forward and studied the calendar on his desk. When he spoke again there was an edge to his voice. "There are six months and ten days until graduation, Conrad. Discipline yourself. Pretend to believe, and belief may come to you. I don't want to see you in here another time."

"OK." Conrad thought again of the paddle.

"When you go back to class, your buddies are going to ask you what happened."

"Yes, sir."

"Tell them it's none of their business."

"Yes, sir. Thank you, Brother Hershey."

By the time school let out it was raining hard. Conrad got his books and ran out to wait for his bus. A little ninth-grader was talking about how it would snow most likely and all the teachers would be in a bus and have an accident and then there wouldn't be school for a few weeks while they got all the teachers buried. There were about fifteen boys waiting for the bus and saying when's that son of a bitch gonna get here anyway, hell, we probably won't get out of this place till six. But then the bus pulled up anyway and they all ran through the rain and Conrad stepped in a puddle on purpose, and all the other bus guys were hurrying to get good seats. Conrad sat in back by himself, he felt so cut off and who gave a damn listening to the bus guys all excited about parties or cigarettes or getting drunk. He felt like a cold hand was grabbing his guts and squeezing them. The bus started moving and all the bus guys were shouting, not out of joy, but to get everyone to look at them, but nobody really noticed each other, except some of the guys who were really bugged about not making the scene were laughing at all the right times. Then the bus was really going, and Conrad was sitting at the window looking at the road all black shiny wet and being amazed at how humans move by going past stationary objects and not hitting anything. He was hungry as hell because of no lunch. He felt like vomiting, but instead he spat on a bunch of little white worms which lived in a crack in the floor. Looking out the window again, he saw a great big oak tree dripping unbelievable drops into a puddle and blurping up giant bubbles that looked like jellyfish until they popped, but the whole time all the guys in the bus were shouting. The guy in front of Conrad had picked a scab off his face and was dabbing at the blood with a piece of paper, and the guy he was talking to didn't even notice it, and Conrad was the only one who saw it except for a little kid across the aisle, and when Conrad stared at his eyes he wouldn't look back, and acted like he saw something outside the window, and when Conrad looked out he saw that the gutters were overflowing and there were big brown triangle puddles on the road.

FOUR
friday, march 15, 1963

L et's stop here for supper, gang."

"Yay, Jeannie!"

Conrad felt dazed and confused. This was the first time he'd been allowed to go out in three weeks. An outing of the church youth group, on their way to an all-state Episcopal youth jamboree. The girls had been singing for eighty miles, singing with hysterical good cheer. The only other guy was named Chuck Sands. He read the Bible, had pimples and greasy hair. Strong, jolly Jeannie—a woman who often helped with youth group activities—was driving this van, and Conrad's father was driving another. What a nightmare.

They piled out of the van in front of a family restaurant in some tiny Kentucky town. The girls rushed ahead and got a table by the window. There were four of them. Butt-faced Patsie Wilson; a distant, chain-smoking girl called Dee Decca; and two "hot" gigglers named Sue Pohlbog-gen and Randy Kitsler.

"Come on, Bunger," urged Chuck Sands. They were still out by the van. Inside the bright window's yellow space, Sue Pohlboggen was fluffing her blonde curls, and Dee Decca was lighting a Newport. Patsie was whispering secrets to Randy. Jeannie was in the ladies' room.

"I need air, Sands. I'll just get something at a supermarket and eat outside, OK?"

"Fine," said Sands. "That gives me more room to maneuver."

Conrad hurried around the corner and walked a few blocks. Seed store, drugstore, dentist, bank. It felt good to be alone, in the middle of nowhere, free from the relentless pressure to conform. He flared his nostrils and breathed in alienation. This was a time to be thinking deep thoughts.

What is it all about? he asked himself. *Why is all of this here? How can human beings be so blind?* The girls primping their hair and waiting for food. Didn't they see the nothingness which underlies everything?

For the last few months, Conrad had had a strange feeling of having just woken up. His early childhood . . . he could barely remember anything about it. Later, as an adolescent, he'd simply taken things as they'd come, the good with the bad, no questions asked. But now . . . he was cut off, awkward and posturing, a *self* in a world of strangers. And what lay ahead? A meaningless struggle ending with a meaningless death. How could anyone take rules seriously? His parents, the brothers at school, the cool party-boys and the horny youth-group kids . . . how could they act like they knew the answers?

Conrad tripped on a crack in the sidewalk just then. Something strange happened as he fell. Some special part of his brain cut in, and instead of falling, he . . . hung there, tilted forward, in defiance of natural law.

The instant the miracle dawned on Conrad, it was over. He fell the rest of the way forward and landed heavily on the cracked cement. For a full minute, he lay there, trying to bring back the state of mind that had let him float. He'd had the feeling before . . . on New Year's Day in the pasture with Hank. And he often flew in dreams. But now the feeling was gone, and Conrad didn't know how to bring it back. Maybe he'd just made the whole thing up. Maybe he was going nuts.

He got to his feet and walked around the corner. There was a lit-up supermarket. He drifted in. Muzak washed up and down the empty aisles; the fluorescent lights oozed their jerky glow. *Someday I'll be buying food for my children*, thought Conrad; *someday I'll be dead*. He found a package of bologna and a small bunch of bananas. *This car trip will never end; I'll be in high school for the rest of my life.*

"He had the strangest supper I've ever seen," Conrad could hear Jeannie telling his father next morning. "He just bought lunchmeat and ate it out in the street."

Dee Decca sat next to Conrad at breakfast. She was impressed by Conrad's bid for freedom. "Where are you going to college next year?" she asked him.

"I don't know yet," said Conrad. This Dee Decca had short dark hair and a reasonably pretty face, though there was something odd-looking about her body. "Harvard already turned me down and I haven't heard from Swarthmore. Georgetown is my ace in the hole. They're dying to have me because I go to a Catholic high school."

He paused to light one of Dee's cigarettes. "I sort of wish they'd all turn me down. Then I could go off and bum around."

"I want to go to San Jose State in California," said Dee. "I want to join a big sorority and go to a lot of parties. I missed the boat in high school."

"A frat house with an ever-present keg of beer," mused Conrad. "Surfing. That sounds cool."

"Listen up now," yelled leather-lunged Jeannie. "It's time to divide into our discussion groups. We're going to share our feelings about the liturgy."

"What's that mean?" whispered Dee. She had a husky, sophisticated voice.

"Let's sneak off," answered Conrad. "I'll meet you outside by the pavilion."

The Kentucky State Episcopal Conference Center was a collection of buildings something like a summer camp. Two groups of cabins, a dining hall, an administration building, and a large outdoor pavilion. The buildings were perched at the top of a long empty hill that bulged down to a forlorn brown river. It was almost spring. The ground was wet but not muddy. The pale sun was like a chalk mark on the cloudy sky.

Conrad took Dee's hand; she let him. They walked downhill, lacing their fingers. Her face was creamy white, with two brown moles. Her mouth had an interesting double-bowed curve to it.

"Question," Dee said after a while, saying it as if she were in a college seminar.

"Yes?"

"Where are we going?"

"To make out?" As Conrad said this, he released Dee's hand and put his arm around her waist. They were over the brow of the hill now, and the buildings were nowhere in sight.

"I hope you don't have W-H-D."

"What's that?"

"Wandering Hands Disease."

"Oh. That's . . ." *too stupid of you to even talk about*, Conrad wanted to say. On the other hand, it could be a come-on, couldn't it, that she would bring up *petting* right off the bat? He steered them into a grove of trees and slid his hand up from her waist and toward her bra strap.

"Stop that, Conrad." She planted her feet and turned up her face. He kissed her. She pushed her tongue in his mouth. She tasted like tobacco. He pushed his tongue back. Her mouth was cool inside. The taste of her spit. Her smell.

They were hugging, hugging and French kissing, not wanting to stop, afraid they wouldn't know how to start again.

"*CONRAD!!!*" The voice was rough and distant.

"Don't worry, Dee, that's just my father. They won't come all the way down here. They'll give up in a minute."

They kissed some more. Conrad didn't bother trying for her tits again. This was plenty.

As Conrad had predicted, the grown-ups gave up on them. He and Dee made their way down to the river and walked along the bank. Apparently the river flooded frequently, for the shore was littered with sticks. There were big sycamore trees. In one spot the river had eaten a great dirt cave into the hillside. Conrad and Dee sat on a rock in there and talked.

"Did you have a happy childhood, Conrad?"

"I guess so. I can hardly remember anything about it. My mother used to give me hay-fever pills. The first thing I remember really clearly is my tenth birthday. It was the day my family moved to Louisville. My brother and I saw a flying wing."

"A *what*?"

"A plane that was just a wing. Anyway, I was happy for a while, but recently . . . It's like you said before. *I missed the boat in high school.* I'm not cool, and I don't know what anything means. I'll be glad to go off to college. Everything here seems so stupid and unreal."

"I'm not unreal." Dee gave Conrad a little nudge. "And not everyone is stupid." She paused, then glanced over. "I'm quite intelligent, you know."

"Well, fine. I used to date a girl who couldn't understand anything. Have you heard of existentialism?"

"Yes. Existence precedes essence. You are what you do."

"That's good," exclaimed Conrad, a little surprised. He'd never heard it summed up so simply. "And nothingness is behind everything."

"I wrote a term paper on existentialism."

"Did you read *Nausea*?"

"Yes. You have too?"

"It's my favorite. The part where he's in a park looking at the roots of a chestnut tree, and the *persistence of matter* begins to disgust him . . . ugh!" Conrad looked at a nearby tree, trying to summon up Roquentin's nausea.

"This river," said Dee slowly, "it's been here for hundreds of years. It'll be here for hundreds more."

"We could live in this cave," observed Conrad. "Build fires and catch fish."

"Not in the winter."

"Do you believe in God, Dee?"

"Don't you?"

"I . . . I don't think so. Not really. Not like in church, anyway. Maybe the universe is God?"

"That's called pantheism. Everything fits together into a whole, and that Whole is God."

"That's like my own theory." Conrad explained about death and the life-force.

"Are you always so deep, Conrad?" She was smiling into his eyes. He'd caught her fancy.

"I . . . I think I'm different from other people. I think maybe I can . . ."

"Can what?"

"I think I might be able to levitate. You know? Fly."

"Let's see."

Conrad strained, and rose up maybe an inch from the rock they were sitting on. But he fell back right away, and then it wouldn't work at all.

"You just stood up a little," laughed Dee. "You're wild, Conrad." She paused and gave him a pert look. "You know what I thought you were going to say at first? When you said you're different from other people?"

"What?"

Dee's voice grew flat with tension. "I thought you were going to tell me that you . . . *masturbate*."

"Uh . . . well, I do, as a matter of fact."

"So do I. Most girls do."

"You do?"

"I do it every night."

This was incredible. "So do I, nearly. We call it 'beating off.' I found out about it when I was twelve. I'd be lying in bed, and for some reason I'd start thinking about naked women with big breasts. A whole stream of them—each woman would march into my room, smile, and march out. One after the other. And my bee would get real hard and I'd rub it."

"Your what?"

"We called it a bee. What did your family call your . . . your . . ."

"We called it the cushy. I used to rub my cushy way before I was twelve. I did it even when I was real little. I used to think of it as 'my bestest spot.'" They both giggled wildly.

This was just incredible. Conrad grabbed Dee and pushed his tongue deep into her mouth. He took one of her hands and pressed it in his crotch to feel his boner. She drew her hand back, but she kept kissing him. They kissed for so long that Conrad came in his pants. Dee noticed the stain.

"Is that what I think it is?"

"I like you, Dee. All trillion of my sperms like you."

They joined the others for lunch. For the whole lunch, Conrad was on a cloud. Dee knew he had a dick, and she'd seen him come. Maybe he wasn't going to have to wait for nuclear war after all.

When Conrad got back to Louisville and told Hank about his new girl, Hank made fun of him.

"Decca? That phony? And you didn't even get tit off her?"

"Look, Hank, I made out with her for a long time. I even came in my pants. And she's read *Nausea*."

"Bo-way. I heard the cops caught her naked with Billy Ballhouse in a car last fall."

"Oh, shut up. Do you know what pantheism is?"

"Sure. It's a bunch of dumb shits kneeling in front of a rock." Hank began laughing uncontrollably, and offering *salaams* to his radio. "O voice from sky, please speak me heap truth."

Conrad waited for his friend's laughter to die down. "What if I told you I could fly, Hank?"

"Is this one of your *Twilight Zone* stories? Remember the one you made up about coming from a flying saucer?" Hank's mood of mockery had passed. "I'm all ears, Conrad. For my money, you're a fucking genius."

"It only lasted a second. It was on the way down to the conference center—we all stopped for food, and I was walking to the supermarket. I tripped on the sidewalk, and instead of falling, I just hung there. Maybe I'm some kind of mutant, Hank."

"Did you tell Decca?"

"I mentioned it. She was excited, but she didn't believe me."

"That's just as well. You know, if you really did turn out to have any superpowers, Conrad, it wouldn't be a good idea to tell everyone. People hate mutants." Hank was laughing again. "Gunjy mue."

saturday, may 4, 1963

B latz beer, I don't believe it. I thought that was only a
kind of beer in comic books." Conrad threw back his
head and laughed. God, he felt wonderful. Drunk on the
first Saturday in May.

"We've got Falstaff, too," said Jim Ardmore with his dark
sly smirk. "Not to mention Mr. Leggett's liquor cabinet."

"You all stay out of the liquor," cautioned Donny Leggett. "Somebody stole a bottle of peppermint schnapps
last week, and my father was really . . ."

"That was Bunger on a rampage," chortled Ardmore.
"He came up here with his friend Hank Larsen and stole
a bottle from your house. It's the gospel truth. The good
word."

Conrad shrugged and opened his beer. It didn't matter.
Nothing mattered. It was Derby Day, and all the grown-
ups were at the track. Conrad and a bunch of Chevalier
guys were getting drunk together at Donny Leggett's
house, a hilltop estate with a swimming pool.

"This is only my third beer," said Conrad. "And I already
feel plowed. You know where I feel it first?"

"In the backs of your *thighs*," groaned Ardmore. "You've told me that a dozen times, you wretched sot."

"When I know I'm going to have a chance to get drunk, I get all twitchy, like a junkie, and then after the first drink, I'm so relaxed." Conrad grinned. "This is great. I'm going swimming." He chugged the rest of his beer, stripped down to his underwear, and dove into the Leggetts' pool.

Some of the cooler Chevalier boys were there, too. Billy Ballhouse, Worth Wadsworth, and Custer Buckingham. They didn't like the way Conrad was acting. It was ungentlemanly.

When Conrad lurched out of the pool and began trying to open his fourth Blatz, Ballhouse spoke up.

"Take it easy, Bunger. You've got all afternoon."

"You want money for beer, Ballhouse? Maybe you should make a run. Where's the beer opener?"

"I mean, Donny's parents live here, Bunger. You can't just throw up all over the place and act like a wino."

"Eat shit, Billy. You're a goddamn candy-ass. You don't know about death." Conrad walked over to where Ardmore and Leggett were sitting. He remembered having seen the beer opener there.

He put all his attention into getting two triangles punched into the top of his beer can. But then someone was shoving him. Ballhouse.

"You can't talk to me that way, Bunger. Apologize."

"Sure, Billy. I'm sorry you're a dipshit."

Ardmore howled with delight, and Leggett burst into giggles. Ballhouse shook his head and gave up.

"Come on," he called to Wadsworth and Buckingham. "Let's go pick up some stuff."

"Would you get me a half-pint?" put in Conrad.

"I'm sorry, Conrad." The contempt on Ballhouse's face was profound. "Girls don't come in half-pints." Pause. "I'm surprised Dee would have anything to do with a drunk like you."

There was a whole fridge of beer, and the three remaining boys spent the rest of the afternoon working on it. At some point the Derby was on TV. Watching it, Conrad realized he was seeing double. It was time to leave. He and Ardmore decided to go to Sue Pohlboggen's house.

"Can you drive?" asked Ardmore.

"Sure, Jim. I used to race these things in South Korea." Conrad revved the VW's engine to a chattering scream.

There was a long gravel driveway leading downhill from the Leggetts' house to River Road. It felt like a crunchy sliding board. So that he wouldn't have to use the brakes, Conrad began slaloming, swooping back and forth from left to right, faster and . . . suddenly everything was wrong. The steering wheel jerked like a living thing, the wheels locked sideways, Ardmore was yelling and—

WHAM!

A sound that Conrad felt, rather than heard, a sound and a brief moment of frenzied motion. His power. Jerkstop to blank. Black. The horn was blowing. The horn was stuck. He was in a barbed-wire fence and the car was wrapped around a black locust tree and Jim was lying still.

"Hey, Jim," Conrad screamed. The horn wouldn't stop. The bleat of that stuck horn was driving him nuts. "Jim, wake up!"

"Don't get hysterical, Conrad." Ardmore sat up and looked around. He hadn't been thrown as far as Conrad had. "Let's tear out the wires to the horn."

They did that, and things got a little better. Some time passed. Conrad's parents came, and they took him home. So that he wouldn't have to face them, he went to bed early, but it took him a long time to go to sleep. It was the black space that bothered him the most, the black space when he'd been unconscious.

If I had died, thought Conrad, *it would have been just like that . . . except I wouldn't have woken up.* Dead black nothing with no time left.

He flinched away from that and began struggling to reconstruct the details of the accident, trying to fit it into some rational frame.

The tree had been on the right side of the road. The VW's left front fender had hit the tree. Momentum made the car slew to the left, and Conrad had been thrown out of his door. He'd flown past the tree and landed in that barbed-wire fence.

The funny thing was that the tree had been blocking the path from the car to where Conrad had landed. By all rights, Conrad should have sailed into the tree and broken his neck. He struggled to remember the details. How had he managed to miss the tree? The power. Somehow he had *levitated his way around it.* Yes.

Just as he was dropping off to sleep, Conrad realized he was floating above the mattress again. He flash-jerked, and jolted back down. All night he dreamed about the flame-people.

"You should thank God you're alive," his mother told him the next morning on their way to church.

"I don't think God has anything to do with it," said Conrad, trying to keep a quaver out of his voice. "I made *sure* to stay alive. Like a cat landing on its feet. I think maybe I have psychic powers, Mom. What does God have to do with it?"

"Plenty. God is everything, Conrad. God takes care of us in different ways. You should stop imagining that you're so great, and thank Him for saving your life."

"If He's so wonderful, then He doesn't need my thanks, does He?"

"No, God doesn't need your thanks. Praying is something you do for your own self."

"But what good is praying? There's no afterlife. I saw yesterday. When I hit that fence, everything just got black. It wasn't like dreaming or like being asleep. It was just black nothing. I think that must be what happens when you die, no matter what. *Nothing*. You don't believe in heaven and hell, do you, Mom?"

"I think heaven and hell are right here in our own lives. And that's enough. What happens after you die doesn't matter."

Conrad was surprised that his mother had such definite opinions about these questions. But why did she bother going to church if there was no afterlife? *Praying is something you do for your own self.*

Conrad's father took him for a walk after lunch.

"I'm sorry about the car, Pop. It's practically totaled."

"I don't care about the *car*, Conrad. I care about *you*."

When the Bungers had moved to Louisville, Conrad's father had started calling him *Sausage*. "Where's my Sausage?" he might shout when he came home from work. That first Louisville summer had been hot, and old Caldwell had bought Conrad a giant wading pool. On Saturday, the two of them would soak in it, Conrad with the hose, and Pop with a long-necked bottle of Oertl's beer. The old man's amazing bulk took up most of the pool, but happy Conrad would splash in the empty spaces, yelling whatever popped into his head.

"I don't care if you don't go to church, Conrad," his father was saying now. "You're free to rebel and think whatever you want to. But *don't get yourself killed.* If you're too drunk to drive, then phone me up."

"You'd get mad at me."

"Conrad, I was a teenager, too. I got drunk and made trouble. But my father always told me, *The main thing is don't get killed.* Call a cab if you have to."

"Did you ever call a cab?"

"Once or twice. There was one morning when I woke up and I didn't know where the car was. My father was waiting for me at the breakfast table. He was the kindest man, Conrad; I wish you could have met him. That morning he just looked up at me and said, 'Well, son, let's go find the car. What's the last thing you remember?'" Mr. Bunger's distant gaze wandered back to Conrad. "Don't do this again, Conrad. Don't get killed. All my and Mom's relatives are dead. It would destroy us to lose you."

"OK, Pop. It might not look that way, but even yesterday, I was careful not to get killed." Conrad wondered if he should try to explain about his power ... oh, why bother, it would only sound like crazy bragging. "You really don't care if I don't believe in religion?"

"You wouldn't be much of a person if you believed everything that grown-ups tell you, Conrad. It's natural to rebel. But you've also got to learn to control yourself, instead of wrecking cars, and spouting this silly stuff that you wish the Russians would blow us up. You can't just tear down. If you're going to rebel, it's up to you to find something better than what the grown-ups have."

"I guess that makes sense," said Conrad. This was not the time to say what he really thought, to say that nothing made sense at all and that it would be better for everyone to admit it. This was not the time to push his father any further. "I guess I should be grounded for wrecking the car?"

"Three weekends."

"Counting this one?"

friday, july 5, 1963

"You do know who Bo Diddley is, don't you, Dee?"
They were in Conrad's mother's car—repaired to the
tune of $700—and on their way to a holiday-weekend
rock and roll show at the State Fairgrounds.

"He had that hit on the radio. *Hey, Bo Diddley.*"

"And the new one. *You Can't Judge a Book by Lookin' at
Its Cover.* He's the best. He even builds his own guitars.
You know I have four Bo Diddley albums at home, Dee?"

"That many! Tell me about the deeper meanings of Bo
Diddley, Conrad." Dee looked pretty good tonight. She
wore a thin white cardigan, and a print dress with a Vil-
lager collar. Usually she wore sweatshirts.

"Well, my favorite song of his is called *Crackin' Up.* It
goes like this."

Conrad proceeded to sing the first few lines of the song,
capturing the sense, if not the exact sound of Bo Diddley.

He sang it loud, with just the right number of *dit-duh-
duh-dit-duuh-dit-dit-dits*, his voice rising to a hoarse shout
on the last line "You crackin' up."

"What's *buggin'* you?" said Dee repeating the line from

the song. "I should play that for my parents." Dee's father was a career engineer for GE. He and his family were due to be transferred out to California in only one month. Conrad's family was moving at the end of the summer. It was all ending fast.

"I first got that record when I was fourteen," said Conrad. "I remember listening to it one day; it was the day that I really got the idea of rock and roll. I was alone at home, and I put on *Crackin' Up* real loud, and I went and stood in front of my parents' full-length mirror and danced a little, singing along, you know. As I watched myself, I realized that someday I'd be cool."

"Are you cool yet?"

"I thought people might think I was cool after I wrecked the car. But no one outside my parents cared, not even Ardmore. And my parents didn't exactly think it was cool."

"How about your friends at St. X?"

"Oh, them. Thank God graduation is over."

"Sue Pohlboggen told me you took her to the senior prom. She said it was awful."

"She said that?" Conrad paused, remembering the prom. Normally he never socialized with the St. X boys. It had been strange to see them all at a dance, probably with girls they were going to marry and not use rubbers with. A mixture of hope and cynicism had led Conrad to bring Sue Pohlboggen instead of Dee. Sue was supposed to be easy. "Are you good friends with her?"

"She was in my humanities class. She's smart, you know. Did you make out with her?"

"Well, I . . ." Conrad broke off, unable to tell the story. On the way from the prom to the St. X breakfast, he'd parked with Sue Pohlboggen. She'd put up a struggle, but he'd gotten his hand down naked in her crotch. The problem was that she was wearing such a tight girdle that his hand had gone numb before he could figure out where her cunt actually was. He'd given up on that, and dry-humped her for a while, which was OK until the end, when her body started making strange, wet *lowing* noises. Noises from her cunt, like it was farting! Ugh! Was this how grown-up sex worked? And then at the prom breakfast he'd thrown up after about three beers.

"The thing about Bo Diddley is *communion*," said Conrad presently. "You can lose yourself in the music, you can be Bo Diddley, instead of all lonely and cut off. I like Flatt and Scruggs, too. Anything but Muzak."

"Inauthentic," Dee agreed and lit a cigarette. "Who else is going to play tonight? Besides Bo Diddley."

"Lots of people. The Shirelles, James Brown, Avalon . . . or maybe it's Fabian, and I think U.S. Bonds is coming, too. It'll be great."

The stage was in the middle of the big arena-auditorium at the Kentucky State Fairgrounds. When he was ten, Conrad had come here to see the Shrine Circus. Today they had a lot of flags up, since it was the day after the Fourth of July.

Some people had reserved seats down on the coliseum floor, but everyone else was up in the bleachers. It was a very mixed crowd. There was a middle-aged black guy with baggy pants right behind Dee and Conrad, and when the Shirelles came out, he danced so hard that you could hear his dick slapping his leg. Some lesser-known black groups played next, and then some white singers came on. One of them was Dee Clark.

"Same name as you," observed Conrad.

"Let's go over there in the empty part of the bleachers," said Dee. "I want to really listen."

The song was *It Must Be Raindrops*. Over in the empty seats, Dee and Conrad got into a kind of follow-the-leader game, balancing along on the seatbacks, childlike and free. The wonderful music spread out to fill all space and time, music for Conrad and Dee alone, centered in the eternal Now. Conrad felt like he could fly Dee to the top of the coliseum, if he wanted to. Fly up to the top where the flashing circus acrobats had whirled, years ago.

Suddenly, finally, Bo Diddley and his band were out on the stage, red sequined tuxes and all. Conrad dragged Dee back to their seats. Diddley struck up a steady chicken-scratch on his git-box and began trading insults with his drummer.

"Hey."

"What dat."

"I heard yo' daddy's a lightbu'b eater."

"He don't eat no lightbulb."

"Sho' 'nuff."

"Whaah?"

"I heard every time he turn off the light, he *eat a little piece!*"

Conrad howled, and the man behind them stood up and slapped his dick against his leg again. Dee began looking around to see if anyone else from her class was here.

"Isn't that Francie Shields down there?"

"Shhh."

Now the band was blasting an old tune called *'Deed and 'Deed and 'Deed I Do*, with the incredible Diddley sex-beat, and over it, the soaring alienation of Bo's strange, homemade guitar. Bo Diddley, the man, right there, in the flesh, black as they come, sweating and screaming—for a few minutes, Conrad forgot himself entirely.

Bo Diddley was the last act before intermission, and Conrad hurried down behind the stage to get a closer look at his hero. Incredibly, Bo Diddley was right there, standing around talking to some black women. He was shorter than he looked on the stage, and uglier.

"Are you Bo Diddley?" blurted Conrad, pushing his way forward.

"Yeah. I'll do autographs after the show."

"Can I shake your hand?"

"All right."

They shook briefly. It was incredible, to be touching the actual meat-body, the actual living person that made the music Conrad loved so well. During the moment he touched Diddley, everything seemed to make sense. And then the moment was over, as usual, every moment over, over and over again. Conrad mumbled his thanks and wandered off, a bit dazed, looking for Dee.

He found her with Francie Shields and Hank Larsen. Conrad had known Hank was coming but had decided not to double-date, since Hank and Dee didn't like each other, although right now, Dee was *glad* to see Hank. It seemed like he was the only other white boy here who wasn't a tough yokel soldier from Fort Knox. Hank, for his part, was drunk.

"Turd-rad," he called genially. "How is your wretched ass?"

"Cool it, Hank. I just shook hands with Bo Diddley. What are you doing for our generation?"

"Feeling pretty good," said Hank. "Around the edges. You want a belt, Conrad? Let me see that hand."

Conrad had meant not to drink tonight, but he heard himself asking Hank, "Where's the bottle?"

"Francie's purse."

Hank and Francie and Dee had all gone to the regular public high school together. Hank had been voted most handsome, and Francie had starred in the senior play. She was a bit overweight, but pretty in a straight-mouth-straight-nose-straight-hair way. Her voice was a lovely, purring lisp.

"Conwad. Do you like it heyuw?"

"It's communion," answered Conrad. "You know? We're all people, and Bo Diddley's a person, too. Let's go over in those dark bleachers and have a drink."

"Well, Conwad, I just saw Sue Pohlboggen and Jackie Pweston. Dee and I can wait with them." Francie liked to stir up trouble. It seemed like everyone in town knew about Conrad's gross prom date with Sue.

Hank took a half-full pint of gin out of Francie's purse and stuck it under his untucked shirt. "Let's roll, Paunch."

"I'll come with you," said Dee. "I'll get drunk, too."

"Fine," said Conrad. "It's existential."

They went halfway up the dark bleachers behind the stage and passed the bottle around. For some reason, Conrad was feeling a little desperate. He sucked hard at the bottle, forcing down four or five big slugs in a row. As always, the hot poison set his face-holes to running—he leaned over a railing and retched some spit. Dee took a few sips, Hank some more, and then Conrad finished the bottle.

"Listen," he told Dee, as they started back down to the main floor. "The incredible thing is that I'm not drunk yet, but by the time I get down there, I will be. Can you feel it, too? With each step . . ." He paused to retch again, and Hank started talking. He was all worked up.

"Bo Diddley is right here, and all these crazy blacks are having a good time. Jesus! The sixties have begun! Why should we be all white at college and *learn stuff* to be faceless Joe bureaucrat with kids like us? I want this summer to last forever! Are you on the Larsen bandwagon, folks?" Hank trumpeted briefly with his lips. "I want to be black, I want to go hood!" Just then he tripped and fell down the last few steps.

"Do you feel it yet?" Conrad asked Dee. Everything was hot and roaring. Another band had started up.

"Yes," said Dee. "I do."

They stood there for a few minutes, leaning on a railing, Conrad staring upward, mouth open, staring up at the spot high overhead where he'd once seen the acrobats, the spot where, in his dreams, the flame-people always flexed and flickered, *showing* Conrad, telling him what he'd need to know during his long mission, *know to forget*, in search of the Secret, the Answer to a Question unnamed, the Question whose annihilation is, in some measure, the Answer, for a time at least, though, no matter what, the Question always returns, making a mockery of yesterday's Answer, but just here and now, at the Kentucky State Fairgrounds, July 5, 1963, wiped-out, drooling, and staring, Conrad has it, Conrad knows . . .

SEVEN

wednesday, september 11, 1963

Zzt-bing-boinggg. "And now the WAKY weather report, September 11, 1963. Carol?" Rrrrwwaaafzz. "Thank you, Chuck. We're expecting more of the same today, with late-evening thundershowers and possible—"

Conrad turned off the clock-radio and sat up. It was barely light out. Five A.M. No time to lose. He got dressed and took the cream pie off the kitchen counter. It had defrosted nicely overnight. Hank was leaving today. High school was all over.

Hank was out in his backyard, by his ham-radio antenna, waiting for Conrad. He had his pie ready, too. The idea had been that instead of saying goodbye, they'd push pies into each other's faces. But now, at five in the morning, they just stood there, the two of them, holding their sad, flat frozen pies.

"Have fun at Columbia, Hank. Look out for the dipshits."

"You think you'll make it down here at Christmas?"

"I hope so." Conrad's parents were about to move to northern Virginia. Moving and college, this was really the end. "It's been great, Hank, all these years."

"Right." Hank's face was stiff and tight, the way it always got when he was upset. "Goodbye, Conrad buddy. I'll never forget any of it."

Conrad took his pie home and threw it in the garbage. It was all over. He'd always known the end was coming, but now it was here. Dee gone, Hank gone, his family about to move, and four years of hard college work coming up— hard work to be followed by marriage and a real job. No slack, no slack in sight. If only he could learn to control his powers of levitation. The only time he was really sure he'd flown was the time he'd wrecked his mother's car.

Just yesterday, he and Hank had had a last talk about it. Hank was half-inclined to believe his old friend's claims— the problem was why Conrad was not, in fact, able to give a demonstration. "Maybe it's a kind of vestigial survival mechanism," Hank had suggested, drawing on their common store of science-fiction wisdom. "Maybe, in ancient times, some races could fly, but it was eventually bred out. Say that the flying-genes happened to crop up again for you, Conrad, but you can only be sure of flying when it's a matter of life and death. We could test it by going downtown and having you jump off the Heyburn Building!"

Instead of that, they'd settled for having Conrad jump out of a tree, but the catch was that unless there was a real chance of dying, then the power wouldn't necessarily cut in . . . and Conrad wasn't willing to take a real chance at dying. After a while they'd given up on the project and gone to a movie instead.

And now it was over, and Hank was gone, and Conrad's parents were moving, and he had to go college, and . . .

He went back to bed and slept till his mother woke him by coming in and shaking his foot.

"Get up, lazybones. It's twelve o'clock!"

"Aw, Mom . . ."

"You have to help get ready for the movers. Your closet is a *rats' nest*." Conrad's mother always used idioms like "rats' nest" with a special gusto. She thought language was funny, especially English. She'd grown up in Germany.

"I don't want to get up. I don't want to do anything."

"Poor Conrad. Aren't you glad to be going to Swarthmore next week?"

"I'm scared."

"Eat something and you'll feel better." Another shake of his foot. "And then I want you to go through your junk and decide what to keep. I have a cardboard box for you."

After some milk and a bologna sandwich, Conrad got to work sorting his stuff: the shell collection, the butterfly collection, the fossil collection—all worthless garbage now—the school papers (going back to sixth grade), his recent poems, the letters from girls (Linda, Dee, and even Sue Pohlboggen), the model rockets, the photographs, the Gilbert chemistry set, the Electroman electricity set, the Brainiac computer set, the Walt Disney comics, the old schoolbooks with their enigmatic graffiti, the lenses and knives and coins and combs and pencils and matchbooks and pieces of wax. Too much. He drifted down to the basement to paunch out.

His big brother Caldwell's room was down here. Caldwell had been off in the army since last summer. He'd gotten kicked out of college after freshman year, and Big

Caldwell had made him join the army. He was stationed in Germany.

Caldwell's empty basement pad was a pleasant place on a hot day. He had interesting college books, and a full two years' run of the *Evergreen Review*. Conrad picked up an issue and turned to a sex-poem he remembered seeing: two lovers sleeping, with spit-out watermelon seeds on the floor, and *"the mixed fluids slowly drying on their skin."* The mixed fluids. Conrad jacked off on that, and then started going through Caldwell's desk.

In the bottom drawer, he found a flat wood case with two little dueling pistols. He'd seen them before, but he'd forgotten about them. Caldwell had traded one of his drunk college friends a record player for the guns.

Conrad took out one of the little pistols and looked it over. It was a one-shot .22 caliber derringer, with a fat, short barrel, and a nicely rounded little wooden stock. There were bullets in the case as well. On an impulse, Conrad pocketed the pistol and a bunch of bullets. *In case anyone gives me a hard time.*

He had a date that night, with an eleventh-grader called Taffy Sinclair. They'd met about a week after Dee left town and had been going out ever since. Taffy's father was a psychiatrist. He didn't like Conrad.

On the way to pick up Taffy, Conrad stopped by Tad's Liquor Store and got a half-pint of gin. If Tad was in the right mood, he'd sell to anyone. Gordon's gin, with that red boar's head on the yellow label.

It was still a little early to pick up Taffy. Conrad took a back road down to the river, to play with Caldwell's pistol.

You had to load it one bullet at a time. Conrad fired it out over the water, missed seeing the bullet splash, and tried again. *There*, right out in the middle, halfway to Indiana. He reloaded and shot a tree trunk from point-blank range. The little bullet bored right in.

Imagine shooting yourself, Conrad thought. He took out the empty cartridge, made double-sure the gun was empty, and put it to his head. *What if I were going to kill myself right now?* He psyched himself up into half believing it and pulled the trigger.

Click.

The dry little sound made Conrad shudder. I *don't want that. I may be miserable, but at least I'm alive.* But with the click had come a sudden feeling like a muscle unclenching at the center of his brain. *He could fly.* He'd tricked his survival mechanism! Right now, for the first time, he was going to be able to fly as well as he wanted!

Conrad pocketed Caldwell's gun and angled out over the river. Twenty feet, thirty . . . He was out over the real current now, looking back at his VW on shore. Somehow it felt very natural.

But then, all at once, the power was gone. Conrad plummeted into the brown Ohio. It took a few minutes of real struggle to get back to shore. Good thing he hadn't flown up higher—though if he'd been higher, then maybe the power wouldn't have dared to cut off.

Fortunately, Conrad's mother had left a load of clothes for the cleaners in the backseat. Conrad got into a dry outfit and sat there thinking. *Why me? What makes me so special?*

He wondered if he should open up the gin. Better not yet. Mr. Sinclair would meet him at Taffy's door and try to smell his breath. A few weeks ago, Conrad had made the mistake of trying to talk to Mr. Sinclair when he was drunk. "Everything's meaningless," Conrad had slobbered. "God is dead." The line usually went over great with girls, but Mr. Sinclair took it too seriously. "You're suffering from extreme depression, Conrad." Conrad was lucky that Taffy was still allowed to go out with him.

Tonight they were going downtown to see *To Kill a Mockingbird*. Taffy looked great, tan and blonde in a spaghetti-strap blue dress. She had a solid little figure and pink bubblegum lips. She liked to talk about her horse, Tabor. Thinking about his plunge into the river, Conrad hardly knew what he was saying.

"Do you ever get hot, Taffy, bouncing on that horse?"

"Oh, Conrad."

There was a weird preacher outside the movie theater. A pale, wild-eyed Negro with big freckles splotched on his papery skin. He had some red-and-yellow signboards about the end of the world, and he was passing out gospel tracts. Conrad stood in front of him for a minute, soaking it up, and thinking, *I can fly*.

"You *be* lookin' for meaning and the words fall away! The *Son* don't come in time till time run *out*. These *are* the last times, my friend."

Conrad took a tract and let Taffy drag him into the theater. He'd brought along his unopened half-pint of Gordon's. Once he'd gotten popcorn and settled down with Taffy, he excused himself to go to the bathroom. *I can fly*.

He sat down in a stall and sucked down a third of the bottle. Just like at the Bo Diddley concert. The buzzing started. He drew the wild man's tract out of his pocket and studied it. It was dull bullshit—a straight pitch for getting saved by Jesus—with none of the weird resonances that the actual preacher had. Conrad took another slug and squinted to see who'd printed the pamphlet. "Gospel Tract Society, Shoals, Indiana." No good.

After the movie, Conrad stopped to talk to the preacher. "What do you mean, 'the words fall away'? How do you make it happen?"

"You hide it to find it," said the man, smiling. He was glad to answer questions. That's what he was here for.

"Conrad, come *on*," urged Taffy. This evening wasn't working out properly.

"How can you hand out crap lies like this?" demanded Conrad, gesturing at the tracts. "Who pays you?"

"I tell you," said the preacher, putting his hand on Conrad's shoulder and drawing him close. "The world take care of the world. And *you* a fallen angel."

All at once, Conrad felt dizzy from the red-and-yellow Gordon's and the preacher's red-and-yellow signs. His head was roaring and it was as if everything were bathed in flames. Flame-people. Flying wing.

In the car, Taffy was really angry. "Just take me home, Conrad. I don't want to go to our make-out spot tonight. You can kiss me in the driveway."

"Thank you, Taffy. I'm sorry I'm acting crazy. I love you. I can fly."

"You can what?"

"Fly. On the way to pick you up, I flew out over the Ohio River. I think maybe I'm not human."

"My father's right, Conrad. You really are crazy." Her voice was cold as ice.

On the drive back to his house from Taffy's, Conrad opened all the windows, hoping the air would wash the gin fumes away. The bottle was on the seat next to him, not quite empty. He felt really strange.

Just then a car full of hoods pulled around him as if to pass. Little greasers, all worked up. Instead of passing, they locked speed and began yelling curses and giving him the finger. Two cars speeding along side by side, the kids on the left yelling at Conrad.

With one swift gesture, Conrad snatched up his bottle and flung it into the other car's windshield. There was a lot of noise. He stepped on the gas and sped the rest of the way home. The hoods were behind him, he could see their lights following him.

Conrad zipped up the Bungers' long dark driveway, loaded the little derringer, and went partway back up the driveway on foot. The other kids had stopped at the end, scared of an ambush. They were yelling things. It was too dark to see. Conrad leveled the pistol at the sound and paused.

He was just drunk enough to consider shooting. *That* would show them. And if the cops came—well, he could just fly away and . . .

As Conrad deliberated, the whole dark world began to flame and shudder. A voice was running in his head, a memory tape. *If you misuse your powers, you will discorporate*, said the voice. *Remember why you are here!*

Slowly he lowered the gun to his side. The car full of hoods was driving off.

"Why I'm here," murmured Conrad. "To find the secret of life."

He unloaded the gun and went to bed. It was time to go to college.

part two

That's living. But everything changes when you tell about life; it's a change no one notices: The proof is that people talk about true stories. As if there could possibly be true stories; things happen one way and we tell about them in the opposite sense.

—Jean-Paul Sartre, *Nausea*

part two

tuesday, october 1, 1963

F or one thing," said the political science teacher, "I'm sure that all of us here agree on the basics. We're all liberal Democrats. Is there anyone here who isn't?"

Conrad and the only other Southern boy raised their hands. The other boy had red hair and came from Mississippi. The teacher called on him first.

"Liberalism has just about ruined America," the red-haired boy drawled. "The conservative philosophy is not only for fools and bigots. It represents the only truly progressive response to the realities of the late twentieth century."

The other students tittered, and the teacher smiled. He was extremely tall and skinny. He wore a tweed jacket and a hand-tied bow tie. "Very well, Pound. And what about you, Bunger?"

This was the first time that Conrad had spoken up in any of his college classes. His heart was beating so hard he could hardly speak. He wanted the teacher to like him.

"Well, I believe in anarchy, Mr. Bonner. Isn't that really the best system? I mean, politics is always so dirty.

Wouldn't we be better off if everyone in Congress was shot, so they'd leave people alone?"

There was a silence. Professor Bonner frowned. A prim-faced boy in a work-shirt turned to glare at Conrad and then raised his hand.

"Yes, Pennington?"

"Anarchy is the *absence* of a political system, sir. There's no point in discussing it here."

"Very good."

Conrad's face burned. After class a very short, dark-skinned boy came over and spoke to him.

"Where are you from?"

"Louisville."

"In Kentucky?" The boy blinked and adjusted his glasses. "I'm from Long Island. Chuckie Golem. You going to have lunch?"

"Sure."

Over lunch, Golem told Conrad about his roommate, a wild character called Izzy Tuskman. The boys discussed the few girls whose names they knew. It turned out that Chuckie lived in the same dorm as Conrad.

"You want to play some Frisbee?" Chuckie asked as they ambled back from lunch. He seemed so kind and gentle.

"What's Frisbee?"

"It's a plastic flying saucer. You throw it back and forth."

"OK. Though I do have a lot of homework . . ."

"Just a half hour, it'll do us good."

It was a brilliant October day, hot as summer. Chuckie patiently demonstrated the Frisbee until Conrad was able to throw it a little.

"The Frisbee looks neat when it hovers against the sky," observed Conrad presently. "It'd be perfect for a UFO movie. Did you see *Earth versus the Flying Saucers*? It came out in 1957, the same year as Sputnik."

"I didn't go to those movies," said Chuckie. "I listened to folk-music instead. I guess they have a lot of UFO sightings in Kentucky?" The precise, hesitant way he said, "Kentucky," made it sound wild and unpredictable . . . if not actually crude and benighted.

"Waal, shore," said Conrad, putting on a hick accent. "There's a gentleman down the road from where we lived— old Cornelius Skelton—he always tells as how one night he seed a flying saucer make off with one of his hawgs. He fired on it, but twarnt no use. Only good come out of it was next day Cornelius found him a big mineral crystal spang where the space vehicle had landed! Still hot, it was. Mr. Skelton keeps that crystal on his mantel, for to show folks. I've seed and touched it myself, I have." The story was more-or-less true, but Chuckie didn't seem to understand that it was supposed to be funny as well. If anything, he looked a little sorry for Conrad. Conrad wished he hadn't told the story. The fact of the matter was that, for whatever reason, he thought of Mr. Skelton's crystal quite often.

They threw the Frisbee some more while Conrad tried to think of something else to talk about. "What's that around your neck?" he asked finally. Chuckie wore a kind of silver tube attached to a chain around his neck.

"It's a *mezuzah*." Chuckie laughed happily at Conrad's confusion. "A religious thing, against the Angel of Death. I'm Jewish."

"Oh, are you?" In his embarrassment, Conrad dropped the Frisbee. He'd never met any Jews before, though he'd heard his brother Caldwell talk about the ones *he'd* met at college. Caldwell said Jews were untrustworthy.

"You don't *look* Jewish," Conrad said politely.

"Are you kidding?" Chuckie gave his dry, humming laugh. "That reminds me of a joke. There's a guy on the train, right, and this old Jewish woman keeps coming up to him and asking, 'Are you Jewish?' 'I'm not Jewish,' the guy says, 'so leave me alone.' 'Are you sure?' says the woman. 'Are you sure you're not Jewish?' She keeps doing this for about an hour, right, so finally he gives up and says, 'All right, lady, I admit it, I'm Jewish!' Big pause, and then she says, 'Funny . . . you don't look Jewish.'"

"That's good," laughed Conrad. This sure was different from Louisville.

"There's a lot of Jewish jokes. Jewish humor. Have you read *Stern*? By Bruce Jay Friedman?"

No.

"I'll lend it to you. It's a panic."

Over the next week, Conrad came to realize that most of his new Swarthmore friends were Jewish. His roommate Ron Platek, and Cal Preminger across the hall, and most Jewish of all, Chuckie and his roommate Izzy Tuskman.

Tuskman and Golem had been wrestling stars at different Long Island high schools. This was one sport that Swarthmore competed seriously in, so the two had been recruited and billeted together in a one-person room. To make space for their desks, the college had installed bunk beds. Often, after supper, Conrad and Preminger would squeeze into

Tuskman and Golem's room to trade jokes and insults. They all liked to tease Conrad for not being Jewish.

"Hey, Conrad, you know what *schmuck* is?" This from Tuskman, a five-foot two-inch, thick-lipped elf who looked and talked like Chico Marx.

"Well, in German it means 'ornament.'"

"He even *speaks* Kraut," marveled Golem.

Conrad knew some German from listening to his mother's relatives. "Ornament," he repeated. "Like jewelry, you know?"

"Dat's poifect," exclaimed Tuskman. "*Ohnament.*" He doubled over in glee. His whole face squeezed into lumpy wrinkles. "Ohnament," he gasped. "Tell him, Chuckie."

Chuckie had a more scholarly demeanor than his roomie. "*Schmuck* in Yiddish means 'penis,'" he explained, adjusting his glasses for emphasis. "If you call a person a *schmuck*, it means you think he's a jerk."

Tuskman had fallen onto the floor now, and the kicking of his legs drove him around and around in a small circle. "Ohnament. Ohnament." Conrad felt a little put-upon. No one had ever called him a Kraut before. He wished he were Jewish, too.

"Come on, Conrad," said Izzy, still giggling on the floor. "Don't be an *ohnament.*"

It was fun having strange new friends, but it was just as much fun to go off and be alone whenever you liked. Conrad felt like he was really getting to know himself. He liked to walk down into the Crum woods, or sit with his books on some isolated corner of the great front-campus lawn. When his parents had brought him to Swarthmore on a tour-of-the-colleges last year, Conrad had been impressed at the sight of blue-jeaned students sitting on the lawn with books. And now that was him.

He didn't study too much out there; mostly he just looked at the clouds and trees, the birds and the squirrels. One day a squirrel got mad at him—he was leaning against its tree, and perhaps it wanted to come down—the squirrel got mad and began making noises at Conrad. Odd, chirr-chucking noises; it was a noise he'd heard in trees before, but he'd never realized that it was squirrels doing it. He threw sticks at the squirrel to keep its scolding going. The noise sounded almost like speech, and faint memories of some higher-energy language flitted across Conrad's mind.

Often, thinking or studying, he had the feeling of being close to some great realization. He'd forgotten something, something big, but always it escaped him. He felt closest to the big answer when, staring up at clouds, he forgot himself entirely. It was so sweet to be a creature living here on Earth.

Conrad didn't pay much attention to his roommate, Ron Platek, for the first few weeks. The guy was clearly a schmuck. Tall, uncoordinated, thick-lipped, hook-nosed, he wore heavy black glasses with Coke-bottle lenses. He looked and acted like an old man. He came from Brooklyn. Seeing Ronald William Platek's address on the list of roommates, Conrad had expected him to be a Negro. Platek, for his part, had expected Conrad von Riemann Bunger to be a Nazi. They finally got to be friends when they rearranged the room's furniture.

"Push that desk over there, Conrad. I'm sorry I can't help you, I've got a bad back."

"OK, Ron. That looks good, doesn't it? How about putting the bookcases together like this?"

"Beautiful. Would you help me nail up my bulletin board?"

"Sure. Do you think we could get some travel posters?" Caldwell had had travel posters in his college room.

"Please, no travel posters. This isn't the University of Kentucky, Conrad. How about some art reproductions from the bookstore?"

"Yeah."

They got in the habit of having long talks in the dark, after going to bed. They were both such provincials—each in his own way—that each found the other's strange accent endlessly fascinating. Ron had an insatiable appetite for facts about the Southern high-school scene, and Conrad did his best to make it sound interesting. In return, Ron told about his gritty life in Brooklyn.

Ron's parents were poor immigrants who'd fled Poland to escape Hitler. The neighborhood they'd settled in was half-black and very tough. Ron had been robbed at knifepoint several times. One of his friends had an older brother who'd paid a woman to shit on his chest. The parks were full of junkies, and the sidewalks were littered with used rubbers. "Some of these guys have *no mind*, Conrad. With the mouth you got, you wouldn't last two days."

Eventually, Conrad got on to the inevitability of death, and they both grew mournful at the prospect of dying without ever getting laid. "With my luck," complained Ron, "my wife will be frigid. Can you believe that? I'm working my ass off, and the whore won't put out. I'll *kill* her!"

After a while, the only thing Conrad didn't like about Ron was his first name. Finally, one night, an appropriate nickname hit him. Ron was tossing in his bed, worrying about a big astronomy test, and suddenly Conrad had the image of Ron as a great dingy *platter* with food sliding back and forth. "Hey, *Platter*," he giggled. "What toothsome victuals do you bear?"

"What are you talking about, Bunger?"

"That's your name. That's what I'm going to call you. *Platter*."

"Fuck you."

"You can call *me* Platter, too. We'll be like the Jackson twins." Conrad was referring to a newspaper comic strip about twin teenage girls.

"Oh, my God, the Jackson twins. With the little brother . . . *Termite*?"

"Yeah."

"Christ, what I'd give to fuck the Jackson twins. Even just one of them. I'd give my left dick."

"I remember I actually jacked off on a *Rex Morgan* comic strip once. There was this real hot woman waiting for Rex in a motel room. You could see her thighs."

"Jesus. Soft, creamy thighs quivering with uncontrollable lust."

Another night, they got onto the differences between the Jewish and Christian religions.

"Is it true that you all are still waiting for a Messiah?" asked Conrad. "I read somewhere . . . I think it was in

Ulysses . . . that every time a Jewish man has a son he's all excited thinking it might be the Redeemer."

"Ah, that's bullshit."

"Did *you* know that Christ was really a Jew, Platter?"

"Of course! What do you think the Last Supper was? *Pesach!* The feast of Passover. My family does it every year. Real good food, Platter, you ought to try it." Platter paused in fond recollection, then went on. "Sure, Christ was a Jew. A nice guy like me! *My* father's a carpenter, you know, he lays parquet floors."

"What if you were the Messiah, and you didn't even know it? What if you thought you were a regular person, but you were really something else?"

"Guys like you and me don't have to worry about that, Conrad. Nobody thinks we're regular persons anyway."

friday, april 10, 1964

Conrad took all the LifeSavers out of the package and shuffled them around on the desk. He closed his eyes, picked one, and tried to guess what color it was. Couldn't tell. Took it out and looked at it: green. For a second he couldn't remember what *green* was supposed to taste like.

His attention wandered back to the paper in his typewriter. Page nine. The fine arts teacher had insisted that all papers be ten to fifteen pages in length. Conrad had been up all night trying to satisfy him. It was 7:15 and the papers were due in class at 8:00. Everyone was supposed to write about the new science library.

"All in all," Conrad typed desperately, *"the new science library is a real plus for the Swarthmore College campus. As one cute freshman coed was heard to say, 'Wow! This building really turns me on!'"*

Still just nine pages. Struck by sudden inspiration, Conrad rubbed the page numbers off the Corrasable Bond page-corners and then retyped them, skipping the number *4*. That brought him up to ten pages. He went by the fine arts class, laid his paper on the teacher's desk, and headed back to his dorm. He didn't want to think anymore. He wanted to sleep.

When Conrad woke, it was late afternoon. He'd been dreaming about flying. For the thousandth time he thought back to the time he'd flown out over the Ohio River. That had really happened, hadn't it? But now, here at Swarthmore, he never felt any of the old power. He was just an awkward Kentucky boy with not too much to say for himself. He winced, recalling the wretched climax of his art paper. Another C for sure.

At least it was Friday. And tomorrow was spring vacation. Conrad was planning to get drunk tonight. There was going to be a bonfire party down in the Crum woods, and he'd arranged for an older student to get bottles for him and Platter. The pickup was supposed to be at five.

Looking to kill a half hour, Conrad wandered out of the dorm and into the quad. There, sitting on some stone steps, was Izzy Tuskman. He was drawing a detailed sketch of a still-leafless Japanese shrub. The rendition was excellent. Tuskman seemed to twinkle with energy as he looked—really *looked*—at the strangely twisting branches.

"That's a good drawing, Izzy."

Long silence. Tuskman was not averse to milking a moment for all it was worth. "Sure," he said finally, looking over with a shrug and a quick smile. "I'm an ahtist. Did you finish your paper?"

"Yeah, it's terrible. It took me all night. I'm going to get drunk."

"Wit what?"

"I'm getting a pint of vodka from Oates. And some Manischewitz for Platter."

"Manischewitz?" Izzy's face tensed in silent laughter. With his mouth open in the pale spring sun, he looked for all the world like a lizard. "Ron is an old Jewish man."

"Oh, he's OK. He's funny. Look, I'll go get the stuff and pick you up here. We can go to my room and get loaded before supper."

"Wonderful." Tuskman turned his attention back to his picture. When Conrad returned in twenty minutes, Izzy was in exactly the same position. The drawing had acquired more detail and more shading; it seemed done.

"Got it?" said Izzy, getting to his feet.

"Yeah. But it cost more than I expected. I don't have any money left for mixer."

"My treat," said Izzy expansively. Conrad followed him into the dorm basement where the vending machines were. No one else was down there. Izzy set down his drawing pad and kicked the glass out of the cigarette machine. "Help me turn it over, Conrad."

They turned the machine upside down, and all the change came out of the change box. You could reach in through the broken-out glass and get money, and cigarettes, too. Izzy bought them three orange sodas, and Conrad took sixteen packs of cigarettes, all brands. They went back to Conrad's room and made themselves drinks.

Just about then, Conrad's roommate showed up.

"Come in, Platter, my good man!" exclaimed Conrad. "Welcome to the Kentucky Tavern."

Platter glanced around, taking in Tuskman and the

sixteen packs of cigarettes. "Are you the guys who broke the machine?" he demanded. "I was just down there."

"Here's your wine, Ron."

Briefly mollified, Platter studied the Manischewitz label. It had a picture of a white-haired old Jewish man with phylacteries.

"He looks so wise," marveled Platter. "He looks like one of the six sages on my postcard." On Platter's bulletin board there was a color picture of six robed rabbis sitting at a table. They all had white beards. Conrad was tired of hearing how smart they were. How could Platter believe in them, when Conrad couldn't believe in anything?

"Those guys don't know anything," he told Platter flatly. "They're not sages. They're stupid old men who can barely talk English." He was really saying this for Izzy's benefit.

"I'd like to see you tell them that," shouted Platter. He pulled the postcard off the bulletin board and shoved it in Conrad's face. "I'd like to see you walk up to that table and tell those guys they don't know anything! *Meshuggeneh gonif!* Crazy thief!"

"Take it easy," interjected Izzy.

"I will *not* take it easy," raved Platter. "And I do not want you guys drinking in here. The drinking is for the Crum party tonight, not for pigs before supper." His anger was half-real, half-burlesque. In any case, it would be unwise to provoke him further.

"Hey, let's get out of here, Izzy," said Conrad. "Let's skip supper and go down to the Crum early."

"OK. I'll buy some peanuts."

The Crum woods surrounded a meadow and a creek adjacent to the Swarthmore campus. A train-line, the Media Local, passed through the woods and crossed a high trestle over the creek. The Swarthmore students often held bonfire parties in the Crum meadow. People would play folk songs, and in the dark you could drink or make out.

But now it was only six. Izzy and Conrad perched on a bank overlooking the train tracks and drank some more.

"What do you want to do in life, Conrad?"

"Uh, I don't know. Be happy."

"*Happy*," spat Tuskman. "You know what I think when I hear *happy*?"

"No." All this was as interesting as anything Conrad had ever heard. He smiled happily at Izzy. Izzy lay on his back and stuck up his arms and legs for emphasis.

"*Happy* is a toad dat's buried in da mud. Just snugged down there under da water and every now and then it opens its mouth and goes *blup*. Dat's *happy*."

"Well, of course I'd like to achieve something. Be creative. But I'm not very good at anything, Izzy. I can't draw or wrestle like you."

"Dere's got to be something dat only Conrad Bunger can do. Find it and work on it."

Conrad decided to tell the truth. "I want to learn the secret of life. That's why God put me here, Izzy, I've got a feeling. I'm supposed to find out what it's like to be something that dies." The alcohol was filling him with the old philosophical excitement.

"You're *flyin*', Conrad."

"What is reality? Why does anything exist? Shouldn't there be an answer? I mean, humans all *die*, you dig that?"

"You know da wrestling coach, Palmer?"

"I've seen him. He teaches my phys. ed. class. Once when we were playing touch football, he told the fullback to think of himself as 'the apex of a triangle.'"

"Yeah, dat's Palmer. A real deep thinker. He was asking Chuckie and me why we're so *cynical*." Izzy said the word like it was a joke.

"Yeah?"

"I told him dat we're da first kids to have grown up under da threat of da *bomb*."

They laughed over that for a while. "That was about as mad as I ever saw my father get," said Conrad. "When I told him I wished they would go ahead and drop the bomb. I mean, I didn't want to have to take my SATs and apply for college and everything."

"One time my Dad stuck a fork in my back," said Izzy, hitching up his shirt. Sure enough there were four tiny dots in a row, down near his belt. "I called him a petty bourgeoisie—and an asshole to boot—and he started chasing me all over da house. We'd been eating supper, so he still had da fork in his hand. He couldn't catch me, so finally he just threw the fork. Ow!"

"Was he sorry?"

Izzy's face grew lumpy with laughter. "He told me to pull out the fork and get da fuck out of da house. So I took his car and got drunk and wrecked it."

They passed the bottle back and forth, taking small sips. Everything seemed so peaceful and right, here in the woods, alone with an artistic friend. After a while, Izzy leaned forward and threw up between his legs.

"Let's walk across da trestle, Conrad."

"Are you sure . . ."

"I ain't drunk. I just throw up easy. I ruined my stomach with Ex-Lax, getting down to wrestling weight. Come on. Let's go face death."

They got up and followed the railroad tracks to the trestle. There were two tracks, so it was relatively safe, even though there were no guardrails.

The sun had just gone down. A good breeze was blowing. Before long, Conrad and Izzy were out in the middle of the trestle, out over the dark creek, higher than the big, budding spring trees. Conrad took another pull of vodka and whooped with joy.

Just then a train's headlight appeared up ahead.

"Come stand here!" yelled Izzy, planting himself in the middle of the left-hand track.

"That's wrong!" screamed Conrad. "That's the track he's on!" The train was already rumbling onto the other end of the trestle. It was loud, and Izzy seemed not to understand he was in the wrong place. Conrad jumped over, grabbed Izzy, and shoved him to the right side. Just then he stumbled.

Conrad was lying on the track, with the train bearing down on him, sounding its horn. *Fly*, he told himself, *Fly!*

In a flash he'd whipped out into midair, ten yards to the left of the trestle. He hung there, scared to look down, while the commuter train's four cars roared past. As soon it was safe, Conrad whisked himself back onto the trestle.

"Conrad!" hollered Tuskman. "You're OK! I thought . . ."

"I flew out of the way."

"Bullshit."

"Believe it." It was dark now, and down in the meadow some people were lighting the bonfire. "I forgot to tell you before . . . that's the one thing I can do. I can fly."

"Den fly down to da fire."

"I'm scared it might not work." Conrad drained the vodka bottle and threw it out into the darkness. Bright shapes were moving behind his eyes. It seemed like a long time till he heard the bottle break. Crazy Izzy grabbed his arm and made as if to shove him off the edge.

"Hey, take it easy," protested Conrad. This was going to be too much trouble if it got out. The power *meant* something; for now, it was better kept secret. "I can't really fly, Izzy. I lay down between the rails when the train came. Don't *push* me like that, shithead, I'm only a regular guy."

TEN

saturday, april 11, 1964

I t's Bunger!"

"Hey, Conrad, wake up!"

Conrad was confused. He was at an angle, and there was a crumpled umbrella over his face. A half-full quart of beer skidded out from under him when he tried to sit up.

Ace Weston and Chuckie Golem were standing over him. It was dawn, it was April, it was the morning after the Crum party. Conrad had fallen asleep in some bushes. Down in the meadow you could see last night's bonfire still smoldering.

"You guys want some beer?"

"Look at him," marveled Ace. "He looks like a college professor turned derelict."

"Ace and I sat up talking all night," explained Chuckie in his taut, dry voice. "We saw something on the hillside here, and we couldn't figure out what it was."

"I didn't want to walk all the way back last night," explained Conrad. "I took someone's umbrella in case it rained. Where are my glasses?"

"The bottle by your stomach is the perfect touch,"

chuckled Ace. He had an unkind sense of humor. "Like a piglet with its mother sow."

"*Pig*," said Chuckie thoughtfully. "That should be his nickname. Pig Bunger."

"I like it," agreed Ace. "Here's your glasses, Pig."

Conrad struggled to his feet, and the three boys headed for breakfast. Conrad hadn't seen much of Ace Weston so far this year. Ace had short blond hair and was said to be a mean drunk. Back in the fall, he'd managed to date the prettiest girl in their class. On the way to the dining hall, Ace talked about a book called *The Glass Giant of Palomar*.

"It's about the first twenty-four-inch reflecting telescope mirror," explained Ace. "The guy who made it went crazy. The mirror has to be a perfect parabolic curve, right, and they have a way to test it with interference fringes up to an accuracy of one or two wavelengths of light. So this guy, his name was Huffman, he grinds the mirror for four years and as soon as they mount it, it cracks."

"Jesus," said Conrad politely. Weston seemed a lot more excited than his subject matter warranted. A put-on.

"So he goes to the nuthouse," continued Ace. "And when he gets out he decides to make an even bigger mirror. This time—"

"Have you ever seen *Wound Ballistics*?" interrupted Conrad, not to be out-weirded. "I found it in the library. It's all pictures of guys who got shot in some World War Two battle at Anzio. Legs missing and everything. I used to leave it open on Platter's pillow at night."

"Do you have it in your room right now?"

"No. Platter hid it someplace. I keep getting overdue notices. *The Palm-Wine Drinkard* is another good book. It's by an African called Amos Tuatola. Platter scribbled all over the cover."

"I have a really good porno book," put in Chuckie. "It's called . . . *Confessions of Harriet Marwood, Governess*."

"This year's campus sensation," intoned Weston. "The new *Catch-22*." The three boys burst into laughter.

"Say, look, Ace," said Conrad finally. "Did you ever fuck Mary Toledo?"

"Yeah, Ace," clamored Chuckie. "Did you?" Up till Christmas, Ace and Mary had been the handsomest couple in the freshman class. Ace had even gone to sit-in at a segregated diner to get arrested for Mary's beliefs. While he'd been in jail, she'd started dating someone else.

"You *should* have fucked Toledo," insisted Conrad. "If you were going to sell America down the river for her." He didn't like the group that had organized the sit-ins. One of them had been Pennington, the boy who'd made fun of him in political science class.

"How about you, Pig?" snapped Weston. "How about *your* love-life?"

"I don't have one," sighed Conrad. "I keep getting drunk and scaring them away. I guess it's approach-avoidance. Maybe I'm queer."

"Have you tried sheep?" inquired Chuckie, pausing to push back his glasses. "I read in the *Kinsey Report* that most farm boys fuck animals. The . . . *ewe* is said to be a good approximation to the real thing."

"Shit. Too bad my parents don't live in Kentucky anymore. What with spring vacation starting today."

After breakfast, Conrad went back to his room and packed. Even though he'd slept outside, he felt pretty good. It had been fun talking trash with Weston and Golem. And last night he'd flown again! He helped Platter lug his huge trunk down to the train station and then took his own suitcase out to the Washington bus that Swarthmore had chartered. His parents now lived in Alexandria, just southeast of D.C.

There were already quite a few people in the bus. Conrad spotted a pretty girl and took the seat next to her. She had full red lips and a tight-curled bouffant hairdo. He'd never seen her before. Maybe she dated fraternity guys?

"Do you mind if I sit here?" he asked, wishing he'd shaved.

She glanced over neutrally. "Do you mind if I smoke?"

"No. I smoke too. I started this winter."

"Oh."

Not only had his friends at Swarthmore taught Conrad to smoke, they'd taught him to read *The New York Times*. As the bus pulled out, he began studying his copy. Maybe he could find something to start a conversation with this girl.

"Another person abducted by a flying saucer," said Conrad presently.

"Hmm?"

"In Oldham County, Kentucky. Happens all the time down there."

"That's not true."

"Look, it's right here in the paper!"

They found more and more to talk about as the trip wore on. She even played the same trip-game as Conrad, the game of imagining that your finger is a long scythe that reaches out to mow the grass by the road. Every time there's a telephone pole you have to lift your finger.

"Or sometimes I imagine that I'm running along next to the road," said the girl. "And that I jump over things."

"I can do that," blurted Conrad. "Sometimes I can really fly."

She smiled and lit a Newport. "How do you know?"

"Last night, I was drinking on the trestle, and a train almost ran over me."

"Why would you do a crazy thing like that?"

"Showing off, I guess. I didn't think it would be so dangerous. But, wait, the point is that I flew out to the side of the trestle and floated there till the train was past."

"Oh, sure. Did anyone see you do it?"

"Well . . . I was with a guy, Izzy Tuskman, but he didn't actually see me in the air."

"I've heard of Tuskman. Isn't he supposed to be an artist?"

"That's what he says. Do you like art?"

"In a way. When I was a little girl my parents used to take me the museum every Sunday, so I'm pretty fed up with the old masters. What I really like now is Pop art."

"Yeah, yeah. Me too. I love Andy Warhol. I wish I could look like him, all blank and cool. Did you hear about the show he had where it was just fake Brillo boxes?"

"Yes. And soup-can paintings. I like those because then art is everywhere, and not just in boring Sunday museums. The world is art."

"What do you like to read? Have you read *Nausea*?"

"I *have*," said the girl, brightening even more. "I loved

it. That guy Roquentin is so *crazy*. It's the only good book that Sartre wrote. The others are too theoretical."

"I was really hypnotized by that book in high school. I practically got suspended on account of it. I went to a Catholic high school for some reason—it was supposed to be the best science school in Louisville—and when I tried to talk about life being meaningless, the teachers all got mad at me."

The girl looked him over once again. "Life isn't really so meaningless. I mean, usually I don't think so. Pretty soon all the flowers will come out; that's something to live for. I love daffodils the most of all."

Her parents lived in Geneva, Switzerland, and she was spending spring vacation in D.C. with high-school friends. The reason Conrad hadn't met her yet at college was that she was a junior. A junior! As soon as he got back from spring vacation, he tried to call her for a date.

But the problem was . . . Conrad had failed to get her name. She'd told it to him when the bus trip ended, but in the noise of the station he hadn't heard. He combed the campus looking for her. He couldn't remember what she was majoring in, and nobody seemed to have heard of her. Finally, one day at the condiment table in the dining hall, there she was.

"Oh, hello!" she said, smiling a big lipstick smile.

"I'm so glad to see you!" exclaimed Conrad. "Please tell me your name; I've been looking for you, and I don't know your name."

"Audrey. My name is Audrey Hayes. Come on, you can sit with me and my friends."

Audrey's friends were four other girls, none of them very attractive. But by now, Conrad would have sat with wild dogs to be near Audrey. When Audrey's friends heard his name, they made wide eyes at her. He'd already gotten drunk often enough to have a bad reputation on campus. But Audrey was really glad to see him. After lunch he asked her for a date.

"Will you come to the Folk Festival with me?" The annual Swarthmore Folk Festival lasted four days, with three big concerts.

"Which concert?"

"Uh . . . all of them?"

Thus began a season of sweetness. Conrad saw Audrey at every opportunity—lunch, supper, the movies. The one problem was that she kept refusing to kiss him.

"I don't want to be a sucker, Conrad. I want to be sure you really like me." Audrey was licking and licking at a strawberry ice cream cone as she talked. They were standing under a tree outside the student union. They'd just been to an evening pottery class together.

"I do like you, Audrey. Come on and kiss me, will you?"

Lick. "I don't think I should, Conrad." *Lick.*

Not quite knowing what he was doing, Conrad shoved Audrey's ice cream cone aside and glued his mouth to hers. She let the cone fall and put her arms around him. They kissed once, twice, three times. The next day, white flowers came out all over the tree they'd been standing under.

Audrey was the best kisser Conrad had ever met. If she happened to be in the right mood, they'd sit down on the dark campus someplace and kiss for half an hour or more. Audrey's mouth was so wet and open, her breath so sweet, her tongue so strong.

"Why do you drink so much?" she asked one night, interrupting the kissing and pushing Conrad back a bit. They were sitting in a patch of daffodils near Audrey's dorm. The school year was almost over.

"Uh . . . I don't know. I just really enjoy it. I feel confused and empty a lot of the time, Audrey. When I'm drunk I feel like I can see the answers; I feel like I'm close to the world."

"But that's all backwards. Drinking cuts you *off* from the world."

"From the ordinary world, sure. But there's a deeper reality. I can feel it. With you, I can feel it, as much as with drinking. We connect, we understand each other. It's the secret of life."

"What is?"

"Feeling connected instead of cut off. Under the surface, the whole world is one thing. You and I are like . . . finger-puppets on God's hand. Or eyes on a giant jellyfish."

"That doesn't sound very romantic."

"I don't mean it that way. I love you, Audrey. That's what I want to say. I love you much more than drinking."

"I'm glad." They kissed a little more, and then Audrey thought of another question. "Didn't you once tell me that you can fly?"

"Yes. But only when it's life-and-death. It's some kind of weird survival trait I have."

"Oh, sure."

"No, really. In high school I was in a car accident, and I flew around a tree. And last month I flew off the trestle to save myself."

"Couldn't you fly for me a little right now?"

"You promise not to tell anyone if I show you?"

"I promise."

"OK. Let's sneak up to your dorm room." Audrey lived on the third floor.

"No funny business!"

"Don't worry, Audrey, I'm a Southern gentleman!"

Boys weren't allowed to enter the girls' dorm at night. But people did it all the time. You could climb up the thick wisteria vines, or you could sneak up the back stairs. Audrey went in the main door and opened the back door for Conrad. Whispering and giggling, they hurried up to her room.

It was nice in Audrey's room, tidy and well arranged. There were stuffed animals, and French books, and empty wine bottles with philodendron vines growing in them. Conrad let himself imagine that he lived here with her.

"Don't make any noise, Conrad, I could get suspended for this."

"Just move those bottles and open your window."

"You're going to climb down?"

"I'm going to *fly* down!"

"Don't, Conrad, you might hurt yourself. You don't really have to fly to impress me."

"But I *can*!"

"Have you done this before?"

"Not really. I've been scared. But you make me feel strong enough."

"Well, don't kill yourself!" She cleared off the window-sill and threw open the big sash window. Sweet spring air wafted in. Conrad crouched in the window and leaned forward.

For a second he thought he was flying, but he was wrong. He was crashing down through the wisteria vines that covered Audrey's dorm, crashing down feet-first. He fell about ten feet before he managed to get hold of a thick piece of the vine. The jolt almost tore his arm out of its socket, but the vine held. Moaning softly, Conrad climbed the rest of the way down. He could hear Audrey giggling overhead.

When he got to the bottom, he looked up and gave a jaunty wave.

"See?"

"What happened, Conrad?"

"I . . . I guess it wasn't dangerous enough."

"You're incredible. I'm going to miss you this summer."

thursday, march 4, 1965

"H ey, Pig."

"Say, Ace. Look at this." Conrad was alone in his filthy room, looking at a piece of paper. He was a sophomore now. Last spring's happy love seemed far away. "It's a letter from Dean Potts."

"'Dear Conrad,'" Ace read aloud. "'I received a copy of the bill from the house director concerning room damage in your suite in A section. The amount of damage astonishes me since it is the largest bill of this sort I have seen. I cannot imagine legitimate excuses for this kind of destruction ... '" Ace broke off and handed the letter back. "Do you still have the knife?"

"Oh, yeah. My ninety-three-dollar Target Master throwing knife. Three dollars for the knife and ninety for the damages. It was those holes in the plaster that really got them. They sent bills to my parents and to Platter's parents."

"What did Platter's parents say?"

"They said, 'Ron, that's what happens when you get in with a bad crowd.' You're going to have to pay his half,

Ace. You were the one who always threw the knife at the wall on purpose."

"Let's get drunk."

"Age, wheels, and bread, Ace. We'll need all three."

"Florman's always sells to you, Pig. And I stole Chuckie's car keys."

"Is it still lunchtime?"

"Yeah."

"OK. We'll swing by the dining hall and I'll go through some purses."

"You're a man after my own heart, Pig."

Conrad found six dollars in a purse in the coat racks. He felt bad stealing it, but he really needed to get drunk. Things were going very badly indeed. Audrey was unhappy, the Dean was incensed, and Conrad hadn't been to classes in over a week.

It was snowing. Wet, early March snow.

"Ka-ka," said Ace, squinting through the slush on the windshield of Chuckie's car. "The world is ka-ka."

"We'll get twelve quarts," said Conrad soothingly. "Twelve quarts of Ballantine. We'll take them to your room, and then we'll put them in our stomachs."

"Good. Feel good."

Conrad still roomed with Platter, but this year Ace was sharing a large suite with Chuckie Golem and Izzy Tuskman. Ace had his own bedroom, a nice big room with two windows. One window gave onto a fire escape, the other led out onto a peaked roof. It was a good place to drink. Conrad and Ace had spent most Saturdays there in the fall, drinking and being glad they weren't at the football game. Recently they'd started drinking during the week as well. It was a constant struggle but somehow worth it. It was a way of being cool.

"What's with you and Audrey?" Ace asked after they'd started their first quarts.

"It's like Platter says: 'The little woman is tired of playing second fiddle to Demon Rum.' When I showed up drunk for supper yesterday, she told me she didn't want to see me for a week."

"Doesn't she realize how lovable we are when we're drunk?"

"Less and less people do, Ace." Conrad sighed and rubbed his temples. He was more worried about losing Audrey than he cared to admit. "Let's put on *Cast Your Fate to the Wind*. I love that song. It's like life. Touching gently and not getting through. Laughing drunk and breaking things. Walking quiet holding a girl's hand and looking at the sky and knowing it's all in the moment and—"

"Being happy and ruining it on purpose so you can start over." Ace interrupted. "Jacking off in a used rubber by the roadside while your girl is waiting in the car. Isn't this beer going to get cold?"

"You mean warm. Let's put it in your bed."

"OK." Ace began bustling around, happy and excited. "These are the twins," he said, tucking two quarts under his pillow. "And little Ricky sleeps over here." He wedged a bottle down between the mattress and the wall. "The neighbor kids go here." He put six quarts under the quilt in the middle of the bed. "And Celia has her own room." The last bottle went down at the foot of the bed.

The afternoon waned on pleasantly. When Ace and Conrad got tired of *Cast Your Fate to the Wind*, they began listening to *Chuck Berry's Greatest Hits*. That was an album you could listen to for a long time. So that they wouldn't have to keep getting up to piss, they started pissing in the empty quart bottles. It kept you on your toes—not to pick up the wrong bottle—and you could compare input and output. They started grooving.

Ace: "Dean Potts should be here."

Pig: "So we could slit his throat."

Ace: "And rig it like a junk OD."

Pig: "His twisted body on the tracks."

Ace: "Blackmail snaps of homo love."

Pig: "And books with Platter's name."

Ace: "They'd have a Quaker service."

Pig: "And we could give a speech."

Ace: "Nothing's wrong with being square."

Pig: "Sperm, alcohol, and death."

Suddenly most of the beer was gone and Ace was turning ugly. He lurched across the room and punched out a windowpane. "You see that, Pig? No cuts." Ace held up his white fist. "The thing is to *jerk through*. No wimp hesitation." He punched out another pane.

"Don't go breaking all the windows, Ace. I don't want to get in any more trouble this week."

"Candy-ass. You joke about death, but you're really scared shitless. Dig." Ace opened the window and hopped out onto the roof. There was a thick crust of ice and snow out there. Face set in angry brooding, Ace began tightrope-walking backward along the roof's slippery peak.

"Hey, come on, Ace," said Conrad, leaning out the window. "I *know* you have more guts than me. Big deal, *man*." The roof sloped down to a sheer fifty-foot drop on either side.

Ace made it out to the end of the roof, but then he took one step too many. He disappeared as suddenly as a duck in a shooting gallery. Conrad had been tensed for this. For the first time since the trestle, his power was back. He flew out the window, along the roof, and down to tumbling Ace, still fifteen feet above the ground. He got his arms around Ace's chest, and with a feeling of digging into Nothingness, Conrad managed to brace himself and slow Ace's deadly fall. They touched down on the ground without a jolt.

"Jesus, Conrad!"

"I can't always do it. So don't fall off the roof again, shithook."

They went back to Ace's room and worked on the beer some more.

"Does Audrey know?" Ace asked. He'd calmed down a lot in the last few minutes.

"I've tried telling her, but she doesn't really believe me. Last spring I was going to show her I could fly—I jumped out of her window. But my body knew I could catch one of the wisteria vines, so the power didn't cut in. I can only fly when it's a matter of life and death."

"You could jump off Clothier Tower. That's like a two-hundred-foot sheer drop. Jump off at lunch hour! All the girls will want to fuck you. I'll help you screen the applications." Ace paused to open the second-to-last quart.

"You know, Conrad, in China, if you save someone's life, that means you have to take care of them forever. Will you give me half the money you get from flying?"

"What money? From who? I mean if the government gets wind of it, then they'll just draft me and use me for a suicide spy mission. I could go in the circus and pretend to be an aerialist . . . but who wants to be a freak for dumb hicks? Crime might be a possibility, if I could learn to *control* my flying, but . . ."

"Use it to invent antigravity," suggested Ace. "That'd be big bucks for sure." He pulled at his beer. "I can't believe this really happened. Why should *you* be able to fly, anyway?"

"That's what I can't figure out. Last year I was thinking . . . I was thinking maybe I'm the new Messiah. Like Jesus, you know?"

"Jesus was a great ethical teacher, Conrad, not just some derelict who knew how to fly."

"Well, anyway. I mean if God—or the aliens—gave me this magic power, it must be that I'm supposed to do something important."

"So how come you spend all your time getting drunk?"

"That's part of it. I get drunk to see God, you know? When I'm drunk I feel like I know the secret of life. Know it in my body. The teachers here can't tell me anything— they're old and square. The answer isn't so much a bunch of words as it is a way of feeling."

"The secret of life," said Ace. "I'll tell you when I saw the secret of life. It was the morning star. Venus, you dig? Once after my paper route there was still enough night left to get out my telescope and look at it. It was a crescent like the moon! You understand? Always get your emotions confused in what you're doing and your mind will be sure to develop. If you want to get out and tell anyone."

"Of course I want to get out," said Conrad, just to have something to say. "Venus is really a crescent? I've never seen the morning star."

"It's the same as the evening star, Pig. The bright dot that you see near the moon sometimes. That's Venus."

"Yeah, yeah, I've seen it. I used to look at the sky with Larsen a lot. We'd lie out on the grass and stare up at the stars."

"My big science friend was a guy named Table," said Ace. "Billy Table. His father was an alcoholic stage magician. Poor Table built himself a big reflecting telescope . . . sanded the mirror and everything—"

"The Glass Giant of Palomar!"

"Exactly! And Table's father got mad when he was drunk and he broke the mirror."

"What a prick. My father was never like that. I don't think he ever even hit me. Maybe once when I was drunk. He used to hit Caldwell sometimes, but by the time I was a teenager, he was worn out."

"Yeah, my Dad never hit me either. He always fought with my mother instead. They're getting divorced." Ace said this like it was nothing, but Conrad could tell it meant a lot. No wonder Ace was upset enough to fall off the roof.

"I'm sorry, Ace."

"Can I have the last quart?"

Conrad looked at his own lukewarm half-full quart. He'd had enough for now. "Yeah, OK. I don't see why I can't get laid."

"It's because you're such a stupid pig," said Ace, opening the last beer. "You drink so much because you're too lazy to do anything else."

"What do you mean lazy? It's work getting money and wheels. Lazy. I just saved your life, didn't I? You're so fucked-up you practically commit suicide, and now you're telling *me* how to live?"

"Maybe I'm doing you a favor," said Ace evenly. It was impossible to ever get the better of Ace in any kind of argument—this was one of the reasons Conrad liked him so much. "You talk about the secret of life, Conrad, you talk about finding out some big Answer. Now, what that means is that you'd like to be an artist ... or maybe a scientist. But you're still just a dumb kid from Kentucky, and everyone treats you that way." Ace fell silent, and let Conrad fill in the blanks.

"Except for Audrey," said Conrad finally. "And, you know, I will make it, Ace, someday I'll be a famous intellectual. And I'll still be getting drunk."

"I hope so, Conrad. I hope both."

Chuckie and Izzy showed up about then. Chuckie was a little pissed about his car—he'd had to walk up to campus and back, in the sleet. But then Izzy found a bottle of sherry somewhere, and they all cheered up. Chuckie played his guitar, and they made up a song about Conrad called *Pig, Pig, Pig, What's the Use, Use, Use?* People like

Chuckie thought Conrad was a mess, but at least they could tell he was different. For now, that was enough.

That night Conrad slept on the floor of Ace's room. He'd hoped for another secret chat about his flying, and about his destiny, but Ace had turned mean again. Conrad's last memory of the evening was Ace's mock-sincere voice trying to trick him into wetting his pants. "I just did it myself, Conrad. Ahhh, it feels good. Relax. Go on and do it." Some friend!

When Conrad awoke, he was alone and the snow had melted. He crawled out Ace's other window and went down the fire escape. *Leaving with no love lost*, Conrad thought to himself. He felt purged and happy. The earth was like a vast terrarium, moist and unseasonably warm. Things were growing. Life—not the secret of life—just life itself.

To begin with, he'd get things back together with Audrey. He would give her his signet ring, the von Riemann coat of arms from his mother's dead father.

TWELVE

wednesday, august 25, 1965

C onrad and Audrey were sitting in the balcony of a Paris theater. The lady they were staying with had given them tickets to a girlie show.

"Look at that man over there," said Audrey. "He has a *telescope.*"

Sure enough, a man two rows ahead of them was studying the distant pink flesh through a short black tube.

"He must be a regular. It's all old people here, have you noticed, Audrey?"

"Et voilà!" cried the woman onstage as she peeled off the last layer. She had her stomach sucked in, and her ribs jutted out unnaturally. Her voice was shrill with the effort of filling the cavernous theater. *"Maintenant je fais do-do!"* ("Now I'm going night-night.") Some men in tuxedos danced out and began carrying her around on a huge platter. Her puddled breasts slid this way and that. Conrad didn't want to get interested.

"Do you want to leave, Audrey?"

"Let's do. This is so square."

It was a hot summer night, with Paris sparkling all around them. Conrad had earned enough at a summer construction job to come visit Audrey in Geneva. Her father was a diplomat there. And now Conrad and Audrey were spending a few days in Paris with a Hayes family friend. It was fantastic, an American dream, from basement digger to *boulevardier* in ten short days.

"Your hands are so hard, Conrad." They were strolling down a tree-lined street.

"That's from the tamper. You know what that is? It's a yellow machine shaped like an outboard motor. But at the bottom, instead of a propeller, there's a big flat metal foot. The whole thing hops up and down like a robot pogo stick. Most days, my job was to guide the tamper all around the dirt floor of a new basement to flatten the dirt out. It was exhausting, and then for hours I'd still feel the jerking in my arms. The regular workers—the black guys—stuck me with the tamper as much as possible. They called it *the hand-jive machine*."

"Did they like you?"

"They were nice. They treated me like anyone else. One of them, a guy named Wheatland, he'd throw back his head and scream, 'Ah just loooove to fuck!' He was an older guy. He'd look at me and say, 'When I was yo' age my dick be hard six days a week!'"

Audrey giggled and squeezed Conrad's hand. Ever since he'd given her his signet ring they'd gotten a lot closer. He'd been drinking less, and she'd started letting him fondle her breasts. She had wonderful breasts, with big stiff nipples. Remembering them, Conrad began hugging Audrey right there on the sidewalk. They kissed intensely.

"Should we do it, Audrey? Do you want to fuck?"

"Yes." The simplicity of the answer astounded Conrad. Good thing he'd asked!

They had a couple of drinks in a nightclub and danced a little. It was hard to pay attention to anything. Finally it was late enough so that their hostess was certain to be in bed. They let themselves into the apartment and sat down in the living room. Conrad had a couch in there, and Audrey was sleeping in the guest bedroom.

"Are you sure you want to?" asked Audrey.

Conrad felt like a condemned man. "Yes. Of course." They made out for a while, working themselves up, and then Audrey went to her room.

"You come in in a minute, Conrad."

He changed into his pajamas and got two rubbers out of his travel kit. He'd had those rubbers for a long time. In the confusion of the moment, Conrad's mind kept blanking out. Whenever he closed his eyes he saw snow, clouds of snow.

Audrey was in her bed waiting for him. He got the rubber on and pushed into her. He could hardly feel anything; he was numb all over. But there was warmth and smoothness; he could tell he was in. Her neck smelled like honey. They pushed and bounced. He was going to come. He told her. He told her he loved her. In the dark, his eyes were full of snow, snow that he somehow sensed as *North Dakota snow*. A bugle was sounding, and there in the snowstorm you could see Old Glory rising up the flagpole. The Stars and Stripes. Showing the colors. Here, yes, here. Now.

They did it a second time, just to make sure they really weren't virgins anymore. The next morning, Conrad and Audrey wandered around Paris in a daze.

"We really *did* it, Conrad."

"Oh, Audrey. I can't believe it. I can't believe it finally happened. That's the weirdest thing about time, the way things that you never think will come finally do come. I love you, Audrey. I love you a lot."

"I'm so excited, Conrad, I can hardly see. I feel like I'm going to fall over!"

They found themselves on a deck halfway up the Eiffel Tower. The only other person there was an old woman with a poodle on a leash. She was busy peeling an orange.

"Why doesn't the elevator go all the way to the tip?" Conrad asked Audrey.

"This is high enough for me. I feel like the wind could blow me right off. My head is buzzing."

"Me too. I feel light as air. I bet I could fly around the tower, Audrey." He had already told her about the time he saved Ace's life.

"Don't risk it! I want my darling to be safe."

But now that the idea had formed in Conrad's mind, it was overwhelming him. Last night he'd done an impossible thing—he'd fucked Audrey. Why not do another miracle today? Before Audrey could stop him, he'd jumped up to stand on the deck's railing. Vast windy space out there, a hungry void. *I can do it.*

As he began to teeter forward, the old tightening in his

brain's center began. Yes. He could hold on to space. Conrad did a slow flip and hung upside down, his face in front of Audrey's. From this perspective, it looked like her mouth was in her forehead. He blew her a kiss and drifted off the deck and into thin air. The poodle started barking.

Moving quickly, and not letting himself think about it too much, Conrad flew all the way around the tower and landed back at Audrey's side. The elevator had just brought up a load of tourists. The old woman with the poodle was yelling to the guard, yelling and pointing at Conrad. The guard frowned, turned off the elevator, and took out a little notebook.

"Oh, God, Conrad, they want to give you a ticket for climbing off the deck. It's strictly forbidden."

"I didn't *climb*."

The guard gave a perfunctory tip of his hat and asked for their passports.

"Let's just fly off, Audrey. I don't want any big legal hassle." The power was still humming in his head.

"*No!*"

Upset and shaking, Audrey rummaged in her purse for her passport. This was no way to be spending lunch hour on such a special day. She'd said no to the idea of flying, but she'd said no about other things, too. Conrad put his arms around Audrey's waist and flew the two of them out off the deck. The tourists from the elevator started yelling; someone took a picture. Audrey clung to Conrad's neck in terror.

"Don't drop me!"

Conrad felt his control waver when he looked down. Black asphalt down there, and the vast latticed curve of the tower's leg. Some of the ants on the distant pavement looked up and pointed. This was madness.

Quickly, before the power faded, Conrad headed for the towers of Nôtre Dame. As they went speeding over Paris, with all the cars and people below like a distant movie, Audrey stayed glued to him, her eyes squeezed shut. They angled in low and landed on some deserted cobblestones by the Seine.

"Don't you ever do that to me again, Conrad."

A fisherman/bum some twenty yards away stared at them for a moment, then looked away.

"Let's get the Metro out of here," suggested Conrad.

"The people on the Eiffel Tower know we came this way."

In the subway, Audrey calmed down. They rode until they found themselves in Saint-Germain. They had a good lunch at the Café Flore.

"What's going to happen, Conrad?" asked Audrey over coffee. "Are you going to start flying all the time?"

"Maybe." Conrad felt within himself. "But right now I don't think I can anymore. It's like I told you before, it's a survival trait. I have to risk my life to make it start. On the tower I was so excited to think we actually fucked that I went ahead and took the chance." He took her hand and squeezed it.

Audrey stared deep into his eyes. Her face looked so open. "It's too bad today's our last day here."

"We'll have lots more chances this fall. You can come visit me at Swarthmore; and I'll take the bus up to visit you in New York." Having finished college, Audrey was planning to get a master's in French at Columbia. "We still have to get good at it."

"You didn't think it was good?"

"Of course it was good. I'm crazy about you, Audrey. And I'm going to start studying hard, so that when I graduate, I can get a good job to support you."

"You're planning to marry me?" She looked surprised.

"Of course."

Walking back to the Metro, they passed a kiosk selling afternoon papers. In the middle of page one, there was a photo of a man and woman hanging in midair. The Eiffel Tower's railing was in the foreground, Notre Dame in the background. Conrad and Audrey's faces didn't show.

"What does the caption say, Audrey?"

"'Mysterious Hoax: Two Americans Sought.'" She looked at him in dismay. "I hate having our picture in the paper like that. What would they do to you if they found you, Conrad?"

"It . . ." Conrad's mouth worked wordlessly. "I . . ." He staggered and sat down on the curb. *The picture of him flying.* Something about it . . . He felt like there was Novocain in his head—Novocain and thick, heavy throbbing. *Picture not good.*

"Are you all right, Conrad? What's happening?"

THIRTEEN

thursday, december 2, 1965

"What do you mean, 'levitation'?" Mr. Bulber was bored and impatient. He and Conrad were alone in the physics laboratory.

"Antigravity," said Conrad, lighting a cigarette. "I want to invent antigravity. That's why I decided to major in physics."

Conrad had come back from Paris filled with high resolve. He'd been cracking the books like never before. Audrey was up in New York, doing grad school at Columbia; she and Conrad got together and fucked one or two times a month. It was agreed that they were both free to date others—Audrey had insisted on this point last time they'd been together. Three weeks ago. Conrad hadn't really heard from her since. Three weeks? He'd been studying hard. Three weeks? It was something to worry about, all right; but nevertheless, right now, Conrad's plan was to figure out a way to mechanize his flying ability, revolutionize transportation, marry Audrey, and retire as a millionaire in three or four years.

"Flying without wings," amplified Conrad, exhaling

smoke. "It's an old science-fiction idea. I'm pretty confident I can get it working."

Mr. Bulber grew irrationally angry. He was thirty-two, with a potato-face and neatly oiled dark hair. He had a small pompadour. Back when Mr. Bulber had been a student, he'd been a loner, mocked and reviled by people like Conrad Bunger. He'd just gotten tenure, and the college had promised him a sabbatical for next year. Mr. Bulber was worn out from six years of teaching and in no mood to nurture some shaggy young wastrel's dreams of glory.

"Conrad Bunger. All right. *Fact:* Antigravity is impossible. If you knew tensor analysis and general relativity, I could show you why. But you don't know. You never will. *Advice:* Stop this intellectual masturbation and bring your lab book up to date. At this point, you're working on a D." Mr. Bulber caught Conrad's crushed expression and softened a bit. "It's good to dream, Bunger, don't get me wrong. Every scientist starts with a dream. But physics is *real*. The world is stubborn. Just wishing for something doesn't make it so.

"What if I told you that I can fly?"

Mr. Bulber's face hardened. "I'd tell you to get counseling."

Conrad made a brief effort to levitate on the spot, but the vibes weren't right, down here in a machine-filled basement, alone with an old nerd who thought antigravity was crazy bullshit. And Audrey hadn't written, and she wasn't ever there when he called . . .

He took his books up to the science library and tried to do the homework for Bulber's Mechanics and Wave

Motion course. *Let a 40-kg cannon ball be attached to a 3-m chain weighing 5 kg per m. The ball is carried to the top of a 4-m ladder. How much work is done?* Jesus. Too much work, that's how much. Next question. *A boy on a Ferris wheel is playing with a yo-yo. Find the velocity of the yo-yo, given that . . .* Conrad sighed and closed his book. None of this stuff made sense. Science. He remembered a guy from chem. lab back at St. X. Gary Fitzer, a total screwball. Fitzer had snuck a test tube under the lab bench, pissed in it, and set it over his Bunsen burner to boil. What a stench! Brother Hershey had pounded Fitzer's ass. Antigravity might as well be piss stink, as far as Mr. Bulber was concerned.

"Get a haircut," said a thick voice behind Conrad. "Love it or leave." It was Platter. Despite occasional spats, he and Conrad were still roomies and best friends. Platter did all his studying in the science library. He said it was more boring that way.

"Always tearing down," responded Conrad. "Never building up."

"Orbit," said Platter, smacking his lips and stroking his beard. "Uff, uff."

"Orbit, man."

In the last year or two, it seemed like society had begun to turn against people Conrad and Platter's age. Growing up, they'd been America's Finest, but now all of a sudden they were spoiled brats, Spock-raised squallers, no-good ingrates. Even though nothing had changed. Politicians were picking up on it, and the funnies, too. Platter's "Orbit, man, uff, uff" routine was from a villainous young

longhair now playing in *Little Orphan Annie*. Rex Morgan
was on the trail of a college LSD guru. *Li'l Abner* . . . in
the old days it had been *funny* . . . but now the strip was
always about Joanie Phonie (Joan Baez), and *S.W.I.N.E.*
(Students Wildly INdignant about Everything). Conrad
had never liked people telling him what to think—but if
you had to choose between radicals and uptight old people, there was no contest. If only he could get hold of
some drugs!

"You want to go eat?" asked Platter.

"Sure. That Bulber is such an asshole."

"Why? He expects you to do homework? Take tests?
Go to lab? What a Nazi!"

"Aw, I was telling him this really good idea I have, and
he started dumping all over me."

"What kind of idea?" asked Platter, beginning to smile.
He'd had experience with Conrad's "good ideas" before.

Conrad hesitated. Even though they'd roomed together
for three years now, he still hadn't ever told Platter that
he could fly. Ace and Audrey were the only ones who
knew—and Ace never mentioned it. Actually, Ace had
been so drunk the time Conrad saved him that maybe
he'd forgotten the whole thing. The picture of Conrad
and Audrey flying off the Eiffel Tower had been widely
publicized—it had even been on TV—but no one knew
who it had been, or what had really happened.

"Can you keep a secret, Platter?"

"Like a tomb." They were walking across the campus
now. It was the start of December, raining a little, beginning to get dark. "Let me guess. You've discovered a new

member of the pion family. Fella name of Ed Pion, with a half-life of two picoseconds. A real degenerate particle, Ed is, here today and gone . . ."

"This is serious, fucktooth. I can fly. I can levitate."

Platter's gasping laugh started up. *Haw-nnh-haw-nnh.* "Sure you can, Conrad. And that fascist swine Bulber doesn't believe you." *Haw-nnh-haw-nnh.* "He thinks you're a weirdo. Just because you have long hair!"

Conrad had to laugh along, but he was more than a little disappointed. If only there was some way to convince Platter he was serious. The only time he could be sure of flying was when his life was in danger. . . .

So be it. The two boys were just walking up to the curb of a street that cut through the campus. A heavy delivery truck was chugging toward them. With a well-timed spring, Conrad flung himself in front of the truck, expecting his mind to come up with the usual last-minute life-saving flight. But something even stranger happened.

Conrad was lying there in the street. Platter was yelling, and the skidding truck was only inches away. *Fly*, Conrad was thinking, *I know I can do it.*

All at once, lying there, Conrad realized that he was not going to be able to fly. Something about having his and Audrey's picture in the paper had finished the power off. Was this, then, some kind of suicide attempt?

The truck's left tire, moving slowly as in a dream, bore down on Conrad's face. The low-hanging bumper was about to touch his hip. The right tire was already nudging his foot. There was only one way out: *Get small! Shrink!*

It happened. For the time it took the truck to pass, Conrad shrank down to a length of two inches. His clothes shrank with him. Tiny in the road, he got to his feet and gaped up at the truck's underside—a moving sky of angry machinery. As soon as the truck had skidded past, Conrad got big and took off running.

Platter caught up with him at the dining hall. "Jesus, Conrad. What happened back there? You trying to kill yourself? The tires barely missed you! You need *help*, old roomie. I don't want to wake up tomorrow and find a grinning corpse in the other bed."

"Where's Ace? We gotta talk to Ace."

"He's in there eating supper, Conrad. What's the matter with you?"

They found Ace eating alone in a corner of the dining hall. Ace was in one of his antisocial phases these days. He frowned impatiently when Conrad and Platter set their trays down on his little two-person table.

"No room," snapped Ace.

"Tell Platter," said Conrad, dragging over an extra chair. "Tell him that I used to be able to fly. The time you fell off the roof?"

Ace cut a small piece of Swiss steak and chewed it for a while. He peppered his salad and ate some. "You said not to talk about it," he said finally, squeezing lemon into his tea.

"But it's true, isn't it? I *flew*."

"It seemed that way," shrugged Ace. "We were pretty hammered."

"You know what Bunger did just now?" interrupted Platter. "He threw himself under a fucking truck."

Ace was on his dessert now, vanilla pudding. "Did he fly to safety?" He didn't bother to look up.

"I *shrank*," said Conrad triumphantly. "I stood up under the truck and it just drove over. I was the size of a thumb!"

Platter groaned and Ace began to laugh. *Eh-eh-eh.* "You're all right, Pig, you really are." *Eh-eh-eh.* "You want to get some beer?"

"Well . . . I guess so."

"What about Mechanics and Wave Motion?" protested Platter. "What about Audrey?"

"A man's got to do what he can, Ronnie." Ace made a wise face and waved one of his hands palm-down over his plate. "Even if he's the size of a thumb. Did I ever tell you all about when I worked behind the counter at the Big Woof?"

"Uh . . . no," said Conrad. "Tell us about it."

"The Big Woof?" said Platter. "What kind of place was this, Weston?"

"It was a diner up in Massachusetts. I worked there the summer after high school. All the customers were idiots; I mean who but an idiot would eat food from a place called the Big Woof? One of these guys would come in, sit at the counter, and say, 'Put me on a dog, Chief.' I'd look over and snap back, 'You wouldn't fit.' A lot of laughs. The boss was kind of pitiful. Ned. Ned's daughter was, like, a real slut. Lots of makeup, always with a different guy, and fucking all of them. Ned tried not to think about it. Then in August, all of a sudden, Ned's daughter wanted to get married real fast. She was knocked up, I guess, and was marrying a Puerto Rican. Ned wanted to make the best of it—his wife was dead, and his daughter was all he had. He loved her a lot, and he wanted the best for her, so he threw her a big wedding reception in the Holiday Inn. I was there, too, there was a lot to drink, but the groom's friends and family were real assholes. I mean, it was a wedding reception, and they were all acting like Ned and his daughter were trash. You could tell the groom wasn't going to treat her right; it was like even though she was married, everyone was going to call her a slut forever. Just for wanting to get laid a lot, no different than guys. It was pretty terrible."

"This is really cheering Conrad up a lot," said Platter. "This is just the kind of story he needs to hear."

"No, no," said Conrad. "Go ahead." It was always nice to listen to Ace talk. That was the real fun of drinking with him, listening to the endless flow of his oddly slanted stories.

"Right. So the reception breaks up with the groom slapping Ned's daughter and hustling her into the car. Everybody grabbed a bottle from the bar and split. Ned had left his car at the Big Woof—so he could ride to the wedding with his daughter in a limousine—and I gave him a ride back over there. 'It's all for the best,' he kept saying. 'I'm sure it's all for the best.' It was Sunday, and the diner was closed. As soon as we pulled into the parking lot you could smell it."

"Smell what?"

"All the meat had spoiled. Ned had a big walk-in freezer with three months' worth of meat in there. The motor had blown out maybe Saturday night, and all day the sun had been shining. It was like five thousand dollars' worth of meat—hot dogs, hamburger, steaks, and chickens—all stinking and rotting there, while some prick was driving off with Ned's pregnant daughter. It was like the summary of his life."

"What did Ned do? What did he say?"

"He always called me Westy. 'Westy,' he said, 'you've only got one life. Make the most of it.'"

FOURTEEN

thursday, december 9, 1965

Conrad gave up schoolwork again and spent a week getting drunk with Ace. Audrey seemed more and more distant. Finally all sources of money dried up. It was a gray winter morning, and Conrad was walking around with nothing to do.

He was loath to go back to the dorm.... Platter was on the warpath. Something about pajamas. Ace and Conrad had been drinking ... yesterday ... and Ace had put Platter's green pajamas on over his clothes. Then they'd found Platter's big stash of old porno magazines and showed them to everyone. What a panic.

Some ugly girls had asked Ace and Conrad up to their apartment; the girls had even paid for beer. Some wild scene late at night ... Ace humping a girl in the bathroom ... the landlady coming up ... Conrad scribbling gibberish in a notebook ... forget it.

Conrad wandered into one of the dorms and took a shower. Better. There was a crazy guy who lived here— Freddy Whitman. People said he took drugs. Check it out. These days it seemed like every issue of *Life* had LSD on the cover.

Whitman's door was open, and Conrad walked right in. Surf music on the box. Whitman was at his desk, blond and mad-eyed, his shirtsleeves rolled all the way up to his armpits. He was measuring some thick red liquid into gelatin capsules.

"What are you doing, Freddy?"

". . . Bunger. I knew you'd come by sooner or later. This is mescaline. I boiled a lot of cactus for three days to get it."

"Cactus?"

"Look." Freddy pulled a big cardboard box out of his closet. It was filled with flat green cactus buds. "Peyote. I order it from Texas. Wild Zag Garden Supply. It's still legal. Have you ever tripped?"

"I've never even smoked marijuana, Freddy. How do you know about all this stuff?"

"It's in the comics." Laughing and twitching his elbows, Freddy handed Conrad a Marvel comic. "This is about a *trip*, man."

Conrad flipped through the pages. It was a *Weird Adventure* about a man who gets on a subway at a stop that's boarded up. The train is full of beige snout-monsters and leads to another dimension.

"Freddy, I don't see what . . ."

"And look at this. It's my letter to the FBI." Freddy handed Conrad a closely written piece of paper titled "STOP PERSECUTING FREDRIC Q. WHITMAN." Whitman was strange for sure. He'd been away from college last year, but now he was supposed to be making a fresh start. "Do you want some peyote?"

"Uh, what does it feel like?"

"The best trip is if you shoot up acid." The *S*-sound in *acid* came out sweet and sibilant. Freddy sounded like a kid talking about candy. "I did that last week, and after a while I noticed this *big jewel* stuck to my forearm. It was the syringe."

"But what about peyote? Will I see God?"

"It's a good solid trip. Colors. Lots of physical stuff. Here, eat these. Eat three."

Conrad took the peyote buds and looked at them. They were fresh and moist, with small soft spines. He broke off a piece. It was spongy and white inside.

"Go on," urged Freddy. "Blow your mind."

Conrad started chewing. Very bitter. A definite feeling of crossing a frontier. This was something he'd wanted to do for a long time.

"Be careful not to eat those hairs in the middle of the buds," cautioned Freddy. "They have strychnine."

Conrad chewed and swallowed, swallowed and chewed. It was hard to avoid the hairs. He picked some of them out from between his teeth. "Give me two more buds. I want to be sure it works."

There was silence, there was noise. Freddy was sitting across the room, watching closely. His teeth seemed so white. He was planning to eat Conrad's brain.

"I'm leaving," announced Conrad. His voice echoed in the quiet room. "I want to get someplace safe before it's too late."

"You have to stay. I want to watch you freak out."

"A phone call." Any sign of panic could be fatal. "I just have to make a phone call, Freddy. I'll come right back up."

Conrad went down to the dorm lobby and sat in the phone booth. He wanted to call Audrey, up at Columbia. The receiver was soft and melting. None of the numbers would stay still. You could see the operator inside the handset. It rang and rang. Conrad staggered to a couch and the full trip hit him like a ton of bricks.

The subway. Conrad was in the first car of a subway train, staring out into the darkness ahead. He was the driver and his stomach was the engine, pushing the vision forward with wave after wave of peristaltic agony. Ropy tooth-monsters loomed ahead, huge pink and beige maws. Conrad tumbled forward, ever faster, swallowed by mouth after mouth. It was like a terrifying ghost-house ride, and he wanted to scream; but his mouth was full, full of sour stinking lumpy lava—the faces leered and gibbered, the train swayed and crashed, endless strobing horror visions; and Conrad was too weak to even die.

At some point he realized he'd been throwing up. Puking into a green metal wastepaper basket, and thinking the vomit patterns were faces. Freddy Whitman still waiting upstairs, dig, *I want to watch you freak out*. Help!

Conrad shuffled out to the street. The bare trees' black branches were monsters' claws. Reaching, reaching, reaching, reaching. Should he walk in the middle of the street? But the cars! Those stories about people who went crazy and ran into traffic or jumped out windows . . . *Calm down, Conrad*. "Calm down," repeated a million voices in his head, voices that thinned and twisted into devils' laughter. "Calm down down downdowdowdowddddyyyahha-hahahahaaauuuuugh! You're going going goinnnnnng craaaaaaazzyyyyaahahahahahaaaaaah!" It was beyond any horror Conrad had ever imagined. Why had he gotten into this?

His dorm room was deserted. Everything looked like a face. The desk, the doorknobs, the bathroom sink. Even the blank walls looked like faces, the nightmare faces you can't stand to see. "Kill yourself," whispered the razor on the sink. "Cut your wrists and end the torture."

Conrad rushed out of his dorm. Tried to rush—the air was thick as jelly. Chuckie Golem and some other guys were renting a house across the street this year. *Go there! Be with people!* It took forever. He could barely talk when he found his friends.

"Where did you get it?" Chuckie kept asking. "Where did you get the dope?" Completing an answer was next to impossible. Language had become an infinitely ramifying net—instead of the tame familiar grid. Each word opened onto a new, randomly selected context.

For a moment, Conrad fell into the delusion that he was a physics professor, explaining relativity to the four smiling faces at Golem's kitchen table. The room became a stagelike lecture hall . . . but then the refrigerator beckoned, and Conrad hugged its great white smoothness. Food. Sex. Things grew less hectic.

"What do you see, Conrad?" He and Chuckie were sitting face to face.

"It's like a Renoir. I've always wanted to be in a Renoir painting and now I am. Ma. The horrors. I had the horrors. Pinball. I'm in a pinball machine, *fzzzt*, the light, oh, the colored lights, tunnel dragon, *there*, did you feel it, too, the vomit lava? Love. I'm so happy. I was scared I'd kill myself. Dr. Kildare Morgan. Everything a painting with the tooth teeth under it. It sits very . . .

Conrad had been staring at Golem as he talked, and now the other boy's face began to undergo a series of high-speed changes. Renoir / Modigliani / Cézanne / Rousseau / Roualt / Bonnard / Vuillard / Monet / Léger / Dufy / Chirico / Nolde / Schwitters / Ernst / Braque / Picasso . . . the entire history of modern art compressed into one wonderful rush of variations on Chuckie Golem's face . . . ending with what seemed like twenty minutes of pure Cubist flow.

"Here's Platter," said Chuckie. "We called him to come get you."

Platter took Conrad back to their dorm room but not before Chuckie took him aside to give a thousand cautions. Chuckie knew about drugs; he had friends in the Village.

"God, Platter," said Platter as they walked back to the room. "You look terrible. No wonder they're making this stuff illegal. The pathetic husk of a once-great mind."

Conrad laughed in mechanical bursts. Platter's voice sounded so thick and convincing. Platter got Conrad into their easy chair and gave him a glass of water. Conrad spilled the water.

The visions grew stranger. Conrad felt himself and his thoughts as filling a vast balloon, a floppy sphere that floated up miles above the Earth. He was a great transparent balloon with a long neck that stretched down to suck the gray-white December air. He had a terrible feeling that soon the neck would break. He would stop breathing and die. Being dead would feel the same at first ... but then the balloon would melt and the magpie scraps of C. v.R. Bunger's personality would scatter into bright empty space. He'd get his crystal, and the flame-people would pick him up in their flying saucer. Groovy. Let it happen ...

"*CONRAD!*"

He forced his eyes open. The easy chair's cushion stretched out on every side. His and Platter's room was the size of a gymnasium. He'd shrunk again. Platter was shouting something, lifting the glass of water ...

Splat.

The water. Cold life on cold Earth. Conrad was big again. He was wet all over.

"Conrad," Platter was babbling. "I was really worried. You were shrinking! Like you said you did under that truck. What's going on here, anyway? You were the size of my thumb, Conrad, I swear! Don't take these drugs anymore, it's madness! I'm going crazy just living with you!"

FIFTEEN

friday, december 10, 1965

Audrey shared a New York apartment with two other girls, also graduate students. The apartment was a fourth-floor walk-up, between Broadway and Amsterdam Avenue.

The daylong peyote trip had granted Conrad one short revelation. *Go see Audrey*. As soon as the stuff had worn off enough, Conrad stole a crowbar from the janitor's closet and pried open the dorm change machine. Fifteen dollars in quarters. A round-trip bus ticket to New York was a prohibitive twelve dollars, so Conrad hitched instead. He made a sign saying NYC and got Chuckie to take him to a big highway. Just before dropping him off, Chuckie gave him some yellow granny-glasses to wear.

"Take these, Conrad. They'll help you keep it together."

He slipped the glasses on. Everything looked thick and sunny—like the good part of the peyote trip.

"Do I look cool?"

"You look like a real blown mind."

Conrad didn't have to wait long before an empty moving van stopped. The truck's cab was full of Italian movers. Conrad had to ride in back.

It was weird for Conrad back there, in the rumbling dark, with echoes of the peyote still bouncing around his skull. It took a conscious effort not to start *seeing* things. Fast-flickering flame-people, mind-rays, and chains of hidden cause-effect, *another order of reality* . . .

The truck dropped him off somewhere in Manhattan. It was early evening. The store windows were full of Christmas displays. Taking the subway uptown to Audrey's was the hardest part. The horror-train. Conrad was scared to look out the windows or at the other passengers. Instead he looked at his hands. They were flaking like wet cardboard. The flesh was crumbling off, and he could see the bones underneath.

He hadn't called Audrey, because he was afraid she might say not to come. He had to push the downstairs bell in her building for quite a while before she buzzed the door. And when he finally got upstairs, she was alone there with another guy.

"This is my friend Richard," Audrey told Conrad.

Richard offered Conrad a glass of wine. He'd just brought a bottle over to share with Audrey. She deserved it, said Richard, because she'd let him store his golf clubs here over Thanksgiving break. Flesh was peeling off his head, and Conrad could see sections of his skull.

"Actually," explained Conrad, "I have a date with Audrey tonight. We were planning to go out to dinner, weren't we, Audrey?"

She paused, thinking, then agreed. Richard took his golf clubs but left the wine. It was Almaden Chablis.

"Why didn't you call?" Audrey asked.

"Is Richard your new boyfriend?"

"You look terrible, Conrad. What have you been doing to yourself?"

"I took some peyote. It made me throw up and see visions. I still don't feel quite normal. I feel like I'm from outer space."

Audrey frowned. "Your drinking is already so bad, and now you have to start with drugs. Is that going to be the new thing with you, Conrad?"

"It's better than golf."

Audrey looked down at her lap and began picking at a loose thread on her jeans. She didn't want to meet his eyes. "What if we stopped seeing each other?" she said after a while. "Swarthmore was fun, Conrad, and this summer in Paris was lovely. But couldn't that be enough? Why should I have to marry the very first person I make love to? Life shouldn't be so predictable."

"Having a predictable life is the least of my worries," said Conrad with a short laugh. "Things are constantly falling apart. You're the only solid thing in my world, Audrey, you're the warm center." He knelt by her chair and began kissing her. "Don't drop me, Audrey. I need you so much."

She kissed back with some fervor. He got her breasts out, she unzipped his fly, and a few minutes later they were in her bed fucking.

"Oh, Audrey. This feels so good. Everything's been skeletons."

"It's all right, Conrad. I do still love you."

After sex, they lay in Audrey's bed, talking and drinking Richard's wine.

"What have you been doing all month?" Audrey asked. "I was wondering why I didn't hear from you."

"I kept calling, but you were never home. And then I was getting drunk. Didn't your roommates give you the messages?"

"I was waiting for you to actually show up. That's what counts, you know. Being here."

"I've been broke."

"Can't you *fly* here from Swarthmore?"

"I don't think I can fly anymore, Audrey." He told how the truck had almost run him over—being careful not to mention that he'd jumped in front of it on purpose. "I needed to fly away from that truck, but I couldn't. But listen! Instead of flying, I *shrank*."

"You shrank." They were still naked, and Audrey was nestled on his shoulder. "Can I have some more wine?"

"Sure." He poured out more wine for both of them. "I shrank to the size of a thumb, and the truck went right over me. When you were a kid, did you ever read the book about the five Chinese brothers?"

"I don't think so."

"Well, there's these five Chinese brothers who look exactly like each other. One of them can swallow the sea, one can stretch his legs to be as tall as he wants, one has an iron neck, one is fireproof, and one can hold his breath forever. To do a little boy a favor, the first brother sucks up the ocean so the little boy can walk around on the bottom and look for treasure. But then the little boy won't come back in time, and the brother spits the ocean back up, and the little boy drowns. So the village decides to put the Chinese brother to death."

"They try different ways of killing, and each time a different brother shows up?"

"Right. They throw the one with stretchable legs into deep water, and he just stands there. The one with the iron neck comes and they can't chop off his head. The fireproof one comes and they can't burn him. Finally they decide to smother the Chinese brother in an oven filled with whipped cream, but that day it's the one who can hold his breath. The judge gives up and they live happily ever after."

"Let me see you shrink, Conrad." She was kissing and caressing him.

"I have to be in the right frame of mind. Hold on." He closed his eyes and let the peyote death-fear come welling back up. He was leaving Earth, his breathing was stopping, the saucer was going to pick him back up . . . and right now he was dying, yes, fading out of flesh for . . .

Her skin slid against his as he grew smaller. He was the size of a child, a baby . . . he was the size of a thumb. Audrey's body was a magic pleasure-park, and Conrad was her gardener. They began having fun. Before long she came, and Conrad got big again.

"Oh, Conrad. That was wonderful."

There was noise out in the living room. One of Audrey's roommates, a hyperactive vulgarian named Katha Kahane.

"*Audrey?* Ya here?" The bedroom door rattled.

"Don't come in, Katha."

"Who ya got in there tonight?"

"Fuck you, Kahane!" yelled Conrad.

Audrey winced, then began to laugh. "I'm sorry, Conrad."

"Do you love me best?"

"Chinese brother."

After a while they got dressed and went out. Conrad was still wearing the round glasses Chuckie had given him.

The night city was black and yellow; the streets and buildings etched strange perspectives. A gibbous moon hung over the skyline. *This is really going on*, thought Conrad. *I'm really alive.*

"What were those two rules I used to have, Audrey?"

"What do you mean?"

"Sophomore year. I thought I had it all figured out. Rule 1: *Don't be a phony.* And Rule 2: *Don't be a mean bastard.* Remember?"

"You don't believe that anymore? Now that you've expanded your consciousness? Is that what it feels like to take peyote, Conrad; is it a feeling of *expansion*?"

"Contraction. You have to focus on just staying alive. It's kind of a nightmare."

"I can't believe you shrank like that." A blush stole across Audrey's cheek.

"Did Kahane think I was Richard?"

"She knew it was you. She just wanted to make you suffer. She doesn't like you, Conrad. None of my friends ever have. Liked you. That's something I like about you the most."

"You really do love me?"

"Yes. But that doesn't mean I have to marry you. Reading about the French Surrealists and Dadaists, I always think how wonderful it would have been to hang out with them in cafés. And you're sort of like them. Only now, in America, being avant-garde is so seedy and violent. Sometimes you frighten me, Conrad. What if you're just a drug-addict-bum your whole life? I wouldn't want to live with a person like that. It's too sad." She glanced at him and looked away. "But you were saying about the two rules. If it's not them, what *is* it? What's the answer?"

"Having adventures. Getting out to the edge and jumping off." They turned the corner onto Broadway. "Making it back is important, too. You go way out, further than anyone's been, and then you come back to tell about it." The street was full of people, happy-looking people. Conrad squeezed Audrey's hand. "After that peyote, I'm glad not to be dead or crazy. Even though I'm such a Chinese brother that nothing can bust me."

"I wonder how you got this way."

"It must have been something that happened when I was little. Radiation. Or maybe I'm not human. I keep having this feeling that I come from a flying saucer."

"Oh, sure. What about your brother and your parents?"

"They could have been implanted with false memories. Really, it's starting to seem like our whole generation is aliens. The geezers are just so . . . square nowhere. Roast Beef. Vietnam. Dry Martini. Gross National Product. Do the Twist. Kids These Days. Hot Black Coffee. Is That a Girl or a Boy? They Call That Music?"

"Look at my new shades." Audrey got a pair of aviator mirror-shades out of her purse. With the sunglasses and her long, tangled hair, she looked real gone. "I've been saving them for you. Richard doesn't like them."

"You look *beat*, Audrey."

"So do you. With those yellow glasses, you look stoned."

"We're cool. We've made it. It's time to groove."

SIXTEEN

friday, december 10, 1965

They decided to have supper in a dark-paneled tavern called the Gold Rail. The waiter helped them order food and a pitcher of beer. He didn't card them.

"It's civilized here," said Conrad, filling their glasses. "Just like in Paris."

"Just like."

They toasted each other and sipped the bitter, lip-tickling brew. Audrey took off her shades.

"How are your courses going?" asked Conrad.

"Philology is a lot of fun. Phonetics is awful. And we've been reading this great novel by Diderot. It's all about men having sex with nuns. One man disguises himself as a nun to get into the convent—he's a young shepherd named Valentin."

"Do they catch him?"

"Well, one of the nuns gets pregnant, so they know there's a man. The Mother Superior tells the nuns they have to line up naked and come into her room and be inspected one by one. So Valentin ties his . . . ties his cock back between his legs . . ."

"What does he tie it to?"

"*I* don't know." Audrey giggled and sipped at her beer. "Anyway, when the Mother Superior leans down to look at Valentin, he gets so excited that he breaks the ribbon and knocks off her glasses!"

"Sounds great."

Their food arrived. Sole and crabmeat for her, steak and fries for him. It was delicious. They were in a booth near the bar. There was a good jukebox. The place was dark and loud and warm and full of good things to eat and drink.

After dinner they ordered another pitcher and started smoking Audrey's Newports. Conrad felt looser and looser, more and more plugged into the Now.

"I feel like I haven't been thinking enough, Audrey. At college I've just been drinking and trying to act cool. When I should have been learning more about the secret of life. I used to always talk about it in high school." There were some loud drunks at the bar. Fraternity guys from Columbia.

"So what is the secret of life, Conrad? Drugs?"

"Drugs ... I don't know anything about drugs yet. All I've done is take peyote once and go crazy. Actually, I was already crazy, from missing you so much. But the secret . . ." Conrad raised his glass, feeling for the just-right phrasing.

Just then Hank Larsen appeared, walking into the Gold Rail as if he had been conjured up for the occasion. Fit and tired-looking, he wore a university jacket with a big *C* on it. He and Conrad recognized each other the instant their eyes met.

"Conrad Bunger! My God, it's *Conrad*." Hank strode over and began thumping on his old friend. "Conrad, buddy. You look like John Lennon!"

"I don't believe this, Hank. I was just thinking about you. The pasture? The secret of life? This is Audrey Hayes. She goes to grad school here, and I came up to see her."

"Pleased to meet you." Hank squeezed into their booth and called for beer. "I've just been down at the pool doing laps. *Five miles.* Coach is all steamed up about some big-ass meet we got next week."

"You're on the swimming team?" asked Audrey.

"Yeah . . ." Hank laughed and shook his head. "They've made a jock out of me. A communications major. And I was planning to be a drunk artist. Remember that painting we made, Paunch?"

"What painting?" asked Audrey.

"It was when Conrad and I were twelve," said Hank. "We got this huge piece of Masonite out of his dad's garage and painted it with gesso. Then we took turns throwing black and red paint on it like Jackson Pollock. Conrad had this idea to make it like the Creation, so he read the Book of Genesis out loud while I was flinging paint. It looked damn good."

"You were better at painting than I was," said Conrad. "We each did some small ones, too, remember, and you were trying to paint like Tanguy and Dali."

"I love those guys. That's one of the great things about living here in the Big Noise. I can always cut over the MOMA and look at the paintings."

"I do that, too," said Audrey. "I love New York."

"I first came up here when I was twelve," said Hank. "My dad took me along on a business trip. We went to Radio City. God. They had all the dancers, and this great stage show—there was a kind of big wagon that kept zooming back and forth, with people jumping in and out of it."

"When you got home you tried to build a model of it with your Erector set," put in Conrad.

"Yeah. Another Larsen debacle." He shook his head in a familiar self-deprecating way, and then looked at Audrey. "So you're Conrad's girlfriend? You're making a noble sacrifice for mankind."

"Oh, he's not so bad," laughed Audrey. "If he's not stoned or drunk."

"Stoned," said Hank. "Tsk-tsk. I remember when Conrad read about Benzedrine inhalers in some beatnik anthology—I think it was an excerpt from *Junkie*—and he ran out and bought all these inhalers and ate the shit in them. Despite the fact that they stopped putting Benzedrine in them about ten years ago."

"Well, it was worth a try," said Conrad, a little embarrassed. "You shouldn't let the sixties pass you by, Hank. Especially at Columbia. I keep reading about all the student activists and—"

"Bunch of pears," spat Hank. He sketched a pear shape in the air. "I refer to the body envelope. Don't tell me you're a student radical, Conrad?"

"Well . . . no, not actually. Not in any organized fashion."

"They won't let you join the Party, eh?" Hank started laughing again and began imitating a pear. *"We don't want Bunger at our demonstration, he's liable to show up drunk!"*

"Conrad wants to find the secret of life," put in Audrey.

"We were just talking about it when you showed up, Hank. Remember that time we were in Skelton's pasture talking about the life-force?"

"Sure. I remember thinking that stuff up. I even wrote a paper on it for my twelfth-grade humanities course."

"*You* didn't think it up," cried Conrad. "*I* did. *You're* the one who said pantheism is 'a bunch of dumb shits kneeling in front of a rock.'"

"That's true too." Hank grinned. "As soon as any philosophy gets turned into an organized religion, it's for dumb shits."

"But everyone joins something," protested Audrey.

"Don't I know it," sighed Hank. "I'm even in a fraternity." He refilled his beer glass from the pitcher. "So what are you majoring in, Conrad? You haven't written me since freshman year."

"You were the one who stopped writing. I guess I'm in math."

"Math?" exclaimed Audrey. "I thought you were majoring in physics."

"Well, I didn't get a chance to tell you yet. My physics teacher really hates me. And on the way up here, I realized that I'll have enough math credits if I just take two math courses each semester next year."

"But what about antigravity?" clamored Audrey.

Hank started to laugh, but Conrad cut him off. "I really was able to fly, man. Audrey saw me."

"That's right. Conrad flew us both down from the Eiffel Tower. Didn't you see the picture? It was in all the papers."

"Oh, yeah . . ." said Hank, slowly smiling. "I remember seeing that picture on the news. It was supposed to be a hoax, but . . ."

"That was me and Audrey," said Conrad. "It was a very special day."

"So you jumped off the Eiffel Tower!" exulted Hank. "Remember in high school, when I said you should jump off the Heyburn Building?"

"Yeah, I was scared. I wasn't quite sure it would work."

"But you say you can't fly anymore? You've lost the knack?"

"Yeah. I don't know why. Recently, I've been *shrinking* instead. Right, Audrey?"

Audrey blushed and giggled.

Hank took a long pull from his beer. "I almost believe you, Conrad. Remember how your family used to have the TV down in that musty basement room?"

"Caldwell's apartment."

"Right. And in the summer, you and me'd watch *Twilight Zone* down there . . . sometimes it would get kind of scary . . . and after the show we'd go outside and lie in the grass, looking at the stars and making up our own stories."

"Yeah."

"And you had this story about how a flying saucer had beamed you down and changed your family's memories to think you'd been born in the normal way. You claimed you couldn't remember anything before your tenth birthday. When your family moved to Louisville."

"He was just telling me that on the way over here!" exclaimed Audrey.

"Yeah." Conrad shrugged. "For some reason that story's always appealed to me."

"The year your family moved in was the year of all the big saucer scares," Hank mused. "Nineteen fifty-six. I remember when old man Skelton saw a saucer and found that crystal in his hog pen. Just before you showed up, Conrad. You were supposed to be ten. Maybe the saucer set you down at Skelton's the day the *Bungers* moved to Louisville. Their memories got doctored, and old Conrad walked up from the pasture and joined the gang."

"And ever since," said Conrad, "I've been trying to be a regular guy."

"Is he a regular guy, Audrey?"

"Forget it! Is that true, Conrad, that you can't remember anything from your early childhood?"

"Oh, I have a few memories. There was this dream I used to always have. A kind of nightmare ... but a *fun* nightmare. I'd be at a circus, except all the people and all the acrobats were made of light. They were like flames, swinging around way up in the air. Neon lights. Eventually they'd come after me and push me down through a trapdoor."

"The aliens!" cried Hank. "Your original race. The door in the bottom of the saucer! Do you know why they sent you here?"

"Isn't this getting a little too ..." began Audrey.

"No, no," said Conrad, refilling his glass. "Hank and I always used to do this. *Why the flame-people sent me here.* To find out what humans are like. Our saucers have been monitoring Earth ever since the forties. We have amassed untold amounts of data. Yet a final understanding of the human condition has eluded us. What makes you people tick? Why do you behave as you do? What are your highest goals, and what can we learn from you?" Conrad was spieling all this out in a flat, robot voice. It was a science-fiction rap, a comedy routine. "It became evident that one of us would have to undergo incarnation as a fleshapoid. I was the one."

"'*I was the one*,'" sang Audrey, "'*who taught her to kiss . . .* '"

Hank joined in for the rest of the verse. It was the old Elvis song, *I Was the One*. Conrad joined in with off-key enthusiasm on the song's refrain, "*Well, I taught her how.*"

"My mission," said Conrad, resuming his rap, "is to sample what is noblest in the human intellect. I was, in short, sent here to learn what humans believe to be . . ." He nodded encouragingly to Hank and Audrey.

The three of them shouted out the catch phrase in unison: "THE SECRET OF LIFE!"

It was a gas, making up such a crazy lie; it was a way to get past the dull, false consensus reality of the straights; it was a way of getting down into the fluid, archetypal flow of subconscious reality.

That summer, Conrad would find out that most of his story was true.

part three

The strangest thing is that I am not at all inclined to call myself insane, I clearly see that I am not: All these changes concern objects. At least, that is what I'd like to be sure of.

—Jean-Paul Sartre, *Nausea*

sunday, july 31, 1966

Conrad's big brother Caldwell came back from the army that summer. The parents had a basement apartment all set for Caldwell in the new Virginia house. He was a tall, lanky guy, with small eyes and a wide mouth. Everyone was excited the day Caldwell came back, but after a few minutes, he just went down to the basement and lay on his bed. Kid brother Conrad tagged along to ask questions.

"What's the matter, Caldwell? Aren't you glad to be home?"

Caldwell groaned softly. He was facing the wall. "I just want to *go*."

"Go where?"

"Anywhere. I want to get a fast car and go."

"What kind of car are you going to get?"

"I had a Porsche over there. I should have brought it back."

"Do you have a lot of money saved up?"

"Get serious." Caldwell rolled over and looked at Conrad. "How come your hair's so long?"

"That's the new thing. It makes old people mad."

"Jesus. You're going to be a senior this year?"

"Yeah, I've got a girlfriend and everything. I even took peyote."

"It's all changed out from under me."

"But you must have had fun in the army. You were lucky to be in Germany. If I get drafted, they'll send me to Vietnam."

"You should get married."

"I probably will. But they're getting rid of the marriage deferment. Graduate school still works, though."

"My baby brother in graduate school? Studying what?"

"Math, I guess."

"You like math?"

"It's easier than physics or chemistry. There's nothing to memorize. It all follows logically."

"I thought you wanted to major in philosophy. That's what you and Larsen used to say. How is old Hank, anyway?"

"Oh, he's the same as ever. I saw him up at Columbia this winter one time when I was visiting Audrey."

"*Audrey.*" Caldwell smiled wickedly. "Does she put out?"

"How many girls did you fuck in Germany?"

"Why aren't you majoring in philosophy?"

"Philosophy teachers don't talk about anything interesting. It's just words. Nothing's true, nothing's false, it's all a matter of opinion. But math . . . math is clean. Like a game of pool. Perfect spheres clicking and bouncing just so. Do you want to go to a bar and shoot some pool, Caldwell?"

"You're not old enough."

"The drinking age is eighteen in D.C."

"Ahhh, I don't feel like it. I want to look through my old stuff. Did the movers just throw everything in a box?"

"I think Mom went through your stuff first."

"God." Caldwell groaned again and struggled to his feet. His room was equipped with a built-in bookcase, a dresser, a bed, a Danish armchair, and a battered old desk. Some of Caldwell's stuff was in his desk and bookcase, the rest was in a big cardboard movers' box.

"I don't suppose they saved my *Hot Rod* magazines," grumbled Caldwell, poking through the box. "Jesus. Here's my old cuckoo clock. And the piston from my Model A. My NRA certificates, the bullwhip, Pop's football jersey, the Alcatraz pennant, the whale's tooth, my cowboy hat . . . and the dueling pistols. Did you ever see these, Conrad?"

"Yeah, I used to play with them senior year high school. I almost shot a guy when I was drunk once."

Caldwell frowned and shook his head. "Some people shouldn't own guns, Conrad, and you're one of them. Here's some old pictures. I took these myself." Caldwell began flipping through the stack of black-and-white photographs. "I took these the day we moved to Louisville. I was fifteen and you were ten. Pop took us out and bought a camera for your birthday. Remember?"

"You know how I am, Caldwell. I've got a great memory now, but I can't remember much before Louisville. I think it was those hay-fever pills Mom made me take every morning."

"That's true, you used to be really out of it. We were already in Louisville on your birthday. It was the day we moved in. Your tenth birthday." Caldwell continued thumbing absently through the old photos. "Look at *this* picture. It's the flying wing!"

Gray and black stipple of lawn, a stark tree ramifying up, faint cloud patterns, and there, floating in the sky, a sliver-black aircraft. It has no fuselage or tail-gear . . . it is simply a wing, a stubby boomerang, a fat, warped pancake. Windows dot its leading edge . . . scores of windows.

"Do you remember, Conrad? You were with me. I tried to tell Pop about it, but he . . . Damn! I'd forgotten I took a picture of it! Let me see that again!"

The two brothers pored over the picture of the flying wing. Assuming all those portholes were normal size, the thing had to be hundreds of feet across.

"I've still never heard of a plane like that," said Caldwell wonderingly. "I know they built some *small* flying wings, but never anything like . . . You know, I bet I could sell this picture to *Aviation Magazine!*"

"Don't do that," said Conrad. His voice came out flat and strange.

"Why shouldn't I?"

"It's my picture."

"Hell it is."

"Give it to me!" Conrad snatched the picture away from Caldwell and ran upstairs. Caldwell didn't bother chasing him.

Alone in his room, Conrad studied the flying-wing photo for a long time. It could easily be a flying saucer. *The flying saucer that beamed me down. The day the Bungers moved to Louisville. The flame-people beamed me down in Skelton's hog pen and hypnotized the Bungers, new in town, and with no living relatives. When I came "home," the Bungers threw a tenth birthday party for me. The saucer hung around for a while, and Caldwell took its picture.*

Conrad's mother was tapping on his door. He put the picture in his wallet.

"What is it, Mom?"

"Dinner's ready! We're having roast beef!"

The three others were sitting at the dining table, exactly as they had been sitting the first time Conrad saw them, March 22, 1956.

The saucer makes a terrible noise, a deep slow flutter. The whole house is shaking, but no one cries out. The mind-rays have frozen them in place. It is a Norman Rockwell tableau. Pop is at one end of the oval table. He is carving a roast beef. Light glares off his glasses. Mom is at the other end of the table. She is pouring coffee and smiling at Caldwell. She wears pearls. Caldwell holds his plate out for the red meat. He is gangly, with a wide, grinning mouth. The rumbling of the saucer-drive builds in frequency, and the little family begins to glow. Their minds are being reprogrammed. The door opens, and Conrad approaches the table, carrying a cake with ten lit candles. . . .

"Conrad! Are you with us, my boy?" Pop was staring at him, a half-smile on his face.

"He's probably stoned," chortled Caldwell. "Don't you think Conrad should get a haircut, Pop?" He helped himself to some gravy.

Mr. Bunger proudly took in the sight of his big sons. "Look at these two birds, Lucy! Our boys! How was it in Germany, Caldwell? How was it on the ramparts of the Free World?"

"It was a blast. We only had to work a few hours a day—listening to East German radio broadcasts, and the rest of the time . . ."

"You drank booze and chased women. I shudder to think. This is what my taxes go for, Lucy. A strong national defense.

I have some of these *career* men in my congregation—colonels and generals—and they're always moaning about all the lazy people on welfare. 'You're on welfare, too,' I tell them. 'The army is a huge middle-class welfare system.'"

"Pop's turned into a real radical," Conrad told Caldwell. Mr. Bunger's good humor was contagious. "He wants to go picket the White House."

"Hey, hey, LBJ," chanted their father in his cracked old voice. "How many kids did you kill today?"

"Really, Caldwell," protested Mrs. Bunger. "That's enough. Stop this nonsense and let the children eat."

"Great food, Mom," said young Caldwell, taking another baked potato. "Isn't Mom a good cook, Conrad?"

"Shore is," agreed Conrad. This was reality, too. One way or another, these were his people. "I've been to *New* York, and to Paris, France, and I ain't never et vittles the like of these."

"Did you know Conrad's getting married, Mom?"

Mrs. Bunger stopped eating and put on her glasses. She looked quizzical and excited. "Is that true, Conrad? You're going to marry Audrey?"

"Caldwell, I'm going to kill you." Caldwell's eyes were squeezed into happy slits. He loved putting his little brother on the spot.

"Have you thought about getting an *engagement ring*?" continued Mrs. Bunger. "You should cash in your savings bonds."

"Slow down," cried Conrad. "Is there such a rush to get rid of me?"

"Of course not," said Mr. Bunger. "But if you do want

to marry Audrey after college, we certainly won't stand in your way."

"What does this Audrey look like anyway?" asked Caldwell, stunned by the success of his gambit.

"She's very nice," said Mrs. Bunger. "She came here for Easter."

"Can't we talk about something else?" said Conrad. This was agony. Even if he did come from a flying saucer, the Bungers sure knew how to act like relatives.

"Why don't we talk about how Caldwell got kicked out of college?"

"Now, Conrad."

"Which of you boys wants more roast beef?"

Lying in bed that night, Conrad mulled over the day's revelations. The picture of the flying saucer. The memory flash of how he'd come into the Bungers' lives. Subconsciously, he must have known it all along. Why else would he have always talked so much about UFOs? Why else would he have gone around saying he came from a flying saucer? But up till today, he'd never suspected it might actually be true.

I am an alien. Conrad felt his chest and legs, his face and genitals. Sick horror filled him as he imagined his body splitting open to disgorge a bug-eyed squid-creature from Dimension Z.

But that wasn't what the aliens—what Conrad—really looked like. Those dreams of the flame-people, those were true dreams. They were creatures of energy, beings of light. That much seemed certain.

Thinking back on the dreams, Conrad tried to remember

more. There was usually a feeling of being forced to leave. Pushed down into a body on Earth. But why?

Why did they send me here? Could it be a kind of punishment? But life was—on the whole—sweet. It was fun to be human: to think, and fuck, and drink, and do things—it was fun to be alive. This was no punishment. But why else would they have sent him here?

The secret of life. The secret of *human* life. Conrad considered his years-long obsession with this notion. For some reason the flame-people were unwilling—or unable—to appear directly on Earth. What they knew of humanity would be gleaned from radio and TV. It was probably the spreading shell of Earth's old broadcasts that had attracted the flame-people in the first place.

They'd sent Conrad to find out what it's like. They'd equipped him with his strange powers—flight, shrinking, and maybe others—to make sure that he would be here a good long time. Sooner or later they would come get him. He would remember the old language of the energy-dance and tell them just how it felt to be human. He would tell them the deeper truths that never get mentioned on TV. Fine. But this left one question.

How much longer do I have?

Conrad drifted into uneasy sleep. He dreamed his old flame-person dream, and then he dreamed of the mysterious crystal that Cornelius Skelton kept on his mantel.

L et's you and me drive to Louisville tomorrow, Conrad."

"What for?"

"Kicks, man. Kicks."

Caldwell had to shout to make himself heard over the hot, beating wind. They were speeding along in his new green MG convertible, on their way back from an evening's drinking in D.C. Caldwell had managed to get the car for $700 down, and con man that he was, he hadn't even actually paid the $700 yet.

"That's what I always want to ask Pop," Caldwell was shouting now. "Sure Jesus is great, *but what did he do for kicks?*"

"I wouldn't mind going to Louisville," said Conrad, still thinking about Caldwell's proposal. "Maybe we could get some nooky there. And it'd be great to see Hank. I could probably sleep at his house. But where would *you* stay?"

"Don't worry about me, I'm the one with all the rich friends. I'll find a place for both of us, if you like. It'll be fun, huh, bro?"

For the last few days, Conrad had been waiting for Caldwell to ask why he'd grabbed the flying-wing picture. But Caldwell seemed to have forgotten all about it. He just seemed glad that Conrad was finally old enough to really talk to.

Mr. and Mrs. Bunger—Caldwell referred to them as "the ancients"—gave the trip their grudging blessing. Mrs. Bunger told the boys to be sure to look up this or that old family friend; and Mr. Bunger gave them each $100.

"You don't have to spend it *all*, you know."

"Don't worry, Pop. We'll be good."

"Just be sure to come back in one piece."

They took Route 50 through West Virginia, and picked up Route 42 in Cincinnati. Taking turns at the wheel, they made it straight through in fourteen hours . . . which meant they hit Louisville a little after midnight Friday night. Somehow they hadn't gotten around to calling ahead.

"Where are we going to sleep, Caldwell? Which one of your rich friends' parents do you want to wake up?"

"I thought you said we could stay at Larsen's."

As chance would have it, Hank was still up, playing with his shortwave radio. Over the years, he'd packed a whole wallful of equipment into his bedroom. His greatest score to date was the time he'd picked up a transmission from a ship in McMurdo Sound, Antarctica. Conrad tapped on his window, and Hank hurried to the door.

"Why, come on in! It's the rompin', stompin' Bunger boys! How you been, Caldwell, you get out of the army all right?"

"Well, they told me if I reenlisted I'd get a promotion, and seven dollars twenty cents a week extra . . ."

"But you passed it up. Wise move. Conrad, good to see you, buddy. Louisville's been dead without you. Hey . . . you know who else is back in town?"

"Who?"

"Dee Decca." Hank grinned and rolled his eyes for emphasis. "She's been askin' about you, Conrad; she's hot to trot."

"*I* remember her," put in Caldwell. "A dark-haired girl who wore sweatshirts? Smoked a lot? Not too good-looking?"

"*That's* the one," said Hank. "Only now she's smokin' pot."

"This sounds better all the time," said Conrad. "Any chance of a beer?"

"My birthday's not till next week, but Caldwell here's over twenty-one, and the liquor store up at the shopping center's open till three. I see no obstacle to an efficacious implementation."

"Let's rock and roll."

They picked up three sixes of Falls City and went cruising with the MG's top down. Caldwell drove, Hank took the passenger seat, and Conrad squeezed into the jump seat with the beer. At one in the morning, it was still seventy-five degrees.

"Where's Dee staying?" Conrad wanted to know.

"At *Sue Pohlboggen's.*"

"I'm not going there," said Caldwell flatly. "I want to see some *real women*, not these hippie-dippie chicks Conrad hangs out with. You know of any parties tonight, Hank?"

"I heard Tacy Leggett's havin' a blow-out. Wasn't her kid brother Donny a Chevalier boy?"

"Tacy!" screamed Caldwell. "Tacy Leggett!" He executed a U-turn and headed for River Road.

"Be careful on the Leggetts' driveway," cautioned Conrad.

"That's right," chimed in Hank. "Conrad stacked up your mom's VW there Derby Day senior year."

"My baby brother did that?"

"You missed *all* the excitement," said Hank. "Spending four years in the army. Four years! Dumb pud."

"Laugh it up, guys. You're the ones going to Vietnam."

Tacy Leggett's party was still jumping. Otis Redding and Wilson Pickett blasting, cars all over the yard, people dancing by the pool. The pool had spotlights in it. Tacy recognized Caldwell at once. She held her mouth open and squealed, and then she threw her slim arms around him.

"Cal'well! Mah little soldier-boy! How you *beeyun*?"

Donny Leggett wasn't there. Most of the guests were Caldwell's age: straights with real jobs. Neckties, even. There was an outdoor bar set up, with a white-coated black man mixing drinks. Hank and Conrad drifted that way.

"Peppermint schnapps, Paunch?"

"Gin and tonic."

They got their drinks and sat down by the pool. Clinking glasses, they grinned, remembering the time they'd snuck up here and raided Mr. Leggett's liquor cabinet.

"Where's Audrey this summer?" asked Hank after they'd toasted several other high-school escapades.

"Back in Geneva. I was gonna go, but I couldn't face digging basements again."

"She's a real nice girl. That was fun seeing you all in the Rail that night."

"Yeah. I want to talk to you some more about the flying saucer thing."

"Oh, no."

"It's really true, Hank. Look at this." Conrad took the flying-wing picture out of his wallet.

"Could be a saucer," agreed Hank after a brief inspection. "Or it could be a plane heading toward the camera. Where'd you get it?"

"Caldwell took it, out in our front yard *on my tenth birthday*."

Hank shook his head impatiently. "I don't see why it's so all-fired important for you to think you're from a flying saucer, Conrad. Your folks aren't that bad. You act like a kid who thinks he's an adopted prince."

"But . . ."

"And what if I *did* swallow the whole story? Then what? A flying saucer puts you here to find out what it's like to be human. So what? For all practical purposes, you're still just crazy Conrad. You say you have superpowers . . . but if all they can ever do is save *your* life, they're not going to mean anything to *me*. It doesn't connect to anything, Conrad. Old man Skelton still writes UFO letters to the *Louisville Times*, but nobody takes it seriously. His friends all tease him about it."

"Old man Skelton!" exclaimed Conrad. "That's it! We'll sneak in there tonight and steal that crystal he has. I've been dreaming about it ever since I found this picture. Maybe I can use the crystal for a definitive proof!"

Hank sipped his drink and gave a slow laugh of appreciation. "OK. Another Bunger-Larsen caper. Just like old times. But *I'm* not going to get caught holding the bag on this one. *You* do the sneaking. Old Skelton shot him a robber just last year, I do recall."

"Don't worry, Hank, I'll go in. Mr. Skelton can't hurt me. I'll just shrink if I have to. I wonder if Caldwell's ready to hit the road."

"Don't bet on it."

The party was breaking up now, but Caldwell and Tacy were still slow-dancing by the pool. As Conrad approached them, he could sense the working of Caldwell's keen mind.

With a sudden lurch, Caldwell managed to pull himself and Tacy into the pool. Great splashing and laughter.

"Ooh, Cal'well, you all right, hunneh?"

"Sure." Caldwell grinned, his eyes slits. "A little chilly, though. And these are the only clothes I brought."

"Ah can toss yoah clothes into our dryer. Can you wait that looong?"

Caldwell gave Conrad a meaningful glance.

"I really have to get back to Hank's," offered Conrad. "He promised his mom he'd be back by—"

"I can't ride in the car all wet like this," snapped Caldwell. Another signaling glance.

"Well . . . uh, I wonder if you could maybe stay here for a while and I'll come back for you? Could you give me your keys?"

"All right. But drive carefully." All the other guests were gone now. Still in the water, Tacy and Caldwell kept touching each other.

"Cal'well can sleep in the gues' room, Conrad. You just go home and call us tomorrah mornin'."

The two brothers exchanged smiles. Everything was working out perfectly. Hank and Conrad got in the MG.

"Hey, Hank, you want me to show you how I slalomed this hill that time?"

"Go, Bo Diddley."

It was three in the morning by the time they went creeping up to old Cornelius Skelton's farmhouse. Conrad had tied his handkerchief over his face, bandit-style; and Hank was carrying the tire iron from the MG. Conrad took the tire iron and began prying at one of Skelton's windows. Hank lent his force, and the window latch gave with a sudden snap and clatter.

The two boys crouched and froze, waiting for a reaction. But all was quiet: Skelton's big brick house, the rolling pastureland, the distant suburban split-levels, the thin crescent moon overhead.

They'd popped open one of the dining room windows. Right in there, not more than fifteen feet off, Conrad could make out a dark patch—the big fireplace, with the mantel where the famous crystal always sat.

"I'm goin' back to the car," whispered Hank. They'd left it around a bend in the driveway. "After you've been in there a minute, I'll back her up for a fast getaway."

"Good. Cover the license plate with one of the bags the beer came in. And don't leave any empties on the ground. Fingerprints."

"Right. And don't you go in there with that tire iron. Armed robbery."

Conrad handed the tire iron over, and Hank melted into the night. Conrad inched the window the rest of the way up, being careful not to touch the panes. He kept pausing and listening, poised to take flight. Nothing.

Another minute and he'd eased himself up over the windowsill and into Skelton's dining room. God, it was dark. If only he didn't knock over a chair! He should have waited to do this sober—though of course if he'd been sober, he wouldn't have tried it at all.

Faintly, faintly, he could see the dining table. *Skirt that, but don't bang into the walls.* His feet were silent on the thick carpet underfoot. Old Skelton had gotten rich from all the land he'd sold off for the subdivisions. Funny he didn't have an alarm system. *Maybe it's a silent system.* Conrad moved faster. He heard the low whirr of the MG, backing up the driveway. *Hurry!*

Another few steps and he bumped into the mantel. He reached out, and with his first grab, he bagged the crystal. From childhood, he knew it by touch: a parallelepiped with hard edges and smooth faces.

Just then, all hell broke loose.

NINETEEN
saturday, august 6, 1966

K*LA-BRAAAANNNNGGAAANNGAAANNG....* an alarm bell was screaming. *SNIKKK...* sudden spotlights blanked out Conrad's vision. In a spasm of terror, he dropped the crystal and shrank to thumb-size. His clothes and his mask shrank along with him.

There Conrad was, right in front of Skelton's fireplace, standing next to the fallen crystal. The crystal looked as big as an icebox. There were fast footsteps upstairs.

Could he carry the crystal? *Yes.* Though tiny, he still had most of his old strength. Conrad hoisted the crystal onto his back and scampered for the window. Hank was right out there in the MG; you could hear him gunning the engine.

As soon as he got out from under the dining table, Conrad tensed his legs and leaped for freedom. He landed right on the windowsill. Glancing back, he noticed something odd. High in one corner of the room, an automatic camera—the kind Conrad had seen in banks—was grinding away. But there was no time to do anything about it; Skelton was already pounding down his staircase.

Another leap and Conrad was safe in the creases of the MG's folded-down top.

"Go, man," shrilled Conrad. "Haul ass!"

Hank peeled out. A load of buckshot whizzed past, but then they were safely around the bend in the driveway. Conrad hopped into the passenger seat and got big again.

They headed straight for Hank's just a few miles off—and hid the car in the garage. A minute later they were in Hank's bedroom, jabbering as adrenaline coursed through them.

Conrad fumbled a cigarette lit, talking the whole time. "There was a camera in there, that's what I can't believe, spotlights and a camera mounted up . . ."

"He got your picture? Little like that? Christ almighty, you looked like Mighty Mouse flyin' out of there; you really weren't shitting me, but . . ."

"It's going to be on TV, I know it; maybe no one'll recognize me, but why in God's name did Skelton have that set up so—"

"For the *aliens*, son. Skelton always knew the crystal comes from a saucer, and he's been waitin' all these—"

"Shit, that's right, my cover's blown, my ass is—"

"Just glad I didn't get shot for this dumb turd—"

"Calm down, won't you, I have to get out of town before the cops and saucers come roaring down to—"

"*You* calm down, asshole, cops can't find us. Skelton couldn't have seen the car, it was too dark, and the plates were covered, you had that silly-ass snot-rag on your face, and—"

"The flame-people aren't going to like it, Hank, they don't want anyone to know that—"

"Skelton's so fucking nuts no one is going to give a squat, they'll say it's fake like any other UFO that—"

"I just hope they don't terminate my mission, is all. I like being on Earth."

They paused to catch their breath.

"Let me see that crystal, Paunch."

Conrad handed it over. "I'd remembered it as being bigger than this. I saw it plenty of times when I was little. Pop was friends with Mr. Skelton, you know. He's a pretty nice guy."

Hank held the crystal up to the light, slowly turning it back and forth. It was clear, with slanting faces, each a parallelogram. It was the size and shape of a big ice cube. At certain angles, it split the incident images in two. Looking through it made you feel like you were seeing double.

"This is *cool*," said Hank after a while. "You know that crystal-set receiver I built back in fifty-eight? That could only pick up NBC?"

"Yeah. It had that part called a *cat whisker*." Suddenly Conrad realized what Hank was getting at. "You mean?"

"*A receiving set*. Based on this specially tuned crystal."

"Oh, my God. Can you rig it now?"

"I'm too fucking wrecked. Let's call it a night. I'll get you the spare mattress from the basement."

While Hank got the mattress, Conrad fondled the crystal, wondering what kinds of signals they might pick up. Saucer transmissions? Messages from the future? A how-to course on antigravity?

Mrs. Larsen woke them up around noon.

"Conrad! Your brother's been phoning for you. I thought he was joking, but then I peeked in. It's so nice to have you here. We had no idea you were planning a trip!"

"Uh . . . hi, Mrs. Larsen. It's good to see you. Is Caldwell on the phone right now?"

"I told him I'd wake you and have you call back. Here's a towel and a washrag. Did Hank make you sleep without sheets?"

"Doesn't matter." Conrad was in his clothes, under a light blanket. His head hurt and he felt greasy all over. "OK if I take a shower?"

"Of course! Do you still like scrambled eggs?"

"Sounds wonderful."

When Conrad came back from the shower, Hank was already up and dressed, laying out equipment on his desk. "Should have *some* kind of Rube Goldberg assemblage runnin' here before too long." The phone out in the hall was ringing.

"Conrad! It's for you."

Conrad went out and took the phone from Mrs. Larsen. "Hello, Caldwell."

"Conrad Bunger!" The voice was high and husky. For a horrible instant, Conrad thought it was Skelton . . . or one of the flame-people. "This is Dee! Dee Decca. Sue's big sister saw you at Tacy Leggett's last night, so I thought I'd try—"

"Dee!" Conrad was hysterical with relief. "Dee baby! Three years! I loved all your letters . . . don't know why we let it slide like that . . . you're in Louisville, too? Hank already told me, come to think of it, and I was gonna call you today. You as smart as ever? Have you seen God?"

"All the time. I'm a California girl now, Conrad, modern-style. I've got some *stuff* to share with you, and so much to tell. Remember the Bo Diddley concert? And existentialism?"

"Oh, Dee. Do I remember. Look, you're at Sue Pohlboggen's? Can I come over? Is Sue willing to speak to me?"

Muffled voices and giggling. "She says, 'At a distance.' Do you have a car?"

"Uh . . . yeah. Got an MG convertible, Dee."

"Cosmic! Why don't you come get me, and we can take a little drive in the country."

"Sure," said Conrad, not missing a beat. Caldwell could take care of himself, and Hank'd be busy putting the receiver together. *Meanwhile I'll be out getting stoned with my high-school girlfriend!* "I can hardly wait."

"See you in half an hour."

"Beautiful."

Over breakfast, Conrad filled Hank in. Hank took it in stride.

"This space-radio I'm building'll take all day anyway. Get a piece off Dee for me, Conrad. We'll look for you around suppertime."

Caldwell was less gracious when he finally got Conrad on the phone.

"What do you mean, *you need my car today*?"

"I've got a date with Dee Decca. Why can't you use Tacy Leggett's car? Let *her* drive you around."

"That's just it, Conrad. Things didn't work out so well last night. I need to clear out of here. As a matter of fact, since goddamn Mrs. Larsen wouldn't wake you up, I already called Tuck Playfair to come get me."

"Old Tuck's still in Louisville?"

"Yeah, he's coming to get me any minute. But look, I need that car."

"You can do without it till tonight, can't you, Caldwell?"

"Oh, Christ, all right. I think I hear Tuck outside right now. Look, let's meet at the Larsens' for supper. Say six o'clock?"

"Yeah, I'll tell Mrs. Larsen. And we gotta be sure to watch the local news at seven."

Caldwell groaned. "What did you and Hank do, Conrad?"

"What did *you* do to poor Tacy Leggett?"

"You screw up my new car and you're dead."

"Six o'clock."

Dee looked pretty much the same. White skin, two dark moles, a cute face with double-curved lips. She wore jeans and a purple T-shirt.

"Your hair's longer, Dee."

"So's yours. Isn't it great? The fifties are dead forever." She hugged him, and they patted each other's backs.

"Hello, *Conrad*." It was Sue Pohlboggen, curly, blonde, and sassy as ever.

"Sue. How is your ass?"

"*I'll* never tell." She let out one of her suggestive giggles. "Dee's been dying to see you."

"Well, here I am. You ready for our drive, Dee?"

"Let me get my stuff." She darted into the house and was back in a second. She held a lit cigarette and a small, paperback book. "You have to read this, Conrad, it's wonderful."

"The Doors of Perception," read Conrad. "By Aldous Huxley. Isn't he the guy who wrote *1984*?"

"Brave New World," corrected Dee. "He died the day JFK got shot. He was tripping on LSD."

"That killed him?"

"No, no. He was dying anyway. His wife gave him an injection, to help him die. I love your car!"

"So do I," chimed in Sue. "Is it really yours?"

"I'll never tell," said Conrad, raising his voice an octave. This was neat, to be here flirting with his old girlfriends. "Uh, I don't guess you want to come along, do you, Sue?"

Sue giggled again. "Oh, it's just a two-seater. Don't do anything I wouldn't do!"

saturday, august 6, 1966

"Shall I roll another joint, Conrad?" They were idling down a two-lane country road. It was a hot, sunny Saturday afternoon.

"Uh ... *yeah*. I'm just starting to feel it. Time slowing down, you know? The song on the radio, I can't even tell what it is anymore, it's been on so long. I don't *believe* those guitars!"

"*Eight Miles High*. It's great to be with you, Conrad. Do you remember how we used to talk about death and God together? We thought we were misfits, but we were just ahead of our time. Things are really far-out in California. Whole crowds of people getting stoned and communicating ... we're not alone anymore."

Dee bent down out of the wind to roll the joint. She kept her marijuana in a little plastic pill bottle. Not *that* little a bottle, really—they'd already smoked two of the thin, yellow cigarettes, and it looked like there was still plenty of *stuff* left.

There were fenced-in pastures on either side of the high-crowned asphalt road. Trees grew by the fences.

Watching the trees go past was . . . too much. Like green spaceships. Flying saucers. *What if there's a saucer hovering right behind the car*, thought Conrad, his stomach tightening. *Full of cops and aliens.*

"How do you feel, Conrad?"

"Uh . . . I . . . I . . . it's hard to decide if this is pleasant or not."

"Yeah. I like that about being high. Not having things be pleasant or not. Just, you know, *there*. Be *in* it. Like a movie. Don't you feel like we're in a movie, Conrad?"

Some cows drifted past on the left. Conrad glanced back at the empty road and relaxed. It was just a movie, one way or another. Let it happen.

"I feel good, Dee. Thanks for doing this. I've never had enough grass to get stoned before. Just . . . you know, six guys sharing one joint. Locking the door, and everybody saying, 'How am I supposed to feel?'" Conrad burst into shrill laughter. "I already *knew* from taking peyote last winter, and I didn't even *want* to feel like that again. But this is different. This is fun. This is a really good high."

"*The Doors of Perception* is about peyote. Mescaline, actually. I've never had a major psychedelic. What's it like? Did you see God?"

The MG hummed down a hill toward a shady stream. Cool . . . dark . . . safe. "You want to stop here and go wading, Dee? I'll tell you about peyote in a second, but right now this requires . . ." Conrad braked and pulled onto the road's soft shoulder. Turned off the engine.

The angry whine of insects. Cow shit all over. Cops coming soon, no doubt, state troopers who would search their car and find Dee's pill bottle and recognize Conrad from Skelton's picture . . .

Conrad restarted the car and pulled back onto the road. "I don't think I want to stop, after all. I'm feeling a little paranoid. What are you majoring in, Dee?"

"Philosophy and religion. It's all one department at San Jose. We've been studying a lot of the Eastern stuff. Lao-tzu, D. T. Suzuki. There's so many wonderful things to read."

"The secret of life," said Conrad. "Have you found out what it is?"

"I feel like I know it when I'm high. It's what we always said. *All is One.*" She reached out and laid her hand on Conrad's neck. "All part of the same thing. That's Taoism, really, and mysticism, too. You know?"

Her little white hand was part of Conrad's neck now, and the hot summer air was blowing right through them as they drove along. The car, alive in its own way, bore them past the plants and animals, beneath the big bright sky, with the flame-people somewhere high overhead. All is One, all the universe is together, no matter what. Conrad decided to stop worrying. If *he* was a flame-person, how bad could the other ones be?

Dee withdrew her hand and lit the new joint. Passed it to Conrad. He sucked at it. The harsh, hot, grassy smoke, and the yellow paper tasting like banana.

"The secret of life," said Conrad again. "It is, really, such a simple thing. *All is One.* I dig you absolutely, Dee. But . . . still. There's so many big fat books about it—don't those books say something? And there's still all the hard questions: Why does anything exist? What is time? What is matter made of?" Stoned and merged as he was, these questions sounded a little ridiculous to Conrad, but he pressed on nonetheless. After all, if his only mission on Earth was to find out the secret of life, then there was no point in finishing the job too quickly. "*All is One* . . . it's great, but there's more, isn't there?"

"There's different levels of knowing it. Two people might *say* the same thing, but mean something different. You end up back where you started, and it looks like a circle, but really it's a helix. I mean, if . . ."

The new joint was hitting Conrad hard. Dee's well-chosen words scattered past him like a school of fish. The road ahead looked utterly unfamiliar, and the car's controls felt strange. Here came another stream, wider and deeper than the last one.

"Let's go wading," said Conrad, pulling off the road again.

"I thought you were too paranoid to stop."

"Not anymore. Now I'm too stoned to drive."

"Times like this I remember my favorite Zen saying," said Dee. "*Once you're born, the worst has already happened.*" She slipped off her shoes and hopped out of the car. "Let's hit the curl, ho-dad!"

"Cowabunga!"

The afternoon passed in a happy blur of sound and color. Dee and Conrad waded, mostly, splashing around and watching the patterns of drops and ripples. There were water striders to chase, and some crawdad-holes to poke in. They made out a little, too. It was just the kind of unproductive, noncommercial afternoon that was beginning to make dope-smokers so unpopular with corporate America. And the cops never even showed up.

"Do you do this a lot?" asked Conrad, as they motored back toward town. "Out in California?" The dope had pretty well worn off.

"The countryside's nicer here. The grass there is *sharp*. You can't sit in it. But there's the ocean, of course, and mountains in the east. There's one boy I go hiking with a lot."

"Your boyfriend? Is he nice?"

"Yes, he's very nice. I'm glad to be settled on one guy. Sophomore year, I really went wild. I was fucking all kinds of guys."

"I wish I'd been there."

"We could have been fucking in high school, Conrad, if we'd just known how. When you get down to it, sex isn't really that big a deal."

"Oh, God, Dee, don't torture me." He leaned over and kissed her. "I know how to fuck now."

"Yeah, only not by the side of the road. But who knows about tomorrow. Do you have a regular girlfriend?"

"She's called Audrey Hayes. I think I'll marry her after graduation. She's in Switzerland now, her parents live there. I miss her, but I'm glad she's not here today." Conrad took Dee's hand and gave it a squeeze. He felt drained and happy. "This has really been a wonderful day."

"You're all set to get married?"

"Yeah, basically. I mean, that's the next thing after college, isn't it?"

"Aren't you worried you'll end up like all our parents? Married, and with a job and children—just slogging along?"

"Yeah, I worry about getting old. But not all old people are robots. Look at artists and writers. Look at scientists. I don't see why I have to end up like our parents."

"I guess. And, when you think about it, who really knows what our parents are like."

"Who knows what anyone's like," Conrad sighed. "Being human is so weird."

"What are you doing tonight?"

"I'm having dinner at the Larsens'. And then . . . I don't know." Conrad remembered the seven o'clock news. He'd be on it for sure, the size of a thumb. And the radio Hank had been working on all day. What if they started picking up saucer transmissions? "I've got to do something with Hank tonight."

"Well, stop by if you go cruising. Bring us some beer. Sue's always been hot for Hank, you know. She says that's the main reason she went out with you."

They kissed some more in front of Sue's house, and then Conrad headed over to the Larsens'. With the Bunger boys as well as her own four children to feed, Mrs. Larsen had opted for a buffet-style presentation. A meat loaf and a great bowl of potato salad sat on her kitchen table with the plates and flatware. Caldwell was on the back porch, already eating.

"Say, bro." Caldwell looked as tired and happy as Conrad felt. "Food's in there."

"I see it. Where's everybody else?"

"They'll trickle in. The parents already got their food.

They're downstairs watching TV. Give me the keys before I forget."

"OK." As he filled his plate, Conrad realized how hungry he was. He took double portions and sat down next to his brother.

"How was your day with Dee?" asked Caldwell.

"It was good. We smoked some grass and went wading. How about you? What was the problem with Tacy Leggett?"

"Oh, there was no problem with *her*. We got in her bed and pumped away for a while . . . but then we fell asleep."

"And her mother found you?"

"Her father. He didn't say anything, but when I came out of her room, he was sitting in the living room drinking a Bloody Mary and cleaning his shotgun."

"Jesus."

"He made me sit down with him and talk about duck hunting. It got old real fast."

"So Tuck picked you up."

"Yeah. We went out to Harmony Landing and played golf. Saw some old friends. I've got a date with Sherry Kessler for tonight."

"A girl a day," marveled Conrad. He ate in silence for a minute, then remembered about Skelton again. "What time is it? I gotta watch the local news."

"Ten to seven. Hank wants to see the news, too. He's in his room building a radio. What are you two guys up to, anyway?"

"I'll tell you later. It's kind of complex." Conrad was still a little apprehensive about telling Caldwell that he wasn't—strictly speaking—his real brother.

Just then Hank came out to the kitchen to eat. "Hey, Paunch," he called out. "You get in Decca's pants?"

"They got stoned and went *wading*," clucked Caldwell. "These hippies don't have enough sense to get laid."

"How about the radio?" Conrad demanded. "Does it work?"

Hank's face took on a strange expression. "Why don't we go back to my room, and I'll show you what's happened. Just let me fill up my plate here . . ."

The crystal sat on a square of pegboard, surrounded by bright little doodads: striped-sausage resistors, plastic-disc capacitors, buglike transistors, and wires of every color. The largest component was a many-finned variable capacitor from an old truck radio. Conrad remembered the day Hank had gotten that capacitor. The truck had been an abandoned hulk in a nearby quarry—Hank and Conrad often went there on weekends to look for the girlie magazines that the quarrymen sometimes left.

"Why aren't any wires connected to the crystal?" asked Conrad. "Why don't you even have it fastened down?"

"That's just it," said Hank, his voice a tense, exasperated whisper. "Look at my thumb, fucker." He held out his thumb for inspection. There was a charred blister on it. "And the other hand, too." Hank's left palm was crossed by a deep, scabbed scratch. "Every time I try to do anything with that bastard-ass crystal, I get hurt."

"The crystal attacks you?"

"*No!*" Hank caught himself and forced his voice back to a whisper. "I burned my thumb with the soldering gun; and I scratched my palm with the screwdriver. But it's the crystal's fault. You don't believe me? Go ahead and try for yourself. It's *weird*. See that masking tape? Try and tape the crystal down onto the pegboard. I dare you."

Conrad picked up the roll of tape and stared uncertainly at the crystal. "If I try, I'll get spastic and hurt myself."

"Go ahead, dammit. This was your idea in the first place."

Conrad measured out a length of tape and tried to tear it off the roll. The tape was tougher than he'd expected. He pulled harder. Just then his thumb slipped oddly. The thumbnail caught in a wrinkle of the tape—caught, bent, and snapped.

"Shit! I just broke my goddamn thumbnail!" Conrad dropped the tape and put his tongue to the wound. "I broke it right down to the quick. I can't believe I . . ." He stopped talking then as he realized what had just happened.

"It's been like that all afternoon," said Hank quietly. "I suggest you pocket that crystal, Conrad, and forget about trying to build anything with it. Sooner or later, you'll find out what it's really for."

"Seven o'clock!" called Caldwell from the kitchen. "Didn't you guys want to watch the news?"

saturday, august 6, 1966

Hank's parents and one of his brothers were already down in the basement. "Conrad here wants to see the news," Hank explained after the greetings. "Catch up on all the big doings."

"The local news is the only thing on right now anyway," said Mrs. Larsen agreeably. "We still only have two channels in Louisville, Conrad. I keep telling Hank's father he should get us an antenna to pick up the UHF channel, but he doesn't think it's worth the trouble."

"There's no sports on that channel," explained Mr. Larsen. He was a distant man with a deprecatory chuckle. "Just violins."

The local news ran along uneventfully: a new candidate for mayor, problems with the sewage plant, a change in zoning, but then . . .

"A bizarre robbery at a farmhouse in Louisville's East End last night." The newscaster was a trim young woman with heavily coiffed brown hair. "When Mr. Cornelius Skelton called police officers at 3:00 A.M., they found a broken window lock and only one item missing: a large, semiprecious mineral crystal which had rested on Mr. Skelton's mantel. Skelton asserted that he had 'expected the robbery.' The crystal was coupled to an alarm system—a very special system which included an automatic movie camera! Here is Skelton's incredible film of the robbery taking place."

"Cornelius Skelton," Mr. Larsen was saying. "Isn't he the rich fellow who has that farm down the road?"

"A jewel heist in our own neighborhood!" exclaimed Mrs. Larsen. "How exciting!"

Caldwell favored Conrad with a hard, questioning stare. The film started: silent, black and white.

A blurred shape, jellylike in slowed time. A young man's back. He jerks grayly, then blurs out into cloud. He's gone? No . . . there he is again, at the bottom of the screen, tiny before the looming fireplace. He's the size of a thumb! He wears a white bandit-mask, the little scuttler, and now he hurries off out of the picture, lugging Skelton's crystal on his tiny back.

The news show cut to Skelton's face, in color. Old Cornelius looked as calm and gentlemanly as ever, laying down his bizarre rap in an emotionless Kentucky drawl. "I've said this time and again. A flahn saucer landed on my farm in the spring of fifty-six. It butchered one of my hogs and left a crystal in its place. I anticipated that the aliens might return for the crystal, and I rigged my camera accordingly. View the film with an open mind, and ask yourself if any human being could *shrink that way*."

They ran the film again in slow motion. This time Conrad could recognize himself. The arms, the eyes. All of a sudden, he was starting to feel funny.

The brunette came back on. "The incredible shrinking man? This afternoon, our WHAS news team showed Skelton's film to Dr. Mario Turin, Professor of Astronomy at the University of Louisville."

Cut to a black-goateed man with a sliding smile. A mellow-voiced male interviewer, off-camera, asked the questions.

"Dr. Turin, what do you think of Mr. Skelton's assertion that his film shows an alien from outer space?"

Turin smiled and jerked his head. "Cornelius Skelton is well known for his strong beliefs in UFO phenomena. I think it's only natural that he would interpret his film in terms of extraterrestrial visitation."

"But you don't agree with Mr. Skelton?" The interviewer's voice was smooth and comforting. It reminded Conrad of the time Platter had come to get him at Chuckie's. His head felt so numb!

"No, I don't. I think it's more likely that Mr. Skelton is the perpetrator—or the dupe—of a hoax. The 'shrinking' effect could easily be produced by an ordinary zoom lens. What we have here is an unusual film . . . of an ordinary robbery."

Conrad was finding it harder and harder to pay attention. It was unsettling enough to see himself on TV—and to have Caldwell angrily elbowing him whenever the Larsens looked away—but his head was filled with a funny, dead tingling, as if he'd just gotten a shot of Novocain in the center of his brain.

It was an odd feeling, yet not totally unfamiliar. Conrad had felt this way once before: in Paris, right after he'd seen the picture of Audrey and him hovering off the Eiffel Tower . . .

That was the last time that one of my powers was publicly recorded. The picture of me flying was in the paper, and then I couldn't fly anymore. His head throbbed thickly. It was the news report for sure. Somehow Conrad was programmed to change his special survival power each time he was unmasked. He was turning into a new "Chinese brother."

The news ended on a light note, and a vaginal-deodorant commercial came on, the one with Dorothy Provine. With the marijuana still in his system, Conrad slid into a heavy paranoid fantasy that Caldwell and the Larsens were all staring at him. In Caldwell's case, this was no fantasy.

"Let's go out to the car," said Caldwell, poking Conrad sharply. "I have to pick up Sherry soon." He thanked Mrs. Larsen for the dinner and hustled Conrad out to the garage. He was really angry.

"What do you think you're doing, breaking into Mr. Skelton's house?" demanded Caldwell. "He's an old friend of the family! Have you turned into a junkie or something?"

"How . . . how do you know it was me?" essayed Conrad.

"I know what you look like, even with a snot-rag on your face. And the way you and Hank have been acting, it's been obvious that something's up. What did you do with the crystal, sell it?"

"No. I've got it right here." Conrad took the crystal out of his pocket and opened his hand a little to show it to Caldwell. "I'm not giving it back, either. It's mine."

"*Why* is it yours, Conrad?"

"Because . . . because it comes from the same flying saucer that *I* came from." Conrad couldn't hold the secret back any longer. "The flying wing! It put me down at Skelton's the day you all moved to Louisville. I'm not really your brother. You were just hypnotized into thinking I am. The aliens picked the Bunger family because they had no friends or relatives."

Caldwell's eyes were blazing—with anger, with fear, with hurt. Conrad backed away.

"Don't try to hit me, Caldwell, I have special powers. If you really can't stand it, then go ahead and turn me in. My life here'll be over, but if that's what you have to do . . ."

Caldwell sat down on the MG's fender and rubbed his face. "Conrad," he said softly, "don't tell me you're not my brother. You're the only brother I have. Even if you *are* an alien. Didn't we grow up together? Don't you look like Mom and Dad?"

"Yeah, yeah. Maybe they even fixed it so that my body here has the right genes. I think they made the body out of pigmeat, as a matter of fact, but they could have doctored all the amino acids to match."

Caldwell lifted his face up from his hands and looked at Conrad with curiosity. "If you're wearing a fake, pigmeat body—keep in mind that I think you're out of your gourd, Conrad, but just for the sake of argument—if the body standing here in front of me is a *costume*, then what do you *really* look like?"

"A stick of light. I remember from my dreams. My race is called *the flame-people*. The other flame-people are in a saucer hovering out past the Moon. They monitor Earth's TV and radio. They snuck me down here to find out what it's really like. Instead of vaginal deodorant ads, you dig?"

"How do you know they're out near the Moon? Do you talk to them? Do you hear voices, Conrad?" Caldwell's voice was taking on an air of strained normality. He'd decided not to believe the story.

"I don't hear voices, Caldwell, and I'm not crazy. I don't care if you believe me, just so you don't turn me in.

"Time to regroup," said Hank, stepping into the garage. "Conrad's television debut has left us all a bit bemused. My mother is askin' questions."

"She knows?" asked Conrad, his voice rising.

"She saw the crystal in my room today. She wants us to give it back."

"Wait," interrupted Caldwell. "Did Conrad really shrink or not, Hank? He's been telling me all this shit about—"

"Flying saucers," said Hank. "I've heard it, too. I *did* see him shrink last night. But . . ."

"Can you do it again?" demanded Caldwell. You could see vague plans for the perfect bank robbery forming in his mind. "Because . . ."

"That's what I was about to tell you," said Conrad. "I *can't* shrink anymore. I'm programmed to like change powers each time I get exposed. I could feel it happening after Skelton showed the movie on TV. The flame-people want me to survive, but I have to keep quiet. We don't want everyone on Earth to know about us, because—"

"Oh, I don't want to hear any more about it, Conrad," interrupted Caldwell in sudden revulsion. "You are so fucking nuts." He got in the MG and fired up the engine. "Open the garage door, would you, Hank? I've got a date."

"Where are you going to sleep?" asked Conrad solic-itously.

"Wherever I get laid; wherever I pass out. Get out of my way."

Hank opened the garage door, and Caldwell backed out. He looked like he couldn't decide what to think. Big brother. He really cared. Conrad ran over to the car, and the two brothers shook hands. Caldwell was shaking his head and grinning by the time he drove off.

"I wonder what your new power is going to be," mused Hank.

"I don't know. It's not really clear to me how many more chances I'm going to get. One more fuck-up, and they might just come get me." Conrad reached into his pocket and felt the magic crystal. "Why don't I take a walk, and you tell your mother I've gone to give the crystal back? Then maybe later we can go over to Pohlboggen's. She's hot for you, and Dee's got more grass."

"Sounds good. See you in about an hour. You're not really going to Skelton's, are you?"

"No way. I'll be over at the Z.T."

Conrad followed Hank's street out of the subdivi-sion and crossed Route 42 to get to the Zachary Taylor National Cemetery. "Old Rough-and-Ready" himself was buried there, along with his wife, and about ten thou-sand World War II soldiers, each soldier with an identi-cal white headstone. The stones seemed almost to glow in the gathering dusk. As Conrad walked among them, they kept shifting into new alignments, like the atoms in a crystal.

Crystal. Conrad took the troublesome stone out of his pocket and peered at it. It lay still in his hand, mockingly inert. What was it for? Why had the flame-people left it?

Here I am, a creature made of pigmeat and a stick of flame. I used to say that I was looking for the secret of life, but now . . .

What could the secret of life mean, anyway? Conrad looked at the vast world around him, remembering Audrey, remembering today's outing with Dee. *How could any one formula ever sum it up?*

The secret of life—big deal. Conrad thought of a poem he'd read in some beatnik anthology:

> The beach night of eternal star
> Sea of possibility and infinite spacetime
> Mists on the Earth—What a laugh
> To sell answers in paperback,
> When you see God
> Only piss to mark the spot.

Conrad lay there, on the cemetery grass, not thinking anything in particular. As full darkness set in, lightning bugs appeared, blink-------------blink--blink---------------------blinking around the cedars and the weeping willows. The stars were out, high overhead. Every now and then you could see the abrupt streak of a meteorite. It was peaceful, peaceful lying there, alone in the Louisville night. Conrad held the crystal in his right hand; somehow its sharp planes and skewed edges made for a perfect fit.

A quarter-hour passed, then another and another. Conrad still felt a little high, lying there in the dry grass, too high to fall asleep. It would be nice with Hank and Sue and Dee later—they could all go to a drive-in or—

ZZZZOW.

A tumbling pattern of red lights swooped down out of the sky and thudded into the ground a hundred meters from where Conrad lay. The object was a good-sized pyramid with a bright light at each of its five corners. . . . *It was a UFO!*

There were houses all around the Zachary Taylor cemetery—and everyone's lights were coming on. Conrad wasn't the only one who'd seen the pyramid land. Was it the flame-people? This ship certainly didn't look like the good old flying wing, but maybe it was a scout ship or . . .

Conrad jumped to his feet, not certain whether to watch or run. If the UFO was from a *different* alien race, would they be friend or foe? If it was from the *flame-people*, what did they want? Unconsciously, Conrad's fist clenched around his magic crystal. The thing felt warm to the touch.

One side of the pyramid furled open. A rod of light darted out, a rod of light with a knob at one end. Dogs were barking, and some of the humans were out in their yards yelling. A police siren sounded in the distance.

Moving rapidly, the stick of light floated over the low cemetery wall and disappeared. One of the barking dogs gave a shrill yelp of terror and fell silent. Conrad stared at the scout ship, unsure whether to run or to keep watching. Just then he noticed a dark shape moving toward him through the gravestones.

A big dog, it looked like, in the light from the houses, a big black dog trotting toward Conrad with a frightening singleness of purpose. The alien had taken it over. It was coming to get Conrad.

Now the dog was only ten yards off. Something glowed at the back of its neck—a large parallelepiped crystal resembling the one Conrad held clutched like a sword hilt in his fist. Moving instinctively, Conrad raised his fist to the back of his neck and . . . drew out a rod of light. Yes. Drew it out like a sword from a scabbard, pulled his flame-person self out of the human spine where it lived!

The dog charged now, and as it leaped, Conrad stepped sideways and slashed downward with his sword of light. It burned the dog in half; for a moment, Conrad thought the fight was already over.

But now alien energy came oozing out of the dog's spine, energy that rejoined its crystal to form a sword-thing like Conrad's. The glowing shape flung itself at Conrad; he hacked and parried as best he could.

It was strange-feeling, this battle—Conrad had double perspective on it. On the one hand, *Conrad* was the human being wielding the sword; on the other hand, *Conrad* was the stick of light in the human's hand. He could feel it either way. Each time he touched the other flame-person, a tingling buzz rushed through him like an electric shock. The main thing was to keep the other from hurting his human body. If he lost his meat, he'd have to go back to the saucer. Thrust and slash, dodge and duck. It was all happening too fast to analyze.

Suddenly the other flame-person knotted itself into Conrad's sword and began to pull. It was talking to him, Conrad realized—that buzzing was a kind of talk.

Come on, Conrad, it was saying, *it's time to get you out of here. People are going to recognize you from TV, and your next powers are going to use up so much of your crystal-energy that . . .*

Conrad braced himself and refused to budge. Just then, four or five spotlights focused on him and the scout ship pilot.

"DON'T MOVE OR WE'LL SHOOT!" Cops—squad cars full of cops.

Oh, #!%*, buzzed the other flame-person. *I give up.* It swooped back to the red-flashing spacecraft and, as suddenly as it had come, the UFO tumbled back up into the sky.

WOZZZZ.

Conrad's bright sword flexed in exultation. Conrad's human body sighed in relief. The big dog lay there on the ground before him, cut right in two. With the same automatic motion that he'd used before, Conrad raised up his stick of light and slid it down into his spine. Like a sword-swallower. Click. He felt whole again. Good and—

"RAISE YOUR HANDS UP HIGH!"

Fly, thought Conrad. *Shrink!* Nothing doing. He pocketed the crystal and raised both hands high as if to surrender. The cop cars were about twenty yards off—they couldn't get any closer, with Conrad in here among the gravestones. Each gravestone cast a dark shadow. It was obvious what to do.

Conrad twitched his left hand and dived down to the right. In a shadow. Good. He scuttled backward, shifted to a new shadow, scuttled further. Further. Bright lights, dark shadows. Someone fired a shot, someone screamed not to. There were more cops, circling up on Conrad's position from behind.

"WE HAVE YOU SURROUNDED!"

Cops in front of him, cops behind him. By now, they'd lost track of exactly where he was, here in a patch of shadow behind one of ten thousand identical gravestones. *If only I looked like a cop.*

The crystal twitched in his pocket, and then Conrad felt his clothes shifting, felt the flesh of his features crawl. All right!

"He's not over here!" called cop-voiced Conrad, getting to his feet. He could change his face! *Third Chinese brother!*

"I'm going to check over by the wall!" His handcuffs jingled, and his pistol slapped against his leg. The other officers wandered this way and that.

There was a low stone wall around the cemetery. Conrad found a spot with no people close by and rolled himself over the wall. *Mr. Bulber*, he thought, as he dropped out of sight. *I want to look like Mr. Bulber.*

When he got back to his feet, he was a nondescript guy in his early thirties—a carbon copy of his Swarthmore physics teacher, Mr. Bulber. Mr. Bulber had the virtue of being very normal-looking: prim mouth, neatly parted dark hair, horn-rimmed glasses, charcoal-gray suit . . .

More and more people were coming to see what was up, but no one noticed "Mr. Bulber" walking off. As he walked, Conrad drew out his wallet and took a peek. Money in there, good, and, even better, IDs with *Charles Bulber* on them.

Conrad started walking along Route 42. But where to? Probably the cops or someone had gotten footage of him dueling with the other flame-person—which meant that his old cover was thoroughly blown. Plenty of people in Louisville would recognize Conrad Bunger from the pictures. He wasn't going to be able to look like his old self anymore at all. It was time to get out of town.

Some teenagers threw a beer can at him from a passing car. Of course. Who *wouldn't* throw a beer can at Mr. Bulber, all neat and square in his charcoal-gray suit? He'd want to pick a new body-look before long; but, for now, this was good and innocuous.

Conrad could feel the crystal in his pants pocket. It was smaller than it had been just a few minutes ago. Strange. He was going to have to get rid of the crystal. Holding it in the Z.T. for that long had somehow energized it—one of its functions seemed to be that of a radio beacon. It had to be the crystal that had enabled the flame-people to home in on him like that.

And what did they want from him anyway? Apparently they thought he wasn't doing too good a job here—they wanted to abort his mission. But unless he was actually holding the crystal, it was too hard for them to find him. *Well, fine*, thought Conrad, *I don't want them to find me.*

He had half a mind to just throw the crystal into the roadside weeds. But wait. What was it the other flame-person had said? *Your next powers are going to use up so much of your crystal-energy that ...* That what? And what was the meaning of "crystal-energy"? The other flame-person had consisted of a crystal and a stick of light. Somehow, the troublesome crystal in Conrad's pocket was part of him—for why else would he have felt such a crazy need to go and steal it? And just as he'd gotten the power of changing his face, the crystal had gotten a bit smaller.

A battery. The crystal was like a battery. His stick of light, after all, had to be living off *something*. The power for his reality-altering wishes had to come from *somewhere*. Such magical power would involve a higher form of energy than anything that humble human meat could provide.

Conrad reached into his pocket and fingered the crystal anxiously. When he was a kid it had been as big as his fist—though, of course, childhood memories were always inaccurate about size. In any case, last night, the crystal had definitely been the size of a big, homemade ice cube. But now—now that he'd had flying, and shrinking, and face-changing—now that he was the third Chinese brother—now the crystal was only the size of a matchbox.

The crystal was Conrad's energy source, but it was also a kind of transmitter to the flame-people. Unless he wanted them to come back and get him, he was going to have to get rid of it. But where would it be safe? Some cops sped past on Route 42. Conrad felt a big pulse of stress. If the pigs got hold of his crystal, it would be all over. If the flamers found him again, it would be all over. What to do?

Why not just take Mrs. Larsen's advice? Why not give the crystal back to Mr. Skelton? Conrad began walking faster.

The highway traffic made a lot of noise, but he kept having a feeling he was hearing that *ZZZZOW* from before. He glanced anxiously up at the sky, looking for a tumbling pattern of five red lights. Maybe as long as he didn't actually *hold* the crystal, the flame-people couldn't find him. But maybe not. In any case, the sooner he got to Skelton's, the better.

Five more minutes' walking down 42, and Conrad came to the Esso station at the corner of Drury Lane. Skelton's was about three miles down Drury Lane, down past where the Bungers' house had been.

Three miles . . . a good half hour's walk. Conrad looked up at the sky once again. This was taking too long. Drury

Lane didn't have the heavy traffic that Route 42 did, he'd be a sitting duck for the flame-people's scout ship. Should he phone Hank from the Esso station's telephone?

Just then a yellow VW bumped up to one of the gas pumps. That looked like Sue Pohlboggen's car, and in it was ... Dee Decca. Yes!

Conrad hurried over and stuck his head in her window. "Hi, Dee, it's Conrad. Can you give me a ride down the road real quick?"

She was so surprised at his new Mr. Bulber-face that it took her a minute to understand what he was saying.

"Conrad Bunger?"

"Yeah, it's me, Dee, it really is. We got high in the country together today, right? All is One, right?" He walked around to the passenger side and got in.

Dee stared at him tensely. "I just saw the news flash on TV. You were fighting some weird ..." She paused and looked around. She seemed quite high. "I phoned Hank, and he said it was true, so I've been cruising around here looking for you to ..." She patted Conrad's knee. "You can change your shape? You're an alien?"

"I'm really just the same person you've always known, Dee." His Mr. Bulber-voice was firm and manly, with a faint Boston accent.

"Yes, ma'am?" It was the gas station attendant, leaning down for Dee's request. Conrad held his breath for what seemed an eternity.

"I just remembered something," said Dee finally. "I'll come back for gas in a little while." They *putt-putted* out of the station and onto Drury Lane.

"Thanks, Dee."

"Where to, spaceman?"

"You remember old Cornelius Skelton? Who has the farm?"

"Sure. I saw him on the seven o'clock news. That was you, too, wasn't it, Conrad?"

"Yeah. It's a mess. The crystal is what attracted the other alien—the one I was fighting. He . . . it . . . was trying to get me to leave Earth. I've got to ditch the crystal with Skelton and go underground."

The warm summer night slid past. "What did you come down to Earth for in the first place, Conrad? What do you really look like?"

"The sword I was holding—that's the alien me. I came down here and got a human body to see what people are like, I guess. My race—the flame-people—they're in a saucer out past the Moon. All they know about Earth is what they see on TV, and TV is all bullshit, so they put me here to get the real picture. Find out the secret of life, you dig? OK, now take a right down this driveway. If there's cops, we just turn around. My name is Charles Bulber. I teach physics at Swarthmore College."

There were lights on in Skelton's house, but no extra cars. Sooner or later the cops and reporters would be coming here, but right now they were still over at the cemetery.

"Should I come with you, Conrad?"

"Why not? Mr. Skelton was always nice to me when I was little. He taught me how to cast a fishing lure. I think he's basically on my side, even if I *am* an alien."

Mr. Skelton stepped out onto his porch as soon as Dee and Conrad got out of the car. Though he was clearly overwrought, Skelton managed to speak with his usual good humor.

"Well, well. A pretty girl and a man in a black suit. Are you-all from the press?"

"Good evening, Mr. Skelton," said Conrad. "I've come to see you in connection with your missing crystal."

"Would you care to show me some identification? And come up here in the light where I can get a good look at you."

"Here's all the ID we'll need," said Conrad, taking the crystal out of his pocket and tossing it up to Skelton. "I want you to keep this for me till I need it again."

Skelton's weathered face became suffused with joy. "After all my waitin'—you're finally here? Come on in!"

Conrad was tempted. He'd always liked Mr. Skelton, and the idea of being a real alien talking to a UFO buff had a certain appeal.

"No," said Dee, taking Conrad's arm. "We can't. We're in a terrible hurry."

"Ah just want to *talk* to you," protested Mr. Skelton. "Ah just want to see how you *look*." The only light was on the porch; Conrad and Dee were in near-darkness.

"No," repeated Dee.

Conrad realized she was right. Anything they told Mr. Skelton might find its way into the UFO magazines, and onto TV. At this point it was too hard to figure out what was safe to tell and what wasn't. He glanced up at the sky once more.

But there were no red lights up there, no flying wing. Tossing the crystal to Mr. Skelton, he'd felt a tangible drop in his energy level. As soon as the thing left his hands, it stopped being a saucer beacon. Really, for now, there were only the cops to worry about. And they weren't looking for *Professor Bulber*.

"We can talk for a minute, Mr. Skelton," said Conrad. "As long as you've got the crystal back, I guess everything's OK. But I'd rather we stayed out here."

"Would you yourself be from the saucer that mutilated my hog?"

"That's me," admitted Conrad. "March 22, 1956."

"You're Conrad Bunger, aren't you?"

Dee gasped. But the deduction wasn't really so surprising. After all, Conrad had been on TV twice tonight and . . .

"Even when you were a little boy, I suspected," mused Skelton. "There was always something . . . *odd* about you, Conrad. My, my. Me readin' and writin' about UFOs these ten years, and an extraterrestrial living right down the street." He chuckled softly.

"I didn't realize it till this year," said Conrad. "I have a kind of amnesia."

"Conrad, come *on*," hissed Dee. "You have to get *out* of here."

"Three questions," said Mr. Skelton, "and I'll let you and the young lady be on your way. UFOs have been my hobby since my wife died. UFOs and fishin' for bass. I've puzzled and puzzled over these questions."

"All right," said Conrad. This was fun.

"Number one," intoned Mr. Skelton. "Is it true that Hiroshima was the event that got you all interested in Earth? Hiroshima was in forty-six, you know, and the first official saucer sighting was by Kenneth Arnold, in 1947. Did you come here to bring world peace?"

"I think it was the radio and TV broadcasts which attracted us, Mr. Skelton, rather than Hiroshima. Our ships are stationed at quite some distance from Earth, too far to observe a nuclear explosion directly. And as far as world peace goes—that's not our problem. World peace is *your* problem."

"Very well," said Skelton with a slight nod. "Question number two. *Why* don't you all just come on down and make friends in an open way?" His voice took on an almost pleading tone. "I'm sure our races have so much to share."

"Well," said Conrad, "my impression is that if our presence were too widely known, then we would be unable to carry out our mission here—a mission which, to the best of my knowledge, primarily involves *observing* and *learning from* the human race in its natural state."

"That's what I'd always imagined," said Skelton. You could tell he'd thought about UFOs a lot. "Your role would be comparable to that of a naturalist who observes a beaver colony from a hidden blind. I understand. I promised only three questions, and here is number three. I'm an old man, Conrad, with my own ideas, but there is one thing I'd like to ask you. How does your race account for . . ." Skelton paused, collecting his thoughts. "Let me put it country-simple. What is the secret of life?"

Dee was nervous enough to greet this question with a wild giggle.

"Ma'am?" said Skelton. "I'm afraid I . . ."

"Don't mind her," said Conrad. "What is the secret of life? Strange as this may sound, Mr. Skelton, I don't know. I said before that my mission involves learning from the human race. More specifically, my mission is to find out what *humans* think is the secret of life. Do you have any opinions?"

"Since you so politely ask, yes, I do. *Life goes on.* That's the secret, as far as I'm concerned. No one person—or being—matters that much, because life goes on anyway."

"Thank you," said Conrad.

"*Life* as the secret of life," interpolated Dee. "Let's go."

"OK. We've got to go, Mr. Skelton. Hang on to that crystal for me. It's *part of me.* Hide it. Don't let the cops get it, whatever you do. And one other thing . . ."

"Anything at all, Conrad."

"Do you have any beer?"

"Just a second." Mr. Skelton headed into his house, leaving his front door open.

"Are you crazy?" demanded Dee. "Is beer all you can think about?"

"I just didn't want him to see me getting into the car," explained Conrad. "So he doesn't see me all lit up by the dome-light. I don't want people to know I've changed my face." He hopped into the car and bent down when Skelton reemerged from his house. Dee took the beer—two cans of Sterling—and got in the car as well.

"Why are we helping you, Conrad?" she asked as they drove off. "What am I doing chauffeuring a nonhuman saucer-creature? Why didn't Mr. Skelton come back out with his shotgun and blow you to bits?"

"Because you've both known me since high school?" Conrad opened the beers and offered Dee one. "Let's get some gas for the car, and then I'd like to go to the train station downtown. I think it's at Ninth and Broadway."

"No beer for me, thanks. I'm confused enough as it is. Does Hank know?"

"Yeah. But you're the only one who knows I can change my face. Please don't tell anyone, OK?"

"Can you change back to Conrad for a minute? I don't like you to be Charles Bulber. You look like a real straight-arrow."

"My powers only work in life-or-death situations. Like at the graveyard just now when the cops almost caught me."

"That fire-stick you were fighting with was one of your . . . race?"

"*Flame-people*, Dee. Yeah, that was one of them. They were trying to get me to come back. They think I've fucked the mission badly enough already. But I dig it here. I like being human."

They pulled into a Gulf station, and while the attendant filled the tank, Dee put her arms around Conrad and gave him a big kiss.

"That's nice of you," she said after a time.

"What is?"

"To dig being human," said Dee. "I don't think Jesus ever said that."

"What are you talking about?" said Conrad. They pulled out of the gas station and headed for town.

"I mean, the way the story goes, Jesus was an extraterrestrial-type being who put on a human body, right?"

"I'm not Jesus."

"*I know* you're not. But you *are* in a somewhat similar situation."

"I never understood why Jesus had to get crucified. Couldn't he just say, 'Fuck this *cross* shit,' and fly off, or change his face? Why should he let the pigs kill him?"

"He had to die so he could rise from the dead. I think the idea was to let the pigs take their best shot at him . . . and then *still* come back."

"Oh, look, I don't want to start thinking this way. It's too sick. I'm just a hippie." Conrad finished the first beer and started on the one he'd opened for Dee.

The news about his being an extraterrestrial seemed to have changed Dee's attitude toward him considerably. Before this, they'd been good friends, but now she was looking at him with . . . veneration. As if he *knew where it was at*.

"You're *not* just a hippie," said Dee quietly. "Listen." She put on the car radio. News, excited news.

"... tentatively identified as Conrad Bunger, aged twenty, formerly a resident of Louisville. Bunger's family have refused comment until ..."

"Who told them my name?" demanded Conrad.

"I ... I think it might have been Sue," Dee said. "I told her not to, but she ..."

Conrad groaned and twiddled up and down the dial.

"... indicate a genuine UFO incident. Positive radar contact was made by air traffic controllers at Standiford Field ..."

"... Fort Knox jets scrambled, but the vehicle evaded them easily ..."

"... photographs seem to show one man—now identified as Conrad Bunger, aged twenty—with two alien beings having the appearance of rods of light. An analysis of the images reveals ..."

"... Cornelius Skelton, who states that Conrad Bunger spoke to him in person, giving assurances that ..."

"... here with Cornelius Skelton, who says he saw Conrad Bunger shortly after the Zachary Taylor cemetery incident. Mr. Skelton?" The old man's voice came on— the reporters must have gotten there right after Dee and Conrad left. "That is correct. Ah spoke briefly with ... the alien. There is every reason to believe that this being's purpose here is of a peaceful and scientific nature. Ah feel—"

Conrad clicked the radio back off.

"God. We're going to have to be very cool at the train station, Dee. There's going to be cops all over the place.

You don't think Skelton gave them your license number, do you?"

"What would be so terrible if the police *did* catch you, Conrad? You haven't done anything wrong. Maybe you should go public." She gave him another admiring glance.

"Look, if the police get me, I'll be on live TV. And any time I'm on live TV, the flame-people will know where to look for me. They want to cancel my mission, Dee. They want to get me out of here. They'll chop up my body, and take my flame back to the flying wing."

"Oh, I don't know, Conrad. Maybe it's nice in the . . . flying wing. What does that mean, anyway, *flying wing*?"

"That's what our saucer looks like. Sure, maybe it is nice there. But I'm scared, all right? I'm scared of a big change, number one, and number two, I have a bad feeling the flame-people might be really mad at me. What if they court-martial me, or something? My instinct is to stretch out this Earth-gig as long as possible. Make the most of it, you know?" They were driving down Broadway now. Conrad glanced back to make sure no cops were following them.

"The flame-people can't find you unless you're on TV, or holding that crystal?"

"Right. It's like a person can't see what's going on in an anthill. You can't keep track of just one ant. Jesus . . . would you look at that?"

There was a police barricade in front of the train station. You had to pass a checkpoint to get inside. Flashing red lights and excited yokel faces.

"Just drop me here, Dee. Thanks for everything. I'll miss you."

"But . . ." She looked at him all wide-eyed, like he was a guru or a rock star. This afternoon it had been *Dee-and-Conrad*, but now it was *Human-and-Alien*. It felt bad.

"Don't look at me that way, Dee. I'm still just Conrad. Give me a kiss now."

Dee's face relaxed into her old smile. "We're all aliens, one way or another, aren't we, Conrad?"

It was hard to stop kissing, but—like everything else, like everything—at some point it was over. Last smile, door-slam, *putt-putt*, goodbye.

Getting past the cops was easy with the Charles Bulber IDs. The next train north was due in forty minutes. Conrad wandered into the train station's large newsstand and bought himself the *Schaum's Outline Series on General Physics*.

part four

I got up and went out. Once at the gate, I turned back. Then the garden smiled at me. I leaned against the gate and watched for a long time. The smile of the trees, of the laurel, *meant* something; that was the real secret of existence.

—Jean-Paul Sartre, *Nausea*

saturday, august 13, 1966

Charles Bulber
23 Crum Ledge
Swarthmore, PA 19084
August 13, 1966

Dear Audrey,

I guess you've read about me in Time—yeah, this is Conrad here—DON'T TELL ANYONE! BURN THIS! I mean it, Audrey, if they catch me, it's my ass. God I miss you. You'll be back in the U.S. on Sept. 2. You see, I remember. It might not be too cool for me to come up to Columbia, but you can come down here and stay with me at Mr. Bulber's house, it's so hard waiting for you, sweet darling.

I hope you don't think I'm icky for being sort of an extraterrestrial. I can hardly wait to run my pincers and feelers all over your ripe young . . . No, wait, it's not like that; it's the story we were goofing on at the Gold Rail with Hank Larsen last winter . . . it's really true. My body is real Earthly meat, but there is a kind of stick of flame in my spine, which is what came from the flying saucer. The flame-people, remember? I mean, it's obvious, really—that's why I had those special powers all along. (Remember the time I shrank for you up in NYC and Katha Kahane starts pounding on the door? Yubba!)

Well, I've got a new power now, which is that I can change my face. That's how I escaped in Louisville, I turned into Mr. Bulber. My physics teacher, the one who hated me so much, Professor Charles V. Bulber, Ph.D.? Do you like older men? With pincers and feelers and a squid-bunch of tentacles under each arm? Genitals of the Universe, Part IX. No, really, I have to stop this or you won't come see me, and if you don't come see me, dear Audrey, I will pine away.

I think it's your lips I miss the most, or maybe the way you giggle. And your shiny brown eyes, and the way you stick your neck out to crane. My new Bulber-body isn't too bad-looking—I'm thirty-two, I have dark hair, I have all my teeth, I'm single, I . . .

"All right, Conrad," I can hear you saying. "What have you done with the real Mr. Bulber?"

Mr. Bulber is in France, Audrey, he's on sabbatical. His replacement here at the college was going to house-sit for him, but I, the pseudo-Bulber, showed up and told the guy to get fucked, I'd decided not to stay in France, I just wanted to spend the year lying around my house drinking and taking drugs. The replacement flipped, and the Chairman came by to see me—I played it cool and just said I was working on some new ideas and they should leave me alone. It's my sabbatical, right? I can do what I want.

Meanwhile, I forward all Mr. Bulber's mail to him in Montpelier, the way the house sitter was supposed to, and I've been getting money by selling Bulber-things off. Sooner or later my cover here'll blow, but for now it's a wiggy scene. Except for one thing: no Audrey. Audrey, Audrey, Audrey. You smell good, you know? All over.

What I'm really thinking, Audrey, is that you should just move in here with me. Mr. Bulber's house overlooks the Crum, it's nice and comfortable, he has a stereo—shitty classical records, but I'm getting some new ones—and I'm planning to sell his car next month. It's a 1965 XKE—the poor guy's big self-indulgence, I guess—I already checked at the dealer's and they say it's worth $6,000 as is! It was up on blocks in his garage, but I've got it running . . . dig it, I'm going to meet you at JFK in an XKE if you'll give me the flight number. Then you move in with me, we sell the car, and we live off the money all fall. Talk about a good provider!

I'm really serious about this, Audrey—I'd hoped to marry you next June—and still want to, if things work out. But I've got a bad feeling that my days here on Earth are numbered. No one means as much to me as you do, baby, and I want to spend all the time I have left with you.

"Why are you so morbid, Conrad? Why do you say your days are numbered?"

Another voice heard from. A high voice, a sweet voice. The problem is this: The flame-people think I've fucked up. The idea was supposed to be that I come down here and find out about people and, yes, find out about The Secret of Life, and then someday I'd go back to the flying saucer and report. The whole thing was supposed to be hush-hush. But—as you must know by now—this guy Mr. Skelton got a film of me shrinking, and the flame-people picked up the TV broadcast of it, and I happened to be holding a kind of homing crystal, and the flamers sent a scout ship down to pick me up, etc., etc.

Right now things are cool because I got rid of the crystal and changed my face. (Third Chinese brother, dig, first flying, then shrinking, then changing. It's all built-in, no matter what the flamers think of me.) But sooner or later the PIG is going to catch up with me, and put me on live TV, and my fiery brethren are going to UFO down here and snatch my ass ... unless they figure out a way to locate me even before the PIG does, in which case I get snatched even sooner. I look at the sky a lot, as you can imagine.

God. I could write you all night. I'm working on a nice bottle of Moselle from the Bulber wine cellar (quite the bon vivant, aren't we, Charles?), and looking out over the Crum—I have WIBG on, they're playing a lot of Motown tonight. Ah, Audrey, isn't life strange? I need someone to rap with.

The last person I've been able to speak openly with was last week, August 6, a girl called Dee Decca, my old high-school girlfriend. (It's not the same with her as with you at all, so don't worry.) Actually, I couldn't really talk to Dee too well, once she realized I was an alien—she was too impressed. But I know you won't be like that, Audrey, you've seen me shrink, you've seen me fly—I just hope you don't think I'm too ugly now. Maybe you remember what Mr. Bulber looks like . . . I've stopped slicking down my/his hair, anyway. All the Swarthmore faculty and staff I run into think, "Charlie Bulber's gone crazy. He's acting like one of those hipniks."

The perfection of this con is that all of Bulber's mail passes through my hands. I mean, it's me (in the role of house sitter) who's supposed to forward things to him; and he's sending his mail back through me in bundles to save money. The only fuck-up will be if at some point he writes directly to somebody here. Even if that happens, I can say, "Well, I wrote you before I came back to America, I didn't like it over in France." And probably, for the first few months, anyway, he isn't going to feel that much like writing anyone over here. I hope.

My real flash of genius in this whole thing was to remember that Bulber is in fact on sabbatical this year. Some of the assholes in my Mechanics and Wave Motion course gave him a going-away party last spring. Ginger-ale-and-ice-cream punch, Tom Lehrer records, a French-English dictionary . . . you get the picture. The whole sordid scene of degenerative douchedom. Kids these days.

It's going to be weird if any of those students try to talk to me. Classes here start Sept. 7. At least I don't have to teach any courses. I bought a Schaum's Outline Series on Physics to brush up with, just in case. You're probably wondering why I'm hanging around Swarthmore, anyway. I mean, really, it would be safer to head out to California or something. But, I don't know, I want to see my old buddies some more—Ace, and Platter, and Tuskman, and

Chuckie—I want to see them, and do some unbelievable prank on the college administration before I split.

But most of all, I'm looking forward to some peaceful weeks here at Château Bulber with my darling darling Audrey Hayes. A.H. Ah. Do you fuck? Do you still know how? You can put a bag over my solemn potato-head if you must. Or a pair of your soiled lacy underwear. Or . . .

All right, all right, I'll stop. What else. Let me just get another bottle of wine and reread this and . . .

"Baby Love" on the radio. The wonderful inevitability of the chord progressions—you remember how at the end of Nausea, he hears a jazz song and it makes everything right? The secret of life. It's when you're just plugged-in, you know, it just happens. I miss you, Baby Love.

Do you think your parents will be very angry when you drop out of Columbia grad school and move in with "Professor Bulber"? Don't answer that, don't even think about it. Just do it. Write me your arrival time; I'll be there to whisk you away to a life of vice and criminal flight.

It's only ten o'clock—I guess I can fill up one last sheet of paper. Do you mind reading this? Do you think I'm too weird? That article in Time was unbelievable, the quotes they got from all the authority figures who knew me when I was little in Louisville. Brother Hershey (assistant principal at St. X) was the worst. I mean, usually, when there's a mass-murderer—like that guy Charles Whitman in Texas—all his old teachers say, "Oh, he was such a nice boy, very quiet, never made any trouble." And here's Brother Hershey saying, "I remember Conrad Bunger very well. Bright, but troubled. He wanted to be smarter than he really was. By the end of senior year, we were just waiting for him to graduate and leave." And everybody felt that way about me, it turns out. The head preacher at St. John's—I never realized he knew it was me that used to steal the wine. And Dr. Sinclair, and then that phony shithead Dean Potts putting in his two cents' worth ... ah, never mind. In a way, I'm proud of it—you know how I always try to seem tough and cool. But in another way, it really hurts, to see them all turn on me like that just because I'm from a flying saucer.

I really don't know what to do next, Audrey. Tell me when you're coming, and I'll pick you up, and you'll come down here for a weekend at least. I do want to do some kind of trip on the straights' heads here, but after that we can split to wherever you like. I'm pretty sure I can change my face again if I have to ... it's like the other powers, it just works when it's life-or-death. Some of the newspaper articles I've seen make me kind of nervous. All this xenophobia bullshit, you know. Like given the right circumstances, I could get myself torn apart limb from limb. And if it's not on live TV, the flame-people wouldn't know to come save me. All this is assuming the saucer is still around—maybe they gave up and left for another solar system.

God, I'm depressed all of a sudden. I've got this image of a bunch of stupid Nazi pigs tearing me to bits, and my little flame sinking into the ground and just dying out, and me being dead dead dead forever ...

Help me, Rhonda!

Look, burn this letter after you read it, I mean it. And send me ("Charles Bulber") the flight info at 23 Crum Ledge, Swarthmore PA 19084. Hurry, Audrey, I miss you and I need you.

Here's a kiss: X.

And a fuck: F.

I love you,
Conrad

TWENTY-FIVE
friday, september 9, 1966

After Audrey left, Conrad got a couple of bottles of wine and walked down to the Mary Lyons dorms. It was Friday, five in the afternoon. Ace would be drinking in his room—the room he'd planned to share with Conrad. God willing, there'd be grass as well—Conrad hadn't had a chance to get high since back in Louisville with Dee.

It was a nice walk, not too far, the mellow September sun sliding down, and a tang of cool winter in the air. Conrad had the wine in a paper bag; he was wearing jeans and a Swarthmore T-shirt in a mock-Bulberesque attempt to look like "one of the guys." He figured to run a real number on Ace's head.

As long as Audrey had been here—a week, a week of bliss—Conrad had lain low. Audrey didn't want people to see her shacking up with someone over thirty—there were still plenty of people around Swarthmore who would have recognized her. So mainly they'd gone into Philly, or hung around Bulber's pad talking and making love. It had felt like being married, having their own little house; every morning they made scrambled eggs together; every night they drank German white wine and fucked. Daytimes they might go to the Philly zoo, or the art museum—it had been paradise.

But Audrey didn't want to miss the start of classes at Columbia; and Conrad could see her point. He was, after all, on the FBI's Top-Ten Wanted List—yes, he and Audrey had actually seen the actual photo in the actual post office. *Felony burglary and immigration violation.* Audrey loved Conrad as much as ever—*more*—but they could both see the possibility of real bad shit coming down, and there was no reason for her to throw her life away. The hope was that things would somehow work out and they'd get married in June as planned.

So now Conrad was on the loose, and all his pals were back, and it was time to push the whole trip another notch further. Before leaving Crum Ledge, Conrad had carefully combed his hair into the same cocky little Vitalis pompadour that had always infuriated him so much on Bulber. Humming slightly, he walked up the ML dormitory staircase and knocked on Ace Weston's door.

"Who is it?" Ace sounded blurred and weird.

"It's Mr. Bulber." A hard grin covered Conrad's face.

"*Who?*"

"Professor Bulber. I want to talk to you about your application for Kutztown State."

"*What?*" Ace's voice was high in bewilderment. The lock rattled, and then Ace cracked open the door to peer out. Dope fumes swirled.

"Hello, Ace, I know this may not be the best moment for an old fuddy-duddy like myself to be butting in this way, but, hey, man, could you get a brother high?"

Ace's bloodshot eye stared out through the crack for what seemed a very long time.

"You look like a hermit crab," offered Conrad. "Come on, Weston, let me in, I won't bite. I brought wine." He clinked his two bottles invitingly.

"Uh . . . sure." Ace opened the door and Conrad stepped on in. Platter was there, and Chuckie Golem, too. They had a hookah in the corner; Chuckie was trying to stand in front of the hookah so Mr. Bulber wouldn't see it.

"Don't worry about the illegal narcotics, boys," said Conrad. "And feel free to tell it as it is. We have a lot to learn from your generation. You should just think of me as one of your friends; you see, I'm on sabbatical this year."

"Yeah," said Chuckie tensely. "That's what I heard. You were supposed to go to France, and you're just hanging around here instead?"

"That's right," said Conrad, brushing past Chuckie to kneel by the hookah. "Who's your connection?"

At some point here, Platter had gotten hysterical with laughter. He lay slouched back across Ace's bed, shaking in stoned ecstasy.

"What's the matter with this fellow?" demanded Conrad, giving Platter's upper thigh a slow, intimate pinch. "Ron Platek, isn't it? Anybody got a match? And you ought to recharge the bowl while you're at it, men. I'm ready to really do my own thing. Do you have any good records, Weston, besides those shitty old blues tracks you always made me listen to? Who wants a blow job?"

The three boys looked at Conrad with pale anxious faces. They'd been stoned when he got there, and now it had all gotten too unreal too fast.

"No blow jobs?" rapped out Conrad. "Then let's start on the drugs."

"Look," said Ace, stepping forward with his face set tight. "You can just get out of here, faggot. We don't need—"

"Relax," said Conrad, smiling. "I'm really your old roomie, Conrad Bunger."

Ace didn't smile. "We don't need this, Mr. Bulber. We don't need you coming down here to try to act like one of us. We don't want to see you around, understand?" Ace grabbed his arm—hard—and began propelling him toward the door. "Conrad hated your guts, you know that, man? You think it's time you got hip ... well, we don't give a shit. You come back here and we'll *kill* you, Bulber, you—"

"Wait," protested Conrad. He'd done too good a job. "I *am* Conrad Bunger, Ace. Remember the time you fell off the roof and I flew down to save you?" Ace's grip on his arm loosened. Conrad turned to Platter. "Remember you telling me about the guy who paid a woman to shit on his chest, Ron? And the night I started calling you Platter? 'What toothsome victuals do you bear?' And you, Chuckie, remember the song you made up about me, *Pig, Pig, Pig, What's the Use, Use, Use?*"

They stared at him openmouthed.

"That's right," continued Conrad. "I changed my face to Mr. Bulber's to get away from the cops. I did it so I could come up here and impersonate Bulber, who is indeed on sabbatical in France; I did it so I could see you guys again."

Ace finally smiled and gave his dry chuckle. *Eh-eh-eh.* "Well, let's charge up the hookah. Are you really from a flying saucer, Conrad?"

"Sure he is," said Platter. "I read it in *Time*. Conrad." He stood up and gave his old friend a hug. "Mr. Bulber." *Haw-nnh-haw-nnh.* "It's perfect. The thing about the blow-job was perfect. 'Tell it as it is.'" *Haw-nnh-haw-nnh.* "Oh, Conrad."

"You blew our minds," said Chuckie, giving one of his rare smiles. He got out a film can of grass and recharged the hookah. "The . . . uh . . . *feds* are in town. What's scary is that they aren't asking questions. They're just . . . fucking . . . *hanging around.*"

"I'm not going to be here too long," said Conrad. "I want to do one big prank on the college before I fade."

"A *prank*," said Ace thoughtfully.

"*Give them a teaching*," amplified Conrad. Just breathing in the room's air, he already felt high. "I got that phrase from an article in *Time*, it was in the same issue as the articles about me. You know the *Bhagween*? The fat kid with the big cult-following in Chicago? It seems there was an IRS guy who infiltrated the organization, and the Bhagween finds out. Bhagween takes his head disciple aside and says, 'Hey, you know that IRS guy—*give him a teaching.*' So the head disciple goes to the

IRS guy and smiles and says, 'You are now prepared to receive truth.' So, OK, they go in a hotel kitchen, and the head disciple stands behind the IRS guy and hits him on the head with a hammer. And in the same issue of *Time*, right, Potts gives a quote like I'm a follower of the Bhagween!"

"'Although Conrad Bunger may indeed have been an extraterrestrial,'" recited Chuckie, "'I think it is also appropriate to view him as a confused young victim of the madness of our times.'" He fired up the hookah and handed Conrad the mouthpiece. "Careful . . . the water cools it off, and it's easy to inhale too much."

"Motherfaaarf'ck'nout." Conrad drew in a big, show-off breath and succumbed to a coughing fit. No matter how hard he coughed, the tickle in his throat wouldn't go away. The rhythm of the cough filled all his body; he was on the floor now, still coughing, coughing for dear life. Finally the spasm passed, and Conrad opened his watering eyes to see his three friends standing over him, conversing in hushed tones.

"A flying saucer, hey, Pig?" asked Ace.

"The real thing," wheezed Conrad. "What happened there?"

"I think you're tricking us." Ace made his mouth a thin line and shook his head. His blond hair was shoulder-length this year; he kept it out of his eyes with a leather shoelace worn like a headband. He looked vaguely like an Indian. "You tricking us, man."

"I'm not Mr. Bulber, if that's what you think."

"I'm not Ace Weston," said Ace. "I'm John F. Kennedy."

"Oh, come on," said Platter. "It's not Conrad's fault that Golem has this shitty green weed."

"If it's shit, Platek, you don't have to smoke it."

"I had some real Acapulco Gold out at my sister's in California this summer," said Platter, his lips thickening in emphasis. "I had *one puff* and I couldn't get out of my chair."

"I know where to get Gold," said Chuckie, pushing up his glasses. "But it's too expensive."

Conrad sat back up, feeling good and high now, everything yellow, everything jellied. "How expensive? For a . . . *key?*"

"You have money?" Chuckie looked really interested.

"I'm selling Bulber's XKE for six thousand dollars. I could afford two or three thousand dollars for a kilogram of Gold. I'd kind of like to turn on the whole campus, you know?"

"That sounds evil and alien to me," put in Ace. "Like Freddie Whitman. Maybe Whitman was from a saucer, too." Ace didn't really approve of drugs, though he tended to take them whenever he got a chance.

"What I was thinking," went on Conrad, "was that I should get a key, and roll up thousands of joints, and then hand them out at Collection next month." Collection was a college-wide assembly that took place on Thursday mornings at ten. Attendance was mandatory. There was always a period of silence, and then someone would talk for an hour. "You're big in Student Council, Platter; don't you think you could get me invited to speak?"

"I like it," said Platter. "Grass Is a Gas, by our own Professor Bulber."

"It could work," said Chuckie, still thinking about the kilo of Gold. "Just give it a more serious title. Experimental Mysticism? How long do you think you can keep up your cover, Conrad?"

"Well, if you guys will . . ."

"We'll each just tell *one person*," suggested Ace.

"Hey, *please!*"

"It's hopeless, Conrad," said Chuckie. "You know how . . . *incestuous* Swarthmore is."

"I hate that expression," said Platter. "Cheeksy Moon is always saying that."

"Who's Cheeksy Moon?" asked Conrad.

"Cheeksy Moon and Titsy Jiggle," explained Ace. "That's what we call these two new girls who've been hanging around with us. Cheeksy's from France, and Titsy is from California."

"Those are their real names?"

"No, Conrad, those are names we made up. Their real names are Madelaine Dupont and Sissy Taylor. They're sophomores. You've seen them."

"Oh, yeah . . . yeah. Let's ask them to come over to Mr. Bulber's house for a big drug party!"

"On Crum Ledge?" said Chuckie incredulously. "In a professor's home?"

"It's Conrad's house," said Ace. "And he's really Mr. Bulber anyway."

There was a knock on the locked door.

"Oh, shit," said Chuckie, crouching over the hookah.

The knocking quickly turned to steady pounding. "Open up, it's da cops!"

"That's Tuskman," Ace said, and opened the door.

"Hi! Am I in time for da beer?"

Izzy wasn't going to Swarthmore this year—he was living with his girlfriend in an apartment in the Village. For Art. But he'd decided to hitch down for this, the first big fall weekend. For Beer. When Chuckie explained that the man who looked like Mr. Bulber was really Conrad in disguise, Izzy insisted that he'd known right away.

"From da eyes. I didn't wanna say nothing."

"We're going to have a big party at Mr. Bulber's house tonight," Conrad told him. "I've been living there and selling off his stuff."

"I like it," said Izzy. "I like it. Tomorrow—get dis—tomorrow we'll have a *yard sale*."

friday, september 9, 1966

The new girls were beautiful. Madelaine had straight ash-blonde hair, a lisping French accent, and creamy white skin. Her face was broad—almost Tartar—and her jeans were swollen and tight. Cheeksy Moon. Sissy had long, smooth dark hair, huge breasts, and a cute puppyish face. She laughed in infectious guffaws, and she liked to dance. Titsy Jiggle.

They were excited to attend a dope party at a professor's house, with all the cool senior boys there as well: Ace, Izzy, Chuckie, and Platter. Of course there were other guests, too—word spread fast on the small Swarthmore campus. Cheeksy and Titsy brought a bunch of friends, and there were all Conrad's old friends, too—Ace's ex-girlfriend Mary Toledo, Southern and sexily unwashed; Bobby Glassman, the speed-freak phil-major captain of Swarthmore's football team; Zeiss Pappas, the worldly Greek exchange student; Stu Mankiewicz, who spent most of his time playing pool; Betsy Bell, with her big smile and straight Texas nose—dozens of people, really, and everyone ready to party.

On the strength of his promised kilo, Conrad got Platter to break out a secret stash of Gold that he'd gotten from his sister. Betsy Bell rolled her own cigarettes and carried a little sack of Bull Durham with paper; Conrad prevailed on her to roll up all of Platter's dope. It made about fifteen big joints. Conrad pocketed them, and circulated around the Bulber living room, turning people on.

It was exciting; the first Swarthmore party where dope was smoked openly. Before this, people had always *sneaked off* to get high, but now it was 1966, and it was all out in the open. By eleven, everyone was blasted; and Conrad, stoned out of his gourd, leaned grinning against a wall. The record player was blasting the Beatles: *Good Day Sunshine*.

What a great song, thought Conrad. *This was worth coming to Earth for.* He'd been drinking beer all evening along with the weed, and the room was merging into a single bright pattern. The music spun on, and people left him pretty much alone—no one wanted to talk to Mr. Bulber. Now the record was *Tomorrow Never Knows*, one of George's intense Indian tunes, with John's crazed karma lyrics. The elliptical words seemed to explain everything.

Just then, one of the younger boys who'd come in with Madelaine approached Conrad. "Do you have any more marijuana, Mr. Bulber?" The kid had a snotty edge to his voice—you could tell he didn't think it was too cool for a teacher to be acting like this.

"Not for you," said Conrad, feeling a twinge of sudden dope-anger. "I don't even know your name, and you're trying to bring me down. Dipshit."

"You are really messed-up," exclaimed the kid. He had symmetrical features and shoulder-length brown hair. "You had me in Physics I-II last year, Mr. Bulber. I'm Cal Benner, remember? You gave me a B, but I should have gotten an A. Don't you think you could get in trouble smoking pot with students?" Benner smirked at Conrad unpleasantly.

"I'm already in more trouble than you'd ever believe, dipshit. I'm Conrad Bunger. Why don't you get out of here? I didn't invite you."

"You're just a middle-aged guy trying to get your hands on some sophomore girls," snapped Benner. "It's sickening."

A fresh wave of dope hit Conrad's brain about then. He looked at the angry face in front of him. What were they arguing about? About who he was? Fuck it.

"Hang ten," Conrad said and stomped off to the kitchen for another beer.

Platter and Ace were in there talking to Mary Toledo and Sissy Taylor. Conrad threw his arm around Sissy, who gave one of her goony guffaws.

"Can you teach me physics, Mr. Bulber?"

"I'm not Mr. Bulber," said Conrad, hoping to convince someone. "I'm Conrad Bunger."

"Wasn't that too much this summer?" exclaimed Mary, not believing him. "I always knew Conrad was weird, but when I saw him waving that light-sword on TV . . ."

"And shrinking," put in Sissy. "I never got to meet him last year. What was he like? Did you know him, Mr. Bulber?"

"Call me Charlie," sighed Conrad, opening a beer. "Yes, I knew Bunger. He was a very poor student."

"All he cared about was getting drunk and talking about the secret of life," said Ace, smiling wickedly. "Basically he was a stupid pig."

"It's strange," chimed in Platter. "Usually you think of alien life-forms as being really advanced. But Conrad . . ."

"Maybe they chose a defective one to send down," suggested Ace. "Or maybe they had to like lobotomize him to bring him down to human level. I felt that way this summer, working at the paper mill . . ."

Conrad got a pint of whiskey out of Bulber's cupboard and took it out on the back steps. This party wasn't fun; he wasn't a member of the group anymore. He'd never really fit in here again. Where was Audrey?

Stoned and drinking on the steps there, staring out into the woods with the noise of the party washing out, Conrad felt very lonely. Time passed. He felt himself fading and reeled back into the kitchen. "Hey, Weston, let's get some more dope. Where's Chuckie?"

The party ground on into the wee hours, and Conrad got more and more fucked-up. After a while it wasn't like he was running his body anymore; it was, rather, like he was *watching himself do things*. Terrible things.

Finally he passed out, and then it was daytime.

"A nightmare of madness and evil," groaned Conrad. "How can I do this to myself, how can I pretend there's anything positive about alcohol and drugs? And those poor girls . . . why did I have to act like that?"

"If you think I'm going to feel sorry for you, you're crazy. That's just part of the payoff for you, the big guilt-and-apology session. You acted like a real pig last night, and I'd rather not have to hear about it today." Ace was grinding black pepper into a big glass of beer with tomato juice. "You want one of these, Conrad?"

"I do, but I don't. What time is it?"

"A little after noon. You know Izzy wants to come over and have a yard sale this afternoon? He wants to sell all Mr. Bulber's clothes and books and dishes."

"He can get fucked. I did enough for you guys last night." Conrad looked around the ruined bachelor quarters. Vomit on the rugs, some of the chairs broken, cans and bottles everywhere ... "Do you think everyone knows I'm Conrad Bunger now? The cops are looking for me, you know, and so are the flame-people. I've got half a mind to just get in the XKE and—"

"You gave the keys to Chuckie," said Ace. "Don't you remember? You told him to go sell it and use the money for dope."

"He can't sell it without me there to sign the papers over."

"You already signed the papers. He made you do it before he'd give you the rest of his ounce. You wanted to impress Sissy Taylor how—"

"All right, all right. I remember. Do you still do cross-country running, Ace?"

"Sure."

"Take me on a nice run down through the woods."

"Four miles?"

"Two. Just enough to air my head out."

Conrad put on an old pair of Mr. Bulber's sneakers. They locked up the house and walked down to the dormitory so Ace could get his special shoes. He'd been on the cross-country team his first three years, though now he just ran for fun.

It was another sunny day, with big bright leaves beginning to drop. The path through the Crum was smooth and sandy; Ace set a nice, easy pace; and before long, Conrad started feeling good again. Although the Bulber-body's joints ached a bit, it seemed to have stronger legs than the Bunger-model had. The stupid Bulber-face had put everyone off last night, but at least Audrey still liked him. Good thing she hadn't been here. Aaauugh. Here he was, with who knew how much time left, wasting his energy on a stupid-ass party to impress some sophomore girls. He'd probably screwed up his cover, too. He was going to have to leave before Bulber came back from his trip—why not just leave right now?

They sloped up out of the woods and onto a dirt road that led among factories and warehouses. Since it was Saturday, no one was about; the junked machinery and the great brick-and-metal buildings seemed like relics of an unknown civilization. The road looped back into the Crum—water and leaves. Running like this, Conrad could, oddly enough, forget his body entirely. At some point the pain always grew so great that the brain simply put the body on automatic. The run ended with a final charge up a steep path up to Crum Ledge and Mr. Bulber's house. There was a telegram sticking out of the mailbox. Audrey?

Conrad tore it open; it took a minute to grasp what it said.

M. MARK HZA234444898 US CONSULATE DGW22891 PARIS FRANCE SEPTEMBER 16 1966 CHARLES VENN BULBER LOST IN AVA-LANCHE ON MONT BLANC STOP BODY UNRETRIEVABLE STOP ADVISE DISPOSITION OF EFFECTS STOP

Just then Chuckie and Izzy pulled up in Chuckie's car. "Hey, Conrad," yelled Izzy. "Ready for da yard sale?"

"Where's my XKE, Chuckie?"

"I . . . sold it. Turned out the guy wouldn't pay six thou after all. I could only get three-five. But we've been into Philly, and I got your kilo. It's in this shopping bag with your change. You get eighteen hundred back."

"No," said Conrad waving his hand weakly. "Wait." He couldn't catch his breath. If Bulber was never coming back at all, and all the mail was going through this address . . . then there was no reason that Conrad couldn't just move into the Bulber role *permanently* here and . . .

"Unlock da door, Conrad," yelled Tuskman, tugging at the knob as if to tear it off. "I been puttin' up signs and I wanta get all the furniture out before—"

"Goddamn you," husked Conrad, as loud as he could manage. "Shut the fuck up! And don't call me Conrad anymore. I'm Charles Bulber, you hear me; I'm Professor Charles Bulber, and I want you off my goddamn fucking property!"

"Dat's no way for a professah to talk," chided Izzy.

"Cool it," said Ace, who'd just finished reading the tele-gram for himself. "Conrad just got some weird news."

Suddenly it was too much for Conrad, all the tension and confusion and bad vibes. A shaking traveled up from his knees and into his stomach, and then he was lying on the ground sobbing—or pretending to sob—into the crook of his arm.

After a while, Chuckie and Izzy left, and Ace helped Conrad into the house. He fixed them a couple of beer-with-tomato-juices while Conrad rolled a jay. Ace had thought to get the shopping bag from Chuckie. Soon Conrad's spirits rose.

"Actually—it's a gift from God, Ace. With Bulber dead, I could move in here for good—hell, I could pick up enough physics by next year—and then I could marry Audrey, and have kids with her, and be safe from the cops and saucers forever. But I had to fuck it up before I even started. Last night I told about ten people I wasn't really Bulber; I was trying to impress those girls and . . ."

"Don't worry, Conrad, I covered for you."

"What do you mean?"

"I told everyone I was Conrad Bunger, too. And so did Izzy and Chuckie and Platter—that's going to be like the big campus joke this week: '*I'm really Conrad Bunger.*' You know: 'Bird lives!' James Dean is disfigured and in hiding!' All those people last night thought you were just a silly middle-aged guy pathetically imitating us students. 'I am Conrad Bunger,' indeed. Have you looked in a mirror lately, Dr. Bulber?"

"Oh, Ace."

"I know, you don't deserve a friend like me. What are you going to do with all this Acapulco Gold?" The bagful of mixed money and marijuana had spilled out onto the kitchen floor. Big bills, big buds, gold and green.

"I'm sure as hell not going to hand it out at Collection. I mean, then I'd have to change my face again, and who knows if I could find another niche as perfect as this. I'll stay away from the students, and start learning science. I really always wanted to be a physicist anyway. I guess I'll freeze the dope. Or why don't I divide it in five, and each of us takes one section, and in return you guys really really forget about this whole thing."

"It might work. But why don't you want to go back to the saucer, Conrad? Isn't it fun out there?"

"I . . . I really don't know. I don't remember that much about it. You know the story. They set me down here when I was ten, with fake memories, and it all came out more or less by accident. I only really saw another flame-person once . . . that was the one who tried to get me in the graveyard. He seemed OK; when we touched it was like talking. But I could pick up a real feeling of envy off him. Life on Earth is a lot more interesting than being an energy-pattern in a flying saucer. I'm kind of in a position like a conscripted sailor who jumps ship to live on a tropical island. Or like a spy who defects and begins to believe in his cover."

"But what about back on the homeworld? Maybe it's real nice there. Do you know where it is?"

"No. I don't even know what *kind* of world it is. Your guess is as good as mine." Conrad was moving around the kitchen now, straightening up. "I'll tell you why I want to stay here. It's simple. I want to stay on Earth because I'm in love with Audrey Hayes. That's the secret of life, man. Love. I want to live out a normal human life here; I want to live a nice long life with Audrey. Maybe she'll marry me and move into this house!"

Someone was knocking at the door. It was Platter, bearded and grinning. He looked like a stoned yak. Conrad ushered him in. "Ron, I'm going to do better than repay you for that weed from last night. I'm going to give you a whole one-fifth of my kilo."

"Far-out! And I thought you were going to hand it all out at Collection."

"No, no," said Conrad quickly. "I've decided to go for the long haul. Low-profile. I don't need to talk to Collection at all."

"But listen! I was just at the Student Council meeting. After that big party last night, everyone wants you to speak. We scheduled you for September 22, and the college already approved it! You can talk on the secret of life!"

Conrad kept to himself for the next week and a half. Giving a speech on the secret of life was something he'd always wanted to do—and he hoped to be ready for it. Dee's simple summation, "All is One," seemed like the core of it, but the problem was that sometimes the phrase was . . . just empty words.

"All is One," Conrad would repeat to himself, jogging along the route that Ace had showed him through the Crum. Sometimes it would click, and sometimes it wouldn't.

Odd things kept happening at Mr. Bulber's house. Sometimes Conrad would come back, and it would look as if someone had been there, moving things around. Paranoia or truth? Other days, there'd be a car with strangers parked across the street. Scary, but what could he do? Nothing except hope that, when the heavy shit came down, he'd have another power up his sleeve. Meanwhile, Conrad kept on thinking, thinking about the secret of life.

He got a lot of books out of the Swarthmore library: Einstein's essays, Wittgenstein's *Tractatus*, good old *Nausea*,

and Kerouac and Suzuki and Eddington and Daumal.
There was still so much to learn. He'd really wasted his
three years here so far—he didn't know much of anything,
and the books were hard to understand. They were just
marks on paper. Most days, hungry for reality, he'd wan-
der off into the Crum woods.

He'd go down the hill behind Bulber's, say, and smoke
a joint and sit there, staring at bugs on a rock. The bugs
were alive, people were alive, the flamers were alive—but
what was it all for? When he was high enough, he thought
he knew; he'd have that fine merged feeling he'd had that
day with Dee, and everything would fit together.

Another day—it was Sunday the eighteenth—Conrad
sat all afternoon gazing at Crum Creek . . . wondering at
the way a given bulge in the water could always be there,
yet always be made up of different molecules of water.
The bulge was a definite form, an *object*, yet it was utterly
insubstantial. There was no molecule you could point to
and say, "This is an essential part of the bulge." On a longer time-scale, Conrad mused, human bodies were just
as insubstantial—eat and shit, cough and breathe—the
atoms come and go. But his flame-stick . . . what was *it*
made of?

Focusing inward, Conrad could sort of feel the rod of
light running down his spine. The flame was something
other than ordinary matter, or it wouldn't fit inside his
flesh so easily. Plasma, ether, hypermatter? Try as he
might, Conrad couldn't pull it out as he had in the Z.T.
graveyard. He needed the crystal to get the flame out; the
crystal was an essential part of him. Crystal and flame,

projector and image, body and mind, log and fire. That was *one* direction; what was the other? What did the flame do for the crystal?

Thinking hard, Conrad got an image of his flame-stick as a kind of *recording device*. His human thoughts and impressions were constantly being coded up as patterns in the flame, coded, perhaps, as tiny knotted plasma-vortices. The crystal could hold a transmitter, a transmitter designed so that whenever Conrad touched it, his memory patterns would be read off and beamed up to the saucer for the flamers to enjoy. Conrad recalled reading that mystics sometimes speak of humans as "God's eyes." Perhaps this was literally true. Perhaps he himself was nothing more than an alien movie camera.

When Conrad got back to Mr. Bulber's that evening, he found that all his preliminary notes for his speech had been stolen. The FBI was onto him for sure. He picked up the phone and listened. It gave off a tinny echo. Bugged? He'd resisted using the phone so far. But, hell, if the feds were onto him so bad they were going through his papers, then what difference did anything make anymore? He decided to go ahead and call up his parents. They'd be worried about him. His father answered.

"Hello?"

"Dad? This is Conrad."

"I don't know who you are, but I wish you'd leave us alone. We've been through enough."

"No, Dad, it really is Conrad. I've been hiding out. Remember how you used to lie in the wading pool and call me Sausage?"

"It's Sausage!" old Caldwell called to his wife. "Pick up the extension, Lucy!"

"Conrad?" came his mother's voice then. "Is it really you? Where are you?"

"I better not say. I'm OK, though. I'm in disguise."

"Is all this business about the flying saucers true?"

"I think it is. I think they sent me down here to find out what people are like. But I'm scared that the police are going to kill me."

"Why can't you turn yourself in peacefully?" asked his mother.

"Don't do that," put in Conrad's father. "I think they really might kill you. They've been by here a lot—the FBI and the Secret Service. Those fellows mean business."

"I'm still your son anyway," blurted Conrad.

"We know that," said his mother. "And we still love you."

"I think my phone is tapped, Conrad," said his father. "So we better keep it short. Is there anything I can do for you?"

"One thing, Dad. What's the secret of life? What does it all mean? What are we here for?"

There was momentary silence. Crackles on the phone line. "Damned if I know," his father said finally. "Nobody knows. It's just . . . Here we are, and we have to take care of each other the best we can." Pause. "Does there have to be a reason?"

"Thanks, Dad." Again the fleeting feeling of understanding it all. "Thanks a lot. I guess I better hang up now."

"Take care, Conrad," said his mother. "Please try and find some way to straighten all this out."

Conrad phoned Audrey next.

"Hi, Audrey."

"Conrad! You finally decided it was safe to call?"

"I decided it didn't matter. Either they're onto me or they aren't. This isn't going to change anything. I was going to write you another letter, but I needed to hear your voice."

"Well, here's my voice," said Audrey gaily, and sang a note. "LOOOOO!"

"Very pretty. Are you going to come down for my speech?"

"Of course, Dr. Bulber. What is the secret of life?"

Conrad sighed. "I had some notes, but somebody snuck in and stole them. I bet it was the cops."

"Unless you lost them. Did you get stoned today?"

"No. But I had a lot of good ideas anyway."

"Well, you see, Conrad? Now just keep thinking, and I'm sure your speech will be wonderful. I can't wait to see you."

"Me too. Will you stay the whole weekend?"

"Maybe."

"I love you, Audrey."

"I love you, too."

As Thursday drew closer, Conrad wrote more and more. He got a notebook and carried it with him everywhere. If only he could break through and find the truth! On the one hand, he didn't want to jeopardize his seemingly solid position as tenured physics prof. Maybe, just maybe, despite all his worries, the police really *weren't* onto him. Maybe he really had just lost those earlier notes, maybe he was only being paranoid. But no matter what, he wanted his speech to say something meaningful. Things looked calm now, but who could tell when the end would come? He'd come here to learn from people; surely he could give them something back.

But what, after all, *was* the secret of life? Drink, and weed, and love, and life, and running, and talk, and water, and air—there wasn't any secret when you got down to it. Like his father had said, "Does there have to be a reason?" This was correct, when his father said it. But said in a certain other way, it was wrong.

To say, "There is no secret of life," in that certain other way means something like, "Get back to work, and watch TV, and believe everything the man tells you, and use vaginal deodorant spray—this is all you get—go to church and cough up some money, it's all bullshit, use women like objects (snigger), don't read—stop looking for more—matter is everything, there's no soul, there's no God up there, there's just a mean old man keeping lists like Santa Claus, death is horrible, buy lots of things to forget about death, commit brutal sex-murders, go to war, build bombs, rape the Earth, try to kill everything with you when you die—only your body matters—winning is everything, don't let people push you around, don't listen to others, friends are to get things from—get your head out of the clouds—art's a waste of time, so is philosophy, science will soon solve all mysteries, art is what they *used* to have, no room for art in today's modern age, technology is the thing, science is for making more goods, goods to help us try and buy off death a little longer, medicine is the only science that *really* counts, how much is that in dollars—follow the rules—innovation is too risky, don't step out of line, what if everyone did that, shape up or ship out, you're in the army now . . ."

Easy to say what the Secret *isn't* but what *is* it? It's not a Secret at all, is the main thing, and it's not anything occult or unusual. It's everywhere all the time, like an ether-wind blowing through our minds and bodies, it's God, it's simple existence, *can't you see it?* No word can really capture the Secret, practically any phrase will do. All is One, *All is One, ALL IS ONE*. One what? One of . . . uh . . . those . . . uh . . . IT isn't like anything else, and IT's like everything else, because IT is everything, IT's the underside of everything—like a papier-mâché topographical map that you turn over, and underneath IT's all brown paper. There're no gods and devils down there, no spells and spirits, there's just . . . oh . . . clear *light*, man, light so bright it's *dark*. Love is a kind of merging, love is humanity's concrete symbol for the Secret, two into one, holding nothing back, together at last, tear down the walls and let it flow. It's all in forgetting your individuality, forgetting you're alive so that IT can remember ITself. The Secret. Some Secret. Dear God.

On the last couple of days, Conrad scribbled page after page of stuff like that—hoping somehow that the intensity of his longing could bring the secret out into print. He wrote in the house, he wrote in the woods, he expanded and condensed. Finally he had something typed up; he couldn't tell anymore if it made sense or not. And then it was Thursday.

thursday, september 22, 1966

You should just get high, Conrad, and let the marijuana do the talking." Platter and Ace and Conrad were walking up from Bulber's house to Clothier Hall, the big gray stone building where Collection was about to take place. Platter was stoned—he'd been stoned since last Saturday—but the other two weren't.

"This is too serious for that," said Ace. "I got a feeling."

"Me too," said Conrad. "I'm scared shitless. You guys sit with Audrey, OK?" Audrey had come down last night so she'd be here for Conrad's big speech on the secret of life. "In case something happens. She'll be in the front row. She went there early to save places."

Conrad said goodbye to his two friends outside of Clothier. It was a bright, windy fall day, but the great gray building seemed gloomy as a church or prison. Ace and Platter went in the rear entrance to get their names checked off the attendance list, and Conrad went on down to the stage-door entrance at the front. Dean Potts was right inside the door, waiting.

"Charlie!" said Dean Potts. "You're right on time." Potts was a tall, dough-faced guy—one of these low-empathy American men who never really gets past being a boy scout. Mr. Bulber had been somewhat the same type, so it stood to reason he and Potts would be friends.

"I'm surprised the kids wanted me to speak," said Conrad tentatively.

"That's 'cause you've been throwing those wild parties, Charlie! The President was a little worried what might happen today, but I told him there'd be no problem. *I know the real Charles Bulber*, is what I told him; am I right?"

Was that mockery on Potts's face? Conrad thanked God he wasn't stoned, thanked God he'd typed some kind of speech out in advance. This was going to be tough. If only he'd had more time!

Potts led Conrad out onto the stage, and they took their seats along with the rest of the faculty and staff. The format was that all the students sat down in the auditorium, and the grown-ups sat up on the stage, facing the students. And then the speaker would stand up in front of the grown-ups, facing the students, and talk. Right before the talk, with everyone still sitting down, they always had a minute or two of silence, a legacy of Swarthmore's Quaker beginnings.

The students seemed unruly today, messy and buzzing— they'd all heard of Mr. Bulber's pot party two weeks ago, and they were expecting something bizarre. Settling into his wooden seat, Conrad noticed a small figure darting up and down the Clothier aisle ... *Tuskman*, oh, Christ, Izzy Tuskman with a stocking over his head, tossing out handfuls of joints as fast as his arms and legs could move. One thing about Izzy, he never gave up. When Conrad had given him his one-fifth kilo, he'd explained to Izzy that the handing out of reefers was definitely canceled, but ... did Izzy care? No. He had it all figured out—that he'd wear a disguise and take off before anyone could—

BAM! That was Izzy slamming the rear door of Clothier. Outside you could hear a car peeling out. *Da get-away cab.*

Conrad buried his face in his hands and tried to merge into the One. The meditation period had started—oh, it was peaceful here, in this empty time—two minutes is as close to *forever* as seventy years is, if you look at it the right way, the old finite/infinite distinction ...

In the vast, thoughty silence you could hear matches scratching here and there—people were lighting up. Conrad peeked out between his fingers—yes, there were plumes of smoke everywhere, a faint blue haze percolating up from the crowd. How was he going to convince the President that this wasn't his fault? Especially since it *was* ...

ARHMMM. Dean Potts at the mike, the two minutes were over. "Today's speaker needs no introduction. I give you Charlie Bulber."

The space between his chair and the lectern seemed so far. Taking the first step, Conrad flashed on his old high-school rap about the urinals, how it seemed you can never cross a room, but you always do: "We're going to *die*, Jim, can you believe that? It's really going to stop someday, all of it, and you're dead then, you know?" Right here, right now, death was very close. This was a trap. Something about Potts's face. Conrad could feel it. And inside himself, he could feel a new power begin to grow.

Now he was at the lectern. A rifle barked. Without even thinking about it, Conrad stepped outside of time.

It was like being in a waxworks—all the students frozen with expectant smiles; the plumes of smoke like cracks in ice; and there, hovering just behind Conrad's head, the bullet.

He peered up past the bullet and into the scaffolding over the stage. Perched there were two men in black—government agents. They'd been onto him all along. No doubt they'd found him in the first place by tailing Audrey; they'd probably opened her mail. Conrad winced to imagine cops reading the silly drunken first letter he'd written her from Bulber's. *I do want to do some kind of trip on the straights' heads here . . .*

This was all a setup. The cable from Paris: a fake, to keep Conrad around. The college's willingness to let him make this speech: a lure, to get him into the pigs' gunsights. All a setup, but it hadn't worked. *Fourth Chinese Brother.*

Conrad could feel that his body had gone back to its old shape—his hair was long again; his joints more flexible. It felt good. Getting out of the Mr. Bulber shape was like getting out of an uncomfortable Sunday suit. His shape-changing power was gone, but now he had a new power: the ability to step outside of time.

He crumpled up his confused, rambling speech about the secret of life and tossed it aside. It hung there in the air, just where he let it go. Time had stopped for everything except Conrad and what he touched. Somehow his personal time-axis had turned perpendicular to the world's time. He was still in our universe's space, yet his time had twigged off into a new direction.

Conrad wondered if he should do something to dough-faced Potts, sitting back there with his finger raised in silent signal to the snipers. Give him the speech, maybe. Yeah. Conrad pried Potts's mouth open and stuffed his wadded speech inside. *Chew on that, man. Do you some good.* Potts twitched momentarily into life at Conrad's touch, just long enough to gag and glare, but then, as Conrad shied away from him, he returned to stony immobility.

Conrad hopped down from the stage and went over to Audrey, sitting there in the front row between Ace and Platter. A smile still broadened her full mouth, and her hands were held up in applause. He took her by the shoulders and kissed her.

"Huh?" Audrey jerked in surprise. For her it was as if Conrad had flown over instantaneously. "Conrad? You changed back! But . . . why's it so quiet?"

Conrad made sure to keep his hand on her, towing her along in his altered timestream. "It's my fourth power. I changed the direction of my time. It's a little like I'm moving infinitely fast. As long as I touch you, you'll move along with me. They were going to shoot me up there. I jumped out of time just before the first bullet hit me."

Audrey got to her feet and looked around. It was an unsettling sight: row after row of faces caught in random flash-bulb expressions. The overall feeling was of being in front of a great, cresting wave about to break. "It's creepy, Conrad. Let's get out of here."

Hand-in-hand they walked out of Clothier. Red-and-yellow maple leaves hung suspended in the air. A starling that had just taken wing hovered three feet off the ground. Frozen in time like this, the bird's body looked strange—like a three-dimensional Chinese ideogram. High overhead, a jet's contrails marked the sky.

"They tried to shoot you?"

"Yeah. The bullet's still hanging in the air back there."

"What would have happened if the bullet had hit you?"

"My body would be dead, and maybe the rest of me, too. There's that stick of light in me, but I'm not sure it can live on its own without that crystal I told you about. I was so scared the flamers would home in on me again that I left the crystal at Skelton's. I shouldn't have done that." Staring at the starling's ragged feathers, Conrad tried once again to understand death. Nothing. In the sudden contrast, Audrey's face seemed unbearably sweet. They hugged and kissed.

"Look," said Audrey, disentangling herself. "Shouldn't we get going? How long is this going to last?"

"When I shift back into normal time, it's probably going to be at the same instant I left. So this isn't going to last any time at all. It's an intermission between two reels of the movie. Maybe I'll decide to be a martyr and go stand by that bullet and step back into real time. Do you think I should do that, Audrey?"

"Don't be crazy. I can't believe they'd want to kill you anyway. All you ever did wrong was break into that farmhouse. You've been here on Earth ten years and never hurt anyone."

"It's kind of weird, isn't it? The government has gotten so paranoid recently. I guess they figured that with all my powers there was no way to capture me alive."

"They were right about that," said Audrey, smiling. "You still didn't answer my question, though. How long *for you* is the time-stop going to last?"

"All my other powers always lasted till I knew that everyone had found out about them. When I saw our picture in the paper in Paris, I couldn't fly anymore . . . remember? And then when Skelton's film of me was on TV, I couldn't shrink. Just now, with those guys shooting at me, I could tell they knew I'd changed my face, so I got my old Conrad-face back. But now, outside of time like this, it doesn't seem like they'll ever know at all. This could last for a long time, Audrey. And for all that time, nothing will move or change except the things that I touch."

"Like me. Sleeping Beauty."

"And the air we're breathing."

"I wonder if a car would run if you touched it."

"What for?"

"We've got to do *something*, Conrad. We can't just vegetate." She tugged at him, and they started walking down the long campus lawn toward the street.

"Uh . . ." Conrad was having trouble getting motivated. He'd tried to figure out the secret of life for the speech, and basically he'd failed. Life was life. The feds had almost killed him for trying to explain it. And now here he and Audrey were, together again for the first time in weeks, moving around in the center of an endless stillness. It was like they were the flickering thoughts of some vast, universal jellyfish. Without time, it wasn't quite real, but how pretty the leaves and sky! Life could end any time, and he still didn't know what it was all about. "Is there a rush? We've got all the time in the world."

"Well, I don't know, Conrad."

"Why don't we go to Bulber's house and make love?"

Audrey twisted coyly away and briefly froze till Conrad put his hand back on her. She seemed not to notice the hiatus. "But the flame-people," she protested. "Aren't they going to come after you? If you can move out of human time, then they can, too."

"Oh, Audrey, I don't know. Maybe I'd be glad to see them. Maybe they could fix it all. I want all this science fiction to be over. I'm tired of trying to be cool, or a genius. I just want to live a regular life with you. Get married, go to grad school, learn stuff, have kids, get old. Is that so much to ask?"

Audrey put her arm around Conrad's waist and squeezed. "Actually . . . we could fuck right here on the lawn. No one can see us. Let's do it right there, by the tree where we first kissed!"

So they did.

And then they went down to the little street of shops at the edge of the campus and filled up a shopping bag with food. It was dreamy, dreamy in the food store and on the sidewalks—everyone still and silent.

"It's nice like this, isn't it, Conrad? Just you and me, and everyone else asleep."

"Yes. It's nice now, but I also know we're going to get tired of living in a cardboard world."

"So what should we do?"

"Let's drive to Louisville and get the crystal from Skelton's. I'll hold it, and then the flame-people will find me again."

"And then?"

"Oh, shit, let's just enjoy this while we're doing it." The street was filled with cars, frozen cars with frozen drivers. "Do you like that Mustang, Audrey?"

"Neat! A convertible! I bet you can make it run."

"Just wait here a second with our food." Conrad stepped back from Audrey, and she stood motionless on the sidewalk. He went over to the Mustang and gave the car a tentative pat. At Conrad's vivifying touch, the car gave a brief jerk forward. So Audrey was right—Conrad could pull machines as well as people into his timestream. Careful to touch the car as little as possible, Conrad reached in past the driver to yank on the emergency brake and turn off the ignition. Then he vaulted over the passenger side to sit next to the driver, a fellow student named Bud Otis. The fully wakened car skidded to a stop, with Conrad reaching over to steer it straight.

"Bunger!" shouted Otis. "Where the hell did you—"

Conrad jumped back out and Otis seemed to freeze again. Conrad went around to the driver's side, opened the door, and grabbed Otis. Under the influence of Conrad's magic touch, Otis flipped back into Conrad's time, protesting loudly. Moving quickly, Conrad hustled him over to the roadside, and let him turn back into stone. Then he went and got Audrey.

Audrey kept her hand on Conrad's shoulder while he restarted the Mustang. It fired up fine, and he drove out toward the main highway, weaving around all the stopped cars.

"Look at that," exclaimed Audrey, suddenly. "Soldiers!"

Conrad and Audrey were a block past the campus, and there, lined up in a residential street, were hundreds of soldiers, armed to the teeth. They had tanks and bazookas, machine guns and armored cars. A fleet of helicopters hovered over the treetops, frozen en route to Clothier. High overhead, you could make out the black, triangular silhouettes of fighter planes.

"Wow," said Conrad. "They were really planning to cream me if those bullets didn't work. I bet there's soldiers on the other side of campus, too."

"And in the Crum! Aren't they going to be surprised when their time starts up. You and I'll have disappeared!"

"I just hope their time doesn't start up any time soon," said Conrad, driving a little faster.

Soon they were out on the main highway and could breathe a little easier. They began picnicking on the groceries they'd taken. Bread, salami, fruit, and cheese.

"What happened to your speech, anyway, Conrad?"

"I stuffed it in Dean Potts's mouth. That's what it was written for, really."

TWENTY-NINE

"thursday, september 22, 1966"

Normally, the drive to Louisville would have taken a day and a half. But with the world's time effectively stopped, the road was often jammed by motionless cars in every lane, so that Conrad frequently had to pull onto the shoulder to get around the photo-finish speedsters. The tunnels on the Pennsylvania Turnpike were particularly tough. Some cars simply had to be pat-patted out of the way. Two or three times, Audrey and Conrad walked into a motel, took a key to an empty room, and got some sleep. With all this, the trip took something like four days.

Of course, really, there was no telling just *how* long it took. Neither Conrad nor Audrey was wearing a watch, and the sun, stuck in the old timestream, forever hung there in its near-noon, September 22, position.

They ran into a rainstorm west of Pittsburgh, which was interesting. Each raindrop that hit their car would join their timestream and slide down to the road. Looking back, they could see a carved-out tunnel through the rain. It was interesting, but Conrad couldn't figure out how to put up the convertible roof, and they were getting wet. So they stopped at a Howard Johnson's, took the keys from the hand of a man about to unlock his Corvette, and proceeded in even better style.

The ease of taking the man's keys gave Conrad the notion of robbing a bank, but Audrey talked him out of it. The trip was dragging on longer than they'd imagined, and it was all getting kind of spooky. It was on the last leg—from Cincinnati to Louisville—that it *really* started to get strange.

They were weaving along from lane to lane—every now and then skidding out onto the shoulder. Conrad was driving, and Audrey was staring out the open car window.

"Is it always so hazy in Kentucky?" Audrey asked.

"Hazy . . ." Conrad realized he'd been squinting for the last couple of hours. Things were getting harder and harder to see. It was like wearing the wrong pair of glasses.

"And look at the sun, Conrad, it's gotten all fuzzy!"

Indeed the sun was fuzzy, and the landscape hazy. The great tapestry of past reality was beginning to fade.

"That's not normal, is it, Conrad?"

"Normal! None of this is normal." He tried to drive a little faster. Pass a car in his lane, dodge a truck in the other lane, skid around a solid block of three cars either way.

"We're getting too far away from the main timestream, Conrad! That's why the world is getting so vague. It's out of focus!"

It got worse and worse—soon nothing was clear beyond a fifty-yard radius around the Corvette. It was like driving through thick fog—with the difference that the fog was *bright*, not dark.

"I'm scared, Conrad."

"Maybe I should let you go. I could put you out by the roadside, and you'd leave my timestream. You'd be out there with all the regular people."

"But it's you I want, Conrad."

"Well, hang on then, Audrey. Once I get that crystal we'll see the flamers, and maybe they'll help me out."

Fortunately, Conrad remembered Louisville's roads well, and they were able to find their way to Skelton's. They pulled up his driveway, and the sun-hazed farmhouse reared up before them like a haystack by Monet. Hand in hand, they left the now-shimmering car and mounted Skelton's steps. At the touch of Conrad's feet, the steps grew satisfyingly solid.

They found Skelton on his back porch, poised over a trout fly in a vise. He was busy wrapping it with yellow thread. Like everything else now, Skelton had the gauzy outlines of an Impressionist painting. Conrad laid his hand on the old man's shoulder. It took him a moment to get fully solid, and then he looked up.

"Conrad! How'd you sneak in like that, boy?"

"I'm outside of normal time. I just pulled you into my timestream. This here's Audrey Hayes, who I'm engaged to. Audrey, this is Mr. Skelton."

"Pleased to meet you, Audrey. Engaged to the saucer-alien, hey? Well, I suppose he can have kids like anyone else."

"This is the first time *I've* heard we're engaged," said Audrey, smiling. "Conrad and I came here to see if you still had that crystal."

"That crystal!" exclaimed Skelton. "If you only knew, Conrad, how the feds have been pestering me. Of course I never even allowed as how I had it back, but they *would* keep poking around. Yes, sir. I've got that crystal hid, and I've got it hid good."

"Well, can I have it?"

"Yes ... if you let me watch you use it. You know how much it would tickle me to see another saucer, Conrad, and—"

"No problem. And the sooner, the better. You notice how hazy everything is getting, Mr. Skelton? If my time-stream gets too far off of the old reality, there's no telling where we'll end up. I want to get that crystal and call the flame-people for help."

"Okey-doke. The crystal's hid out in the smokehouse. I wedged her on into one of my country hams. It was my rolling the hams in rock salt that gave me the idea. It seemed fitting, what with you being made of pigmeat and all in the first place, Conrad."

"*Pigmeat?*" exclaimed Audrey.

"Didn't tell you that did he, hey?" chuckled Skelton. "Yep, that's how Conrad got here. He was a stick of light attached to that crystal. When his saucer landed, he flew on out, stabbed his light into my prize hog Chester, doctored that pigmeat into human form, and walked off to join the Bungers. March 22, 1956. I saw the lights, but all I found was the crystal. Here we are."

The three of them stepped into Skelton's old stone smoke-house. Conrad kept one hand on each of his companions, pulling them along in his timestream. The smokehouse had the good familiar smell of fat and hickory. Skelton fumbled at one of the hams till he got it off its hook.

"Let's go outside where there's some light."

They went out and sat down on the grass. The ham was in the middle, and the three people sat around it. The haziness had gotten so great now that everything outside of a small circle around them was gone. No house, no smokehouse, no sun, and no sky. Just raw color, lively specks of scintillating brightness.

Skelton felt around under the ham's outer hide for what seemed quite a long time. Finally he drew out the crystal, shiny and glistening with fat. It was considerably smaller than the last time Conrad had seen it.

"Here, Conrad. You hold it, and I'll keep my hand on you."

The crystal tingled in Conrad's palm. Where earlier it had been big as a matchbox, now it was no larger than a sugar cube. Even so, it nestled into the curves of his palm in the same tight way it had done back in the Zachary Taylor cemetery.

"This may take a few minutes," said Conrad. "Let's just sit tight." He closed his eyes and concentrated. He could feel his memory pattern flowing down through the crystal and into the subether transmission channel.

"Now, *why* did you say the world's so blurred?" Skelton asked Audrey. "I had a cousin who had glaucoma—the way he told it, glaucoma makes things look something like this. *What* did you say was the reason?"

"It's because we're on another timestream," said Audrey. "We're moving farther and farther away from the old world. Like taking a wrong fork in the road."

The crystal was hot in Conrad's hand; and his ears were filled with buzzing. Closer. Closer.

Mr. Skelton was getting nervous and impatient. "I sure don't like having the real world drift away from us like this. If that saucer doesn't show up soon, I've got a mind to . . ."

ZZZZUUUUUHHHHUUUUUUssss.

Five bright red lights solidified out of the bright haze, coming into focus as they approached. It was a square-based pyramid, two or three meters on a side. Still buzzing, it hovered closer, then touched down on the grass next to Conrad and the two humans.

For a moment the vehicle sat there like a large tent, and then one of its faces split open. Out came a stick of light with a gleaming parallelepiped crystal at one end. Remembering the fight in the graveyard, Conrad tensed himself for battle. He raised his own crystal up to the nape of his neck and got ready to unsheathe his stick of light.

But instead of attacking, the creature slid its flame into the big country ham that lay inside the circle of Conrad, Skelton, and Audrey. The flame-person's crystal stayed outside the ham, stuck to its narrow end. The wrinkles in the ham's skin formed themselves into a facelike pattern, and small feet seemed to stick out from the joint's wide end. Now the leg of pork got up and made a little bow to Conrad. Conrad returned the bow, not knowing whether to be frightened or amused.

"Hello," said the ham. "I see you are on your fourth power. We weren't sure you'd be able to take it this far." It spoke in a precise, hammy tenor.

"Where's your-all's home star?" demanded Mr. Skelton.

"We don't have one," said the ham. "We aren't material beings. The whole stars-and-planets concept is relative to the material condition. I think there's a human science called quantum mechanics that could express where we come from. Hilbert space? The problem is that none of us knows quantum mechanics!" The ham laughed sharply. "That's one of the things Conrad was supposed to find out about while looking for the 'secret of life.'" The ham laughed again, not quite pleasantly. "I must say, Conrad, some of your information is valuable, but on the whole—"

"Well, he's only just starting," said Audrey protectively. "I'm sure that sooner or later Conrad can learn everything on Earth that you flame-people want to know."

"You're Audrey," said the ham knowingly. "Conrad's girlfriend. Of course you stick up for him."

"How do you know about me?"

"See that crystal Conrad's holding?" asked the ham. "Besides being a power source, it's a memory transmitter. Every time Conrad touches it, we get copies of all his prior memories. You're Audrey Hayes, and Conrad is in love with you." The ham paused, bobbing in thought. "Love. Most interesting. It's been a mess from the start, but in some ways this is one of the most interesting investigations we've done. It's just a shame that—"

"Isn't there some way we can undo it?" asked Conrad. "I know I've screwed up—all the humans have heard of us now, and they're hunting for me. But isn't there some last power I could use to undo it?"

"'Fifth Chinese brother,' you call it?" The ham smiled. "It's no accident that you thought of that story. Yes, you could be the 'fifth Chinese brother,' Conrad. And you could, in a sense, live happily ever after. But . . ."

"But what?"

"It might deplete your energy too much. You see how small your crystal has gotten. It's the energy source that keeps your flame going, you know. One more wish and there'll be next to nothing left. No crystal, and your light will stop burning. It could turn into a kind of death sentence for you: live your seventy-odd years on some version of Earth, and then that's it. If you come with me now, we can replenish your crystal and you'll be sure of getting away. There's plenty of other 'planets' to investigate, you know."

Conrad squeezed Audrey's hand. "I want to stay. I want to be a person, and I want to keep looking for the secret of life."

"We knew you'd say that," said the ham. "That's why we picked you in the first place. But I had to ask." Pompously the ham bowed once again and laid itself back on the ground. The wrinkled features began to fade.

"Wait," cried Conrad. "What do I do? How do I make the humans stop hunting me? What is the fifth Chinese brother?"

"You know where you want to be," said the ham, its voice muffled and indistinct. "Just go there!"

Then the light-sword slid back out of the meat. The flame-person waved at them in a last salute, and then it whisked back into its scout ship.

ssssUUUUUHHHUUUUUZZZ.

The red lights faded off into the unfocused blur that surrounded them. "What's going to happen if I try to tell people my ham talked to me?" said Skelton after a moment. "Not even *UFO Monthly* would print a story like that! But you could do a great article, Conrad. Come on out and turn yourself in . . . hell, they'd let you go soon enough, and—"

"All that's what I have to get away from," said Conrad. "I'm not going back to that reality. Didn't you understand what the ham said? I can pick the reality I want and go there. Here like this with everything out of focus, we're nowhere in particular. Audrey and I are going to imagine our world all right again, and go there."

"I liked my world fine the way it was," groused Skelton. "I don't want to forget all this, Conrad."

"Fine," said Conrad. "Just take your hand off me, Mr. Skelton, and you'll go back to the old timestream."

The old man hesitated a moment. "OK," he said finally. "I believe I will. It's been a pleasure, Conrad. Nice to meet you, Audrey. I'll write an article explaining how you all disappeared."

"Thanks for everything," said Conrad. "And be sure to tell Hank Larsen that I came back." Old Skelton nodded and drew his hand away. He froze into stillness and then, slowly, slowly, he dissolved into light.

"Let's head off that way," suggested Audrey, pointing out toward where Skelton's lawn had been.

"OK," said Conrad. "Here, take my hand like this . . . we'll squeeze the crystal in between the two of us."

"And think of where we want to be."

"How about Crum meadow?"

"Yes. And you're starting senior year, Conrad, and everyone's forgotten about the flame-people and all that."

"Yes. You've come down to visit ... it's Friday afternoon."

"And Ace is going to let us use the room."

"I'll ask you to marry me."

"You will? So soon?"

As they walked, the haze shifted here and tightened there. Before long it was the Crum, and everything was just the way they'd wanted. They had no memory that it had ever been any other way.

"Audrey?"

"Yes, Conrad?"

"Have you guessed yet what's in between our hands?"

"Oh, will you finally let me see?"

"Go ahead!"

Audrey drew back her hand and found that Conrad had given her a diamond ring. The diamond was tiny, but very bright.

afterword

The Secret of Life is an example of what I call "transreal science fiction." By this I mean a novel in which I write about my real life, letting fantastical SF notions represent my emotions and psychic undercurrents.

In full-on transreal fashion, *The Secret of Life* started as a Kerouac-style memoir-novel which wasn't science fiction at all. I called this early book *All the Visions*, and it depicts my alter-ego Conrad Bunger's life up until the point when I typed out the *Visions*—this was during two exultant weeks in the summer of 1983. I was thirty-seven, and living as a freelance writer in Lynchburg, Virginia.

All the Visions was a memory dump of tales about my ongoing quest for enlightenment. The characters had made-up names. I meant for it to be a beatnik novel like *On the Road*. To fully mimic Kerouac, I wrote *All the Visions* on a single long roll of paper. I rigged up the roll on a length of broomstick propped up behind my good old rose-red IBM Selectric typewriter. The typed scroll was about eighty feet long when I was done. Nobody wanted to publish it.

No matter. The first part of *All the Visions* served as source material for the SF novel you've just read.

As well as being a love story about me and my wife Sylvia, *The Secret of Life* is a *bildungsroman*, that is, a novel of a young person's education. *Secret* is set during my high-school and college years. Having my character learn that he's a UFO alien is a nice objective correlative for the classic teenage sense that you couldn't possibly be the child of the "parents" you're living with. A sense that became particularly strong in the Sixties.

I spent nearly a year working on *The Secret of Life*. The book felt important to me, as if I were deciphering the patterns of my past. And I was hoping that *Secret* might break me out of the SF ghetto and into the world of mainstream lit. While writing it, I was rereading the existentialist Jean-Paul Sartre's memoir/novel *Nausea*, which happened to be a high-school favorite of mine. And I found four apt quotes from *Nausea* to use as the epigraphs for the four parts of *The Secret of Life*.

I sold *The Secret of Life* to Bluejay Books along with a more old-school SF novel of mine: *Master of Space and Time*. Bluejay published *The Secret of Life* in 1985 in a hardback edition, but soon thereafter they went bankrupt, and for years the *Secret* existed only as an Electric Story ebook.

In 2014 I included *The Secret of Life* in my *Transreal Trilogy* omnibus from my Transreal Books, and in 2016, I reprinted *Secret* on its own. Also I published a new edition of *All the Visions*—which still awaits recognition as a modern beatnik masterpiece. You can read it for free online at http://www.rudyrucker.com/allthevisions/

Rock on.

Rudy Rucker
Los Gatos, California
September 26, 2016

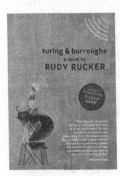

turing & burroughs
a novel by
RUDY RUCKER

mathematicians in love
a novel by
RUDY RUCKER

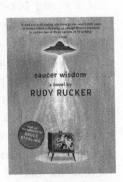

saucer wisdom
a novel by
RUDY RUCKER

white light
a novel by
RUDY RUCKER

million mile road trip
a novel by
RUDY RUCKER

the big aha
a novel by
RUDY RUCKER

spacetime donuts
a novel by
RUDY RUCKER

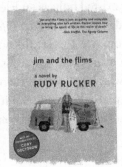

jim and the flims
a novel by
RUDY RUCKER

the sex sphere
a novel by
RUDY RUCKER

also from rudy rucker
and night shade books

Night Shade Books' ten-volume Rudy Rucker series reissues nine brilliantly off-beat novels from the mathematician-turned-author, as well as the brand-new *Million Mile Road Trip*. Conceived as a uniformly-designed collection, each release features new artwork from award-winning illustrator Bill Carman and an introduction from some of Rudy's most renowned science fiction contemporaries. We're proud to make trade editions available again (or for the first time!) of so much work from this influential writer, and to share Rucker's fascinating and unique ideas with a new generation of readers.

Turing & Burroughs
$14.99 pb
978-1-59780-964-1

White Light
$14.99 pb
978-1-59780-984-9

Spacetime Donuts
$14.99 pb
978-1-59780-997-9

Mathematicians in Love
$14.99 pb
978-1-59780-963-4

Million Mile Road Trip
$24.99 hc
978-1-59780-992-4
$14.99 pb
978-1-59780-991-7

Jim and the Flims
$14.99 pb
978-1-59780-998-6

Saucer Wisdom
$14.99 pb
978-1-59780-965-8

The Big Aha
$14.99 pb
978-1-59780-993-1

The Sex Sphere
$14.99 pb
978-1-94910-201-7

Rudy Rucker is a writer and a mathematician who worked for twenty years as a Silicon Valley computer science professor. He is regarded as a contemporary master of science fiction, and received the Philip K. Dick award twice. His forty published books include both novels and non-fiction books on the fourth dimension, infinity, and the meaning of computation. A founder of the cyberpunk school of science-fiction, Rucker also writes SF in a realistic style known as transrealism, often including himself as a character. He lives in the San Francisco Bay Area.